# DEAD IN THE SURF

Jill reached across the table and patted my hand. "So is Justin dead?"

I nodded.

"The news isn't saying much. Just that they're searching for a lost swimmer."

"I hope they find his body."

"What do you think happened?" Jill asked. She offered Matt more coffee. He shook his head.

"I'm not sure. He had a huge gash on his forehead."

Jill squeezed my hand again. "Did he crash?"

"Probably." I looked at both of them. "But something doesn't add up. Everyone said he's the best surfer. He didn't even wear a helmet. What was he doing all the way on the opposite side of the river?"

Jill tapped her fingers on the table as I spoke.

"He had a big gash in his forehead. It almost looked like he'd been hit by something."

"You mean like he was murdered?" Jill asked.

Books by Kate Dyer-Seeley

SCENE OF THE CLIMB

SLAYED ON THE SLOPES

SILENCED IN THE SURF

Published by Kensington Publishing Corporation

# in the
# Surf

## Kate
## Dyer-Seeley

# KENSINGTON PUBLISHING CORP.

http://www.kensingtonbooks.com

KENSINGTON BOOKS are published by

Kensington Publishing Corp.
119 West 40th Street
New York, NY 10018

All Kensington Titles, Imprints, and Distributed Lines are available at special quantity discounts for bulk purchases for sales promotions, premiums, fund-raising, and educational or institutional use. Special book excerpts or customized printings can also be created to fit specific needs. For details, write or phone the office of the Kensington special sales manager: Kensington Publishing Corp., 119 West 40th Street, New York, NY 10018, attn: Special Sales Department, Phone: 1-800-221-2647.

Kensington and the K logo Reg. U.S. Pat & TM Off.

ISBN-13: 978-1-61773-002-3
ISBN-10: 1-61773-002-5
First Kensington Mass Market Edition: April 2016

eISBN-13: 978-1-61773-003-0
eISBN-10: 1-61773-003-3
First Kensington Electronic Edition: April 2016

10 9 8 7 6 5 4 3 2 1

Printed in the United States of America

# Chapter 1

*Hood River, Oregon*
*Somewhere in the middle of the Columbia River*

The swells were relentless. Crashing one after the other and overwhelming the board. I almost laughed. *How ironic, Meg.* The one sport I actually thought I could hold my own in, and now I was holding on for dear life.

I scanned the river for any sign of my instructor or the rest of my windsurfing group. The water and sky blended together in the dull predawn light.

"Help!" I shouted into the wind. A whitecap broke in front of me, sending spray down my lungs. I coughed and grabbed the board tighter. No one was going to hear me over the sound of the wind and raging river.

The current had carried me away from the group so fast, I couldn't get my bearings. *Somewhere in the middle of the Columbia River, Meg. And not where you want to be.*

I forced my mind back to the instructor's directions. I knew I had to maneuver the board so that the sail was downwind. The question was how?

I paddled as hard as I could against the current, trying to reposition the mast. It sunk beneath the waves. My instructor's words rang in my head, "Remember, if you have to drop the boom—and try not to because you'll get exhausted if you have to keep picking it up—always drop it in front of you."

I hadn't planned on dropping it at all. In fact, I had been quite pleased with my ability to hold the "safety position," as he called it. Basically that meant balancing on the board while holding on to the mast with both hands and letting it swing. The problem was it swung in the high wind and quickly swept me far from the safety of the shore.

After paddling with all the force I could muster, I decided I had to give it one more shot. I climbed onto my knees. The board rocked on the waves.

*You can do this, Meg.* I let out a sigh and carefully made my way to my feet.

The freestyle windsurfers I'd been watching earlier made balancing on a board look easy. Trust me, it wasn't.

My feet clenched the grainy board. I extended my hands, trying to keep my center of gravity as low as possible. The muscles in my thighs quaked in response.

*Hang on, Meg.*

I bent toward the sail, focusing on my instructor's

advice to keep my body and back as upright as possible. I grabbed the sail. Then, like pulling a rope, I reached hand over hand, trying to free the heavy sail from the water. It wouldn't budge. I took in a powerful breath and tried to picture what Gam would say. "Find your inner strength, Margaret, and call on your guides for help."

It was worth a shot, right? I took a deep breath, and yelled, "A little help, please!"

It worked. The sail slowly emerged from the water. I got it about a foot high, when another gust of wind hit, sending me and the sail back into the ice-cold water.

My heart rate lurched in response to the shock of the water. *Swim, Meg.* I commanded my arms forward and kicked with all my might. The water was frigid. Every muscle in my body twitched with cold and stress as I climbed onto the board. I had to find a way to paddle back to the other side or I would drift downriver.

The sun began to rise overhead, casting a sepia glow on the dusty hills. I suddenly realized that drifting down the river was the least of my worries. Land was looming on my left. The waves were carrying me straight into the shoreline of the opposite side of the river. In a matter of minutes I would be smashed into the rocks.

That's when I spotted a body dragging along the shore.

* * *

When the opportunity of covering the King of the Hook windsurfing competition for *Northwest Extreme* first came up, I jumped at the chance. Portland, Oregon, had been under a sweltering heat wave all summer. We don't do well with the heat in Portland. Well, at least I don't. The minute thermometers read eighty degrees, there's a mad dash for window air-conditioning units, fans and bottled water. Portland is known for perfect summers with cool morning breezes blowing down the gorge and mild daytime highs. Really the only reason we all subject ourselves to the rain-soaked winter and spring is for summer. *Aw, summer.* It's like the weather gods conspired and offered up a bonus for sticking through all those soggy gray days.

During the glorious summer months the sun doesn't set until nearly ten. Portlanders congregate at parks and spend leisurely evenings strolling through neighborhood shops and stopping for hand-cranked ice cream and late-night pints. There's a youthful vibe in the city as people emerge from their winter hibernation, set aside their rain boots, and revel in the warmth of the sun's return. From farm-to-plate dinners to outdoor concerts under the stars, Portland comes to life.

However, since the Fourth of July, Portland had seen thirty consecutive days over ninety degrees with matching high humidity—something almost unheard of in the city. The weather and complaints about the heat were the hot topic wherever I went. Everyone was talking about the heat wave from the cashier at the grocery store to the brewer at my favorite pub. And no one was happy about it.

So when Greg, my boss and the editor in chief of *Northwest Extreme,* asked who wanted to cover King of the Hook in Hood River, I shot my hand in the air. "I'll do it." A chance to get out of town and watch windsurfers take flight sounded perfect.

Plus, swimming is my sport. This was my chance to prove myself not only to Greg, but to the rest of my colleagues. I'd been focused on continuing my outdoor training during the spring. I was slowly improving, but I still had a ways to go on my practically nonexistent athleticism. But I had to admit I was really starting to enjoy this whole outdoor gig. What started as a job to pay the bills was turning into a bona-fide career. I loved working at *Northwest Extreme.*

Given how my first assignment started out, I couldn't believe I was actually enjoying my job. I'd made some major progress since that crazy hike up Angel's Rest. The idea of covering King of the Hook in quaint Hood River, and escaping Portland's heat, had me ready to pack my bags.

"You sure, Meg?" Greg raised his brow. When I first met him, I thought I would never get used to his ruggedly handsome face and chiseled body, but things had changed between us over the winter. I wasn't sure if I could trust him, and he knew it.

Even though he was my boss, he'd been treading carefully with me. I could have used his caution to my advantage and gotten off without taking a single assignment. Instead the subtle tension between us had spurred me on to make sure my work was top-notch.

Greg looked like he wanted to say more, but shrugged and wrote my name in blue pen next to King of the Hook on the whiteboard.

I spent the next two weeks researching the annual windsurfing event and finding a place to stay in Hood River. The latter proved more challenging than I expected. Not only were surfers descending on the small town from all over the world for the competition, but everyone in Portland was trying to escape the heat wave.

Hood River in the Columbia River Gorge is about an hour's drive east of Portland and is known as the windsurfing capital of the world. The deep canyon stretches for miles, creating a boundary between Oregon and Washington. Winds funnel through the gorge, making it an ideal location for big air.

Temperatures wouldn't be any lower in Hood River. In fact, if anything, it would probably be hotter in the gorge, but there was always the promise of wind. Plus, the rocky banks of the Columbia River were a short walk from downtown. When the heat got to be too much, I could simply jump in the river. It was perfect.

Thanks to a new vacation rental app that I discovered, I scored a bungalow just a few blocks from downtown that was available the week of the event. Greg didn't blink when I showed him my expense report for the three-bedroom house, so I decided I might as well take advantage of the extra space and invite my bestie, Jill, and sort-of-boyfriend/friend Matt to join me for the long weekend.

Jill agreed immediately. She was "on a break" with her boyfriend, Will Barrington. Thank God. Will and I don't exactly get along. I tried to play nice for Jill's sake, but when I caught him with another woman last winter up on Mount Hood, I was done pretending. Jill hadn't said much about their break, but she was painting again, which I took as a promising sign that her heart was on the mend.

Matt took a bit more convincing. Not because he didn't want to join us, but because he'd been slammed at work. Matt covers the technology beat for *The O,* Oregon's largest newspaper. It was the paper I had always assumed that I'd write for after graduation. I was a legacy after all. My dad, Pops, as I called him, had been *The O*'s lead investigative reporter until he was killed two years ago. In hindsight it was probably a good thing that I hadn't landed a job there. Newspapers had been struggling with changing technology. None of my friends read their news on printed paper anymore. They kept abreast of current events and pop culture on their phones. I was the only holdout in our crowd. I still loved the feel of newsprint and how the ink smudged my fingers. Even Matt, who worked for an actual paper, read all his news on his tablet or phone.

*The O* had announced another giant round of layoffs in early June. Fortunately for Matt, the technology department was thriving, but the cuts had decimated the news desk, so Matt had been doing double duty for the summer. When he wasn't covering his regular beat, he was tasked with breaking news when his editor needed a warm body. I hadn't seen much of him, and was starting to wonder if maybe his feelings had changed.

Matt's texts about joining us in Hood River had been noncommittal, so I couldn't believe it when my phone buzzed as I was packing a bag with flip-flops, a swimsuit, rash guard and a collection of sundresses. I answered right away when I saw Matt's face flash on my screen. His shaggy blond hair covered one eye.

"Megs! I'm in." He sounded excited.

"You're in?"

"Yep, I'm coming. I owe Bob in Features a case of my home brew."

"Why?"

"I traded him assignments. He's going to cover breaking news for me while I'm gone and I'm going to do double duty—an event write-up on King of the Hook and a demo of the new GoPro."

"That's the best news! I can't believe you're coming. I'd pretty much written you off."

"Story of my life." He laughed. "I'm going to have to work, though."

"Me too. It'll be fun."

I smiled as I hung up the phone. Yeah, fun. I'd be working with Matt and hanging on the sunny shore with Jill. What an assignment. It was going to be like summer vacation.

Only as I would soon learn, this trip would become the farthest thing from a vacation imaginable.

# Chapter 2

I woke the next morning drenched in sweat. Despite sleeping with every window in my small bungalow wide open, my room actually felt hotter than the night before. The timing of this trip couldn't be better, I thought as I stuffed my clothes, a couple of beach towels and two large bags of groceries into the back of my Subaru.

Even though the clock on my dashboard read 9:00 a.m., I cranked on the air-conditioning. The cool air calmed the heat in my cheeks as I waved good-bye to my empty house.

*This calls for some Bobby Darin.*

I scrolled through my playlist and landed on "Mack the Knife." With my tunes blaring and the air-conditioning blasting, I maneuvered through the narrow streets of Northeast Portland. My neighborhood is quintessential Portland, with tree-lined streets where hundred-year-old maples lean into each other, creating a lush canopy overhead.

A neighbor three houses down tended to the

compost pile and chicken coop in her front yard. Most of the homes on my street were vintage bungalows with charm, character and tiny yards. No one believed in watering grass in the summer. Watering wasted water. Not that Portland was ever short on liquid sunshine. The few yards that had grass looked like brittle straw. Many of the houses had eco-friendly yards where the grass had been ripped out and replaced with rock gardens and organic vegetable beds.

At the end of the block a group of neighbors congregated at the Coffee Haunt for their morning espresso and to dish on the latest neighborhood gossip. I had a feeling I knew what the chatter was about. The neighborhood had been fuming about the new guy on the block who—gasp—had been spotted walking home from the co-op grocery store with plastic bags! Talk about a controversy.

Last week, the sweet but equally nosy elderly woman Mrs. Martins, who lived across the street, had stopped me before I left. "Meg!" She waved a pair of gardening sheers. "Come over here, dear. I have a story for you."

Mrs. Martins seemed to think that since I was a writer, I was her go-to source for neighborhood news.

"You know that young man who moved in two doors down?" She snipped an opaque pink rose.

I nodded.

She narrowed her eyes. "He's using plastic bags. Plastic. How did he even get them?"

"Good question, Mrs. Martins." I tried to match her grave expression.

Portland banned the use of plastic bags in grocery stores a couple of years ago. Being seen with plastic bags was a mortal sin in our neighborhood. I appeased Mrs. Martins by agreeing to look into the story, but I had a feeling that she would stage a plastic bag intervention before I had a chance to meet the new neighbor.

Sure enough as I drove past the Coffee Haunt, there stood Mrs. Martins and a group of neighbors toting reusable bags and offering them to the plastic bag offender. I smiled as I weaved past cars parked on both sides of the narrow street, and turned onto Martin Luther King Jr. Boulevard. My neighborhood was quirky to say the least, but it was a perfect match for me.

The route to Hood River was familiar. Last spring I'd spent a chunk of time driving out to the gorge while on my first assignment for *Northwest Extreme*. Memories of trying to keep up with a group of adventure racers in town and witnessing a murder flooded back as I passed signs along I-84 directing travelers to the old Historic Highway and the Columbia River Gorge National Scenic Area.

*Thank goodness that's all behind you now, Meg.* I let out a sigh.

A layer of brown haze had settled over the foothills and obscured my view of Mount Hood. I wasn't sure if it was due to pollution or because what felt like the entire state of Oregon was burning. The hot, dry summer had sparked forest fires all over the Pacific Northwest.

Hood River was another thirty miles or so east of Oregon's famous Multnomah Falls. I caught a quick glimpse of the falls from the highway. The normally towering cascade looked like a trickle. The effects of the heat were evident everywhere.

Interstate 84 parallels the Columbia River on the Oregon side of the river. The state of Washington sits across the river with stunning striated cliffs, the remnants of geological events a millennium ago. Geology was never my favorite subject in college. I stopped after Geology 101, which was referred to as "Rocks for Jocks" on campus. If my instructor had taken us on field research trips to places like the gorge, I probably would have paid more attention.

I could actually imagine how the towering ridges had been carved from years and years of water cascading down and the giant Missoula floods. Sturdy evergreen trees shored up the hillsides. Closer to ground level deciduous trees lined the freeway, their brittle leaves catching in the air as a semi rumbled past.

After I passed the falls, the evergreen trees became thicker. Some of their branches looked brown and desperate with thirst. I held my breath for good luck as I drove through an ivy- and moss-covered tunnel.

The landscape shifted as I continued east. The forested green slopes began to give way to Oregon's eastern desert land. The hillsides became dry and more barren. Sunlight cast on Washington's cliffs, giving them a golden tone.

My initial research for my feature had involved reading up on Hood River's farming roots. Its organic orchards are nestled in the shadow of Mount Hood, Oregon's tallest peak, with acres and acres of apples, pears and cherries. The farming community remains strong in the region, boasting annual picking parties, farm-to-plate dinners and the famed Fruit Loop tour where visitors can spend the day traveling to u-pick orchards, vineyards, lavender fields and alpaca farms.

Hood River has become known across the globe as a premier destination for outdoor lovers of all kinds. In the summer months, the town becomes the windsurfing capital of the world, but also draws in water enthusiasts of all kinds with paddle boarding, paragliding, kiteboarding, fishing and the annual swim across the Columbia. Hiking trails abound, attracting families and day hikers, as well as more serious climbers who can spend weeks happily lost in the backwoods. In the winter months, Hood River serves as base camp for snow junkies with quick access to the ski runs on Mount Hood, cross-country skiing at Mount Adams across the river, and a maze of snowshoeing and snowmobiling trails nearby.

As I turned off I-84 into town, I caught my first glimpse of the beach. It looked as if the entire state of Oregon had come out to watch the King of the

Hook. The shoreline was mobbed with surfers and spectators.

*This is going to be a real party, Meg!*

I felt giddy with anticipation as I made my way through downtown. There are no stoplights in the charming town of Hood River. Motorists gladly stopped for pedestrians waiting to cross the street. The main stretch of downtown features outdoor shops, pubs, high-end restaurants, tasting rooms and plenty of four-legged friends. *Is owning a dog a prerequisite to living in Hood River,* I thought as I passed pooches lapping up water from dishes placed on the sidewalks by shopkeepers. Even one of the most popular coffee shops was named Dog River Coffee.

The house I had rented was just a few blocks from downtown. I turned off Oak Street and found myself in a neighborhood that looked very similar to mine back home in NoPo (hipster slang for North Portland). The only difference was my place didn't have a panoramic view of Washington's stunning hillsides across a sparkling river.

I parked on the street, grabbed my bags, and walked to the house. I was the first one to arrive. Jill was planning to come after work, and Matt hadn't said when he was leaving. I unpacked the car, arranged the groceries in the kitchen, and snagged the front bedroom with a large bay window looking out onto the street. It would be a great spot to work on my feature. Speaking of my feature, I was due to check in at King of the Hook in thirty minutes.

I hurried to the bathroom to make sure my cheeks weren't too pink.

My face has an annoying habit of flaming up whenever I'm nervous or in any kind of heat. Surveying my appearance in the bathroom confirmed that the blazing temperature was evident on my cheeks. They were at least two shades brighter than my normal color. I tried dusting them with a little powder. That didn't seem to help much.

I scrunched my hair to try to help it curl. I'd been growing it out for six months, a record for me. It reached the base of my chin. I'd had it cut in an angular bob, and with a little product I could achieve a funky look without having to spend hours styling it. As much as I enjoy makeup and accessories, I'm not committed to a style routine. I am, however, committed to my love of vintage clothing. It's kind of a problem. I have a serious addiction to all things vintage and all things pink. My closet is packed with high-waisted dresses and skirts that flare.

It had taken some time to adjust to the culture at *Northwest Extreme* where all of my colleagues rolled in wearing jeans or a fleece. I think more than a few watercooler discussions involved my tendency to overdress. That's okay. I'd gotten used to the teasing and learned to tone down my workday attire a touch.

Thankfully Jill discovered a new beautiful line of women's outdoor clothing that was both functional and fashionable. I hit up the company to write a review of their gear and they sent me a box full of new clothes—all my size. Today I wore a teal knee-length water skirt, made of the most breathable and flattering fabric, a lightweight white shirt with UV sun protection and a pair of black flip-flops.

Even with my glowing cheeks I felt confident. I liked the balance of wearing clothes with a feminine cut, but that wouldn't make me look like a total outsider. I grabbed my phone, notebook and pen, and headed for the beach.

A blast of hot wind flew up my skirt as I stepped outside. I quickly pushed it back down. Whew. The heat was rising. Hopefully, I could snag my press pass, snap a few pictures, and then hit the beach.

Oak Street was jammed with people browsing the boutiques and sipping iced drinks at sidewalk tables. I fanned myself thinking, *Who would want to eat outside in this heat?* I ducked off the main street. At the next corner a group of surfers gathered on the steps of a gaming shop, The Quest. A guy wearing a long druid cape stood blocking the doorway with his body.

"You're not coming in." His voice cracked as he spoke. "Go back to the beach and leave the kids alone."

One of the surfers elbowed the guy next to him. "Nerd alert. What are you going to do, cast a spell on us?"

The surfers broke into laugher.

"Go ahead and laugh. This is my shop. You're not coming in." The druid pulled a plastic sword, at least I thought it was a plastic sword, from behind his back.

This caused the surfers to laugh even harder. The druid held his ground. I slowed my pace. I didn't want to get involved in someone else's journey, as Gam would say, but at the same time it looked like the surfers were bullying the magic shop owner. The surfers definitely had the advantage. They were tall and athletic. The druid was their opposite. Sweat poured from his pudgy face.

One of the surfers lunged toward the druid. The druid's reflexes were surprisingly quick. With one swipe he hit the surfer on the top of the head with the sword.

The surfer took a step back. "Ow." He rubbed his skull. "You want to fight? Where's your backup? That nerd herd?"

"I'm going to tell you one more time. Leave my property, or I'm calling the cops."

I froze in place and stared. Should I call the police? I had a bad feeling that things were about to escalate.

"Oooooh. I'm shaking, how about you, Cruise Control?" the surfer said as he massaged his scalp.

Cruise Control, the ringleader, stared at the druid. I thought he was going to take a swing or something, but then he shook his head in disgust and spit at the druid's feet. "Hey, bras, let's roll. Surf's up."

As he and his gang walked down the hill, he turned and glared at the druid one more time.

"This isn't over, dude." He flashed a hang loose sign and continued on.

The druid lowered his sword as I approached. His gaze followed the surfers down the hill. I cleared my throat. "Is everything okay?"

He jumped to attention and whipped his sword in my direction.

"Whoa." I threw my hands in the air. "I surrender. I just wondered if everything was okay. Were those guys harassing you?"

"Sorry." He held the sword for me to see. "It's plastic."

"I figured. I'm pretty sure there must be some kind of law about brandishing a real sword in public." I chuckled.

"I wish there wasn't." He looked in the direction of the surfers who were now nearly at the bottom of the hill.

"What's up with those guys?"

He shrugged. "King of the Hook. Welcome to hell week in Hood River."

"Not all surfers are like that," I protested, hoping I was right. Otherwise this was going to be a long week.

"Most of them are. Especially to me and my cosplay group."

"Cosplay?"

He motioned to the shop window behind him with his sword. The words THE QUEST were written in gothic script. A variety of costumes and weapons from superheroes with laser guns to knights with real armor were on display. "Cosplay. You don't know it?"

I shook my head. "Never heard of it."

"Actually, I'm not surprised. Cute sorority girl like yourself."

"What does that mean?" I crinkled my upper lip.

"You look like the type. That's all."

"For your information, I'm a professional journalist." I extended my hand. "Meg Reed."

He wiped his hand on his cape and then shook my hand. His palm was still damp. "Sherman, nice to meet you." His face perked up. "You're really a journalist? Maybe you'd be interested in doing a story about the cosplay movement?"

"I might, but you still haven't told me what it is."

"It's a mashup of costume and play. We dress up like a character. Usually from comic books, movies, or anime. You become your character. Create a subculture, plot. It's huge. I can't believe you've never heard of it."

"I have a friend who goes to Comic-Con every year. I know people dress up for that. I just didn't know it was a whole *thing*."

A group of gangly teenage boys in full costumes pushed open the door to the magic shop. One was dressed like a knight, another like a wizard, and two were dressed as elves. I didn't get it. "Sherman, you coming?" they asked.

Sherman, aka the druid, reached into his cape,

pulled out a business card, and handed it to me. "I have to go, but come back by and I'll tell you anything you want to know about the world of cosplay."

"Thanks." I studied the card as he returned inside with the boys. It read: SHERMAN OLIVER, OWNER THE QUEST. COSPLAY KING OF THE DRUIDS.

Between work and play I was pretty sure that dressing in costume wasn't in my near future, but I shoved the card in my laptop bag and continued on. I pulled up a map of Hood River on my phone. Second Street would take me over the freeway and down to the beach. I headed in that direction, along with everyone else. A mob of beachgoers sporting sand chairs and towels funneled onto the narrow sidewalk. I joined the throng and snapped a couple of photos of the crowd in front of me on my phone. This place is nuts, I thought as I fell into step.

The scene on the beach was even more chaotic. Vendors at booths had taken over the large gravel parking lot and were selling everything from energy drinks to ski boats. They thrust free samples of vitamins and brochures at us as the crowd pushed on toward the beach.

Signs directed observers to the grassy hillside on the right and boarders to the beach on the left. Every bench and picnic table in the grass had been taken. A gaggle of geese squawked above. I instinctively covered my head.

It took a bit to find the press tent in the sea of colorful flags and canopies dotting the beach. I had to weave through surfboards lining the grass. The ground was buzzing with bees and dotted with goose poop.

A tanned instructor was teaching a group of young kids how to paddleboard in a shallow, roped-off swimming area. I stopped to watch for a moment. "Push the paddle way out." The instructor dug her paddle into the water to demonstrate. One of her ankles was attached to the board with a bungee cord. She reminded me of a yoga instructor as she posed effortlessly on the board. The class followed her lead, pushing their paddles into the water and gliding forward. A preteen girl giggled, and yelled, "I can't turn my head."

I laughed as I continued on. A giant scaffolding had been erected on the main beach. It was covered with advertising banners and bright yellow King of the Hook signs. An emcee wearing a King of the Hook baseball cap and with a zinc-coated nose announced warm-ups from twenty feet in the air. Thank goodness I didn't have to be up there, I thought. Let's just say that heights aren't my thing. At all.

Out in the water, buoys and ramps had been set up for the competition as well as neon orange flags charting the course. The Columbia River was a mile wide in this section. Its depth was deceptive. A sandbar extended from the beach out under the trussed Hood River Bridge that connected Oregon to Washington. I wasn't sure if the river was normally

low, or if the sandbar was a result of the unusually
dry summer.

A handful of houses dotted the top of the bluffs
on the Washington side of the river, and the small
town of White Salmon looked as if it had been
carved into the cliff side. Train tracks ran parallel
to the rocky jetties below. A coal train rumbled west.
The sound carried across the river.

I looped up to the riverfront path where a blue-
grass band played on the stage and a line queued in
front of a pop-up gelato cart. When I finally spotted
the white awning of the press tent, I dug through
my laptop bag for my ID and business card. While
waiting in line to sign in and receive my press credentials, I noticed a camera crew filming outside the
tent. I listened in to their intro. The reporter spoke
into the mic. "What's up, surfers, are you ready for
some killer wind? I'm here at King of the Hook in
killer Or-y-gun, and you're not going to believe
who is back in town. Hood River's golden boy. The
number-one surfer in the world—Cruise Control.
Give it up for Justin Cruise."

A sinking feeling came over me as the surfer who
had just been bullying Sherman stepped in front of
the camera and flashed another hang loose sign.

# Chapter 3

I listened to Justin's interview while waiting to snag my press badge. Cockiness practically oozed out of him. He'd clearly spent time in front of the camera. Like a model, he flipped his bleached hair and angled his chin as he spoke. He gave the reporter an "I'm cooler than you" smirk as he spoke.

A group of girls about my age—maybe in their late twenties—gathered outside the tent. They all wore bikinis and rash guards and looked like they'd spent ample time on surfboards.

"Can I help you?" A man's voice interrupted my thoughts. He held a clipboard in his arms and wore a shirt that read: KING OF THE HOOK.

I tore my eyes away from Justin Cruise and his group of surfer girls. "I'm Meg Reed. Checking in for *Northwest Extreme* magazine."

"Meg, welcome. We've been expecting you." The man extended his hand. "Kyle Kaspar."

"Right, Kyle. I read up on you." I handed him my ID and press pass.

He tucked the clipboard under his arm and leafed through a stack of file folders on the counter. "*Northwest Extreme,* here you are." He handed me a laminated lanyard with the words PRESS: ALL ACCESS.

I hung it around my neck. Getting press credentials still made me feel official. I wondered if I'd ever get used to it.

Kyle Kaspar founded King of the Hook five years ago. I'd done my homework on him. He had competed in international surfing competitions for years, before officially retiring at the age of forty. In person he reminded me of Greg, only less outdoorsman more surfer. Surfers have a distinct look—natural highlights, uber tan skin, board shorts and flip-flops. I felt like I'd stepped into the pages of a surfing ad. One could mistake the setting for Hawaii if you added some palm trees and subbed the Pacific for the Columbia. Everyone around me sported the look.

"Do you want me to give you the lowdown?" Kyle asked.

"I'd love it, as long as that works for you?" I motioned to the line behind me.

Kyle waved over a woman to cover for him. "Now's good. I always make time for top-tier press."

Top tier. Wow.

I gave the guy in line behind me a grin. "Did you hear that? Top tier. Pretty cool."

Gam wouldn't have approved. She always says, "Margaret, the Universe is never limiting. It's always expansive. There's room for anything and everything. It's our mind that is self-limiting."

Badly done, Meg, I thought as the guy gave me a funny look. Why do stupid things still seem to fall out of my mouth? I was hoping I'd grown out of that.

The guy shook his head and chuckled. He flashed his ID reading, ESPN.

Kyle came around the front of the counter. He spotted the ESPN reporter and gave him a burly hug. "Dude, so good to see you. I'll be back in five and then I'm all yours, man."

*Right. Awesome, Meg.* I believe they call that instant karma.

"Is Greg coming out for the event?" Kyle asked as he lowered a pair of Oakley sunglasses over his eyes and led me outside.

"I think so, but I'm not sure. Greg always has a ton of stuff going on," I said, almost sprinting to keep up with Kyle's long stride.

He stopped and picked up a piece of trash from the ground. "This infuriates me. Stewardship is one of the core pieces of the mission of King of the Hook. Some of these young guys just don't get it." He shook his head and tossed the trash in a nearby garbage can.

"Yeah, I read about that. It sounds like you're really committed to making sure the beaches stay clean and safe." I pulled my notebook and pen from my laptop bag. This was as good a time as any to start my interview.

"It's more than that. I'm not an office kind of guy. I'm a sports junkie. Most of us are. I'm an instructor on the side—I teach underwater diving and skydiving. But this place, this is my sweet spot." Kyle surveyed the beach and crowd of people around us. "When I started windsurfing back in the eighties the sport was relatively unknown. Certainly nothing—nothing—like this."

I paused from my notes. "How many people do you expect this year?"

"Thousands." He brushed a strand of light hair out of his eye. "The sport became really popular in Europe in the seventies. It started making its way here back in the eighties. But I think there were maybe twenty or thirty of us who were serious about the sport. Hood River became kind of a legend. The professionals who were in Hawaii and Europe started hearing about the nuking winds we have here, and they had to come try them. That's how this area became famous. We worked hard to make it professional. It's been gaining respect ever since."

"Yeah, I just met a reporter from ESPN."

"Exactly. But that respect has come from years of stewardship; our mission is more than to provide a venue and competition for surfers. It's to raise the sport to a new level and be stewards of the beaches. Our organization does a ton of volunteering. We do beach cleanups, work with other nonprofit groups to provide access and protect the water. We're always looking to find new sites for windsurfing."

My hand worked as fast as it could to keep up with Kyle's words. I was impressed with his passion.

He pointed to a surfer who looked to be in his mid-forties, too, who was instructing a group of ten-year-olds. They all balanced on boards in the grass. "We also want to train this new generation of surfers to be safety conscious. It's a dangerous sport, but made even more dangerous by surfers who don't follow the rules."

"What do you mean?" I fanned myself with my notebook. The temperature was creeping up. I could smell hot dogs and sausages grilling at a nearby food stand.

"Not paying attention. Most accidents happen because boarders aren't paying attention to their surroundings and slam into someone. Kiters have been pushing the limits on speed, breaking fifty to sixty knots."

"Wow. That is crazy fast."

Kyle nodded. "Yeah, trust me, I've seen some nasty stuff over the years." He stared at the river where a group of newbies was practicing standing on surfboards. "So are you excited to get out on the water tomorrow? The wind forecast looks good."

I smiled, but internally my stomach swirled. "On the water?"

"Right." He pulled a sheet of paper from his clipboard. "I forgot to give you your itinerary. Top-tier press get to participate in a windsurfing demo. You'll actually have a chance to get out in the surf.

Bright and early tomorrow morning. Five a.m. Hosted by yours truly."

"Great." I gulped. Being comfortable in the water wasn't an issue for me. In fact, I was probably more comfortable in the water than on land, but I'd never been on a windsurfing board before and by the looks of the surfers flying out on the Columbia, I wasn't sure windsurfing was for me.

Before I had a chance to say more, we were distracted by a commotion. Justin Cruise and another surfer had their chests puffed out and were shouting at each other.

"Dude, back off!" Justin shoved the other surfer, who held his ground.

"You back off!" The surfer motioned for Justin to come at him. "You wanna go? We'll go."

Kyle swore under his breath. "Sorry, Meg. We'll continue this later. I've gotta go break those two up." He started toward Justin but stopped and turned to me. "I'd appreciate it if you didn't include this in your story. It's not exactly the image I'm hoping to portray."

"Of course." I nodded.

The fight escalated as Kyle pushed his way through the growing crowd. One of the bikini girls had inserted herself into their argument. Justin looked like he was about to knock her to the ground.

What was going on?

I kept my distance but couldn't look away. The

ESPN reporter came over and joined me. "Hey, Top Tier."

I'm sure I blushed.

"So those two are it again. Classic."

"Who's the other guy?" I pointed to the surfer fighting with Justin.

"Ian Schoonmaker. Always comes in second. And as you can see he doesn't like it."

"Ah."

"I can't really blame him. Justin's not exactly a gracious winner."

"You've covered this before, haven't you?"

"Every year, Top Tier." He winked.

"I'm so sorry. I'm an idiot. I don't know why, but somehow I always manage to say the wrong thing."

"Don't worry about it." He gave me a fatherly pat on the shoulder. "It's nice to see a young reporter who's not jaded and burnt-out yet." His press badge caught the sun. I couldn't make out his name.

"By the way, I'm Meg." I squinted and shaded my eyes from the sun. "Or you can just call me Top Tier."

"I like Top Tier. It feels right." He positioned his badge so I could read it. "Ryan Carter."

Ryan Carter. Great. Just great. Ryan Carter happened to be one of—if not the most—well-known sports writer on Twitter. Of course. *Classic Meg.*

We watched as Kyle broke up the fight. He looked less than pleased as he yanked Justin away by his shirtsleeve.

"So I take it Justin isn't well liked?"

The ESPN reporter moved his head from side to side. "I wouldn't say that. He's got his own groupies who follow him everywhere."

"They are groupies!" I pointed to the bikinis. "I knew it!"

"The true sign you've made it as a professional athlete."

"I guess." I grimaced.

"Oh, Top Tier, the fun is just beginning." Ryan winked and excused himself, telling me he'd see me at the demo tomorrow morning.

I spent the rest of the afternoon interviewing vendors and snapping pictures. My mouth was dry from the heat, and my eyes burned from all the dust blowing in the air. After four hours, I decided I had enough material to start my intro and post to our social media pages. Greg had put me in charge of our social accounts, and I was quite proud of the fact that I'd tripled our follower numbers in the past few months.

I crawled back to the house through the heat. Neither Jill nor Matt had arrived yet, so I cracked open a bottle of my favorite Double Mountain red ale and posted the day's pictures on *Northwest Extreme*'s social media pages. I loved coming up with quick and witty captions. Our audience had really started to engage, and I knew that was due to my efforts. Greg and the rest of the team were clueless in that department. It made me feel good that I was contributing something important and tangible.

After I finished with the updates, I spent about an hour typing my notes from the day. Then I curled up on the couch with a book.

I may have dozed off. The next thing I knew, the sound of laughter and footsteps on the front porch startled me awake. Matt and Jill had arrived.

"Megs!" Matt pounded on the door. "Let us in!"

I jumped to my feet as Matt made goofy faces at me through the window. "I didn't know you guys were coming together," I said, holding the door open. "I'm so glad you made it."

"Finally," Jill replied, flinging her arms around me and dropping her bag in the entryway. "This guy took forever." She pointed to Matt.

Matt closed the door behind him. "Hey, blame my editor." He patted a laptop bag slung over his shoulder. "Duty called."

Jill released me and winked at Matt. "I'm messing with you."

"What else is new?" Matt scowled, then grinned. "That's what I get for agreeing to spend a weekend with you two."

"You know you love us." I joined in the banter.

"He totally does," Jill said to me. "Actually, I had a brief to finish." She looked like she had come straight from the office. She wore a charcoal gray pencil skirt, a silk tank top and a matching suit jacket. "I cannot wait to get out of these clothes," she said, surveying the room. "This place is super cute. Nice find, Meg."

Matt nodded in agreement. "I'm impressed that

you found anything to rent. It's supposed be packed here this weekend."

"It is," I said, motioning them into the living room. "I hung out at the beach for a while this afternoon and it was already humming with tourists."

Jill kicked off her pumps and plopped on the couch. "The beach. Let's repeat that over and over again. The beach. My weekend is going to involve reading, sketching, drinking some great beer and planting my body on the warm sand."

"Did someone say beer?" Matt held up his index finger. "Hold that thought." He hurried outside and returned with a cooler. It had a built-in bottle opener on one side. He yanked off the lid and pulled out a bottle of microbrew. "Who wants one of these bad boys?" he asked as he popped the cap off the beer.

"I do!" Jill shot her arm in the air.

Matt handed her the bottle and grabbed another one from the cooler. "Megs?"

"No, thanks." I shook my head. "I have to be at the beach at five tomorrow morning for a lesson."

"Ouch." Matt grimaced as he cracked open the beer. "Five. That sucks for you."

"Tell me about it," I sighed. "Bad boys reminds me of a real-life bad boy I met today. Justin Cruise."

"Why does that name sound familiar?" Matt asked.

"He's one of the best surfers in the world. *The O* has probably run a number of features about him in the sports section," I said. "He's also a world-class jerk."

While they drank their beers, I filled them in on my run-in with Justin at the gaming shop and about him and Ian fighting on the beach.

"He sounds like a real winner," Jill said, finishing her beer and resting it on the coffee table.

"Yeah, and I have a feeling I'm not going to be able to avoid him this weekend," I said, pushing to my feet. "On that note, I've got to get to bed. I'll sneak out early, but let's meet at the beach tomorrow."

Matt held his beer in a toast and Jill blew me a kiss.

As I tucked into bed, I made a little wish that I wouldn't have to interact with Justin tomorrow. Apparently my fairy godmother was already asleep. Little did I know that I was about to do much more than interact with him.

# Chapter 4

Five came early the next morning. I hit the silence button on my phone and tugged on my swimsuit. Knowing that I was going to cover King of the Hook meant that I had to go swimsuit shopping before I left Portland. My usual swimsuit style is vintage, but I didn't think my halter top and swing skirt would fly. I found a sturdy hot-pink one-piece that would keep my ample chest in place and a matching rash guard. I'd never worn a rash guard before, but I decided I might from here on. It made me feel like I was more covered up, and it was surprisingly comfortable.

I tiptoed out without disturbing Jill and Matt, leaving a note on the kitchen table to let them know I'd meet them later.

Hood River sat in a quiet morning slumber. The shops were closed and bistro tables had been pushed inside for the night. As Kyle predicted, the wind had picked up. A strong west wind made the flags flutter and tossed dry leaves in the air. I hoped that wasn't a bad sign for my first windsurfing lesson.

I quickened my pace as I turned onto Second Street. The moon still hung bright overhead, and the air felt thick with the promise of heat. It was going to be another scorcher.

On the beach, a small group of press had gathered in front of Kyle, who was directing everyone into wetsuits and helmets. Unlike tropical locations like Hawaii, in the chilly waters of the Columbia wetsuits were required. I tugged on mine. Thank God it was still dark. I had a feeling the wetsuit wasn't as flattering as the rash guard. The moment that thought escaped my brain, a bank of huge floodlights clicked on, illuminating the beach and half of the river.

Great.

Kyle walked us through how to climb onto our boards, balance, and raise the sail. I tried to ignore the fear rising in my body as I mimicked his motions.

"You want to skim the water like this." Kyle leaned back on his board and mimicked the motion of gliding. He made it look easy. I knew better. Even on land I felt unsteady and shaky.

As we were about to enter the water, Justin Cruise strolled up. "Hey, dudes, wanna see how the pros do it?"

My colleagues all clapped. I caught Ryan Carter's eye. He gave me a knowing look, and mouthed, "Told you."

Justin slipped on his wetsuit in one easy move.

He flashed his signature hang loose sign and sprinted into the water. Before I could blink he was on his board, with his sail raised.

"Helmet!" Kyle shouted after Justin. Justin was already in the air. Kyle shook his head.

The reporter standing next to me started clicking photos of him. Drat. I should have brought my phone. I hadn't counted on industrial lights at o-dark-thirty.

A gust of wind blew down the river. Justin rode it with ease. He launched his board into the air and did a 180-degree turn.

"Whoa." I put my hand to my mouth.

Ryan nudged my arm. "That's nothing. Kid tricks. They don't call him Cruise Control for nothing. Watch."

He was right. Justin took off into orbit. He did an acrobatic summersault in the air, holding on to the board with one hand. After two loops he hit the water—hard.

"Ouch!" I winced. "Did he just break his back?"

Kyle overheard me and laughed. "No way. We live for rides like that." He pointed to the illuminated river. "He's doing what we call the body drag now, and then he's going carve for a minute."

Body drag. I shuddered. That didn't sound appealing.

I watched as Justin caught air so high that it looked like he could reach up and touch the birds overhead. He tacked back and forth on the stretch of river in front us. Then he spun the sail forward and backward until he finally sank into the surf.

"That's impressive," I said to Ryan.

"He's not number one for nothing. I told you he was good."

"And a jerk."

Kyle called us to attention as Justin sailed farther away from us and out of the spotlight. "Okay, the wind's kicking up a bit, which is going to be great for the competition later, but I want to get you out there now before it really starts blowing. The crew has your boards ready to go. Put on your helmets and follow me."

My heart thumped inside the snug wetsuit. What was I thinking? I couldn't do this.

"You can do this, Maggie. You are my water baby." I could hear Pops' voice in my head. After he died it took me by surprise when I heard his comforting voice in my head. Not anymore. Now I'd come to expect that he'd show up whenever I was in need of a familiar voice. For some reason I wasn't able to hear him when I tried. Only in times like this when my nerves were on high alert. Gam would probably say that was because I was able to connect with my higher self. Whatever the reason, I felt reassured (albeit slightly) by his words.

I waded into the cold water. It stung my feet. Every once in a while one of the freestyle surfers would fly into the spotlight and then disappear into the darkness again, like performers onstage at a Vegas show.

"First step. I want you to bring your boards out to waist-deep water," Kyle directed. "Watch those sails."

Some of my colleagues joked around as Kyle demonstrated how to get on the board and raise the sail. I shot them a look to pay attention when he started talking about wind direction and how to stop.

I hoped I would remember everything he said.

"Stay close to shore. The current . . ." Kyle's words were drowned out by the sound of a helicopter circling above.

"Don't worry about that." He shouted. "They're just shooting a preview of warm-ups for later."

Perfect. That was just what I needed. Arial footage of me floundering on a windsurfing board. I could picture the staff at *Northwest Extreme* watching streaming video of me looking like an idiot.

I pulled my board deeper into the water. What had Kyle said about the current? Waves lapped over my board and sail. *You got this, Meg.* I exhaled and climbed onto the board.

While everyone around me made the transition from their knees to standing with ease, I floated on my board, letting it gently bob on the river.

"On your feet, Meg!" Kyle called.

Right. I balanced on my knees and slowly found my way to standing. The helmet made my head feel heavy. I nearly fell off backward, twice. Kyle surfed over to me.

"You doing okay, Meg?"

"Yeah, I'm great," I lied. "I was just trying to get a feel for the current."

"Good." Kyle leaned off his board and held on with one hand. "You remember how to raise the mast?"

"Yep." I didn't move.

"Go ahead and give it a try."

I gulped. Have I mentioned that in addition to not being athletically inclined, I really don't like having to perform with someone watching?

"That's it. Up haul the sail." Kyle urged me on as I reached toward the sail, trying to maintain my balance and not bend forward too far. "Steady. Steady."

It didn't budge. I tightened my muscles and pulled harder.

"Awesome, Meg. That's it. Keeping it coming."

It felt like my biceps might rip in half. I put all my body weight into trying to raise the sail. Did it weigh more than me? I tried to keep my focus as the sail slowly emerged from the water.

"Almost there." Kyle cheered behind me. He was starting to get on my nerves.

Then finally with one last yank, the mast was upright. I couldn't believe it! I had actually done it!

"Nice job, Meg. Okay, follow me out this way, but be sure to . . ." The sound of his voice trailed off as he rode a wave the opposite direction.

Be sure to what? And what about the current? Why did he keep cutting off at the most important moments?

I gripped the mast. The board started moving.

It was working. Amazing! For a brief moment, I reveled in the fact that not only had I raised the sail and balanced on the board, but I was actually windsurfing. Kyle was a good instructor if he could get a klutz like me up and surfing this quickly.

No wonder windsurfing had been gaining popularity in the past few years. I could understand the lure of feeling the wind on my face and gliding gently over the waves. This was amazing!

Maybe this would be my new sport. Imagine how impressed everyone at *Northwest Extreme* would be to see me now. The helicopter circled above. I wanted to wave but figured letting go, even with one hand, probably wasn't the wisest idea.

As Gam would say, enjoy being fully present in the moment. I was definitely present and acutely aware of the sound of my breathing, the dampness of my feet, and filled with pride that I'd finally succeeded in an outdoor adventure.

Suddenly the light changed. Or—went out. I was plunged in darkness. What happened?

I realized that I'd floated past the perimeter of floodlights and was sailing blind.

*You need to stop, Meg.*

That's when I realized that I'd forgotten to get one critical piece of information from Kyle: I had no idea how to turn around.

# Chapter 5

I knew that Kyle had said something about turning, but that was when everyone around me was talking. Plus, I hadn't planned to go any farther than a few feet away from shore. I figured if I needed to turn around, worst-case scenario I could jump in and swim.

That wasn't an option here. I was far from shore. Really far.

Had Kyle said something about holding the sail still and turning the board with our feet? Or was it that we were supposed to let go with one hand and lean in that direction?

Neither sounded like a great option, but I had to do something and soon. Panic rose in the back of my throat. I couldn't swallow. This was bad.

The wind gusted harder, pushing me over choppy waves. Swells came faster and faster. I dug my feet into the board, trying to maintain contact with my toes.

I decided to try to let go with one hand. I was at

least seventy-five percent confident that had been Kyle's instruction.

*Do it now, Meg. Don't wimp out.*

With one hand clutched on the mast, I slowly let go with the other and leaned to the side. For a split second I thought it worked. The board wobbled with my shifting weight.

Then a wave hit and I lost control.

I fell backward into the river. Water flooded up my nose.

Kicking hard to the surface, I gasped for air. The shock of falling and the frigid temperature of the water also cranked my adrenaline into high gear. I paddled as hard as I could. Thank goodness my foot was tethered to the board, I thought as I pulled myself back on.

Now what? I thought as I shivered with fear and cold.

Under the bright lights in the distance I could see the rest of my group. Had anyone noticed that I was gone? Kyle had been right in front of me. If he didn't know that I was missing, he would realize it soon, right? It looked like there was a boat near a sandbar in the middle of the river. I wondered if I could make it in that direction.

Nope. The wind continued to surge. The waves took on an ominous appearance. For the first time I had a pretty good idea why Kyle had warned us about the current. It had swept me at least three quarters of the way across the river. The current was in control. Not me.

I had to get back to the group. Otherwise at this rate I might be swept all the way back to Portland.

The scent of fear and freshwater hung heavy in the air. Time to raise the mast—again.

My entire body rebelled in a series of quivers and shakes as I crawled onto my knees. The board rocked in the surf. *How am I going to do this?*

I tugged, yanked, and pulled—nothing. The water-logged sail wouldn't budge.

Water pounded the mast, making it nearly impossible for me to raise it. The churning waves under the grainy board felt like an evil puppeteer directing me wherever it pleased. I tried one more time, clutching the board with my toes and heaving with all my might.

It worked. The mast, free from the water, caught a giant gust of wind and lifted the board a foot into the air. This time it didn't feel fun.

I held on for dear life as the board came crashing back toward the surf. It hit the water and launched me off into the river again.

I gasped for air as wave after wave assaulted me. Swimming against the current and *into* the wind felt like I was treading water. Despite all the time I'd spent in the pool, I felt like someone who was just learning to swim. For each stroke I took, the wind and waves knocked me back twice as far.

*Meg, focus.*

I kicked with all my might. My legs felt heavy as if the current was intentionally yanking them deeper down into the water.

*Kick, kick, kick. Kick, kick, kick.* I sang the mantra aloud.

Was there a boat nearby? I could have sworn I heard the sound of a motor over the wind.

Climbing back on the board in the worsening conditions wasn't pretty to say the very least. I basically hauled my body on the board.

What to do next? I could try to paddle back across the river, lying flat on the board, but that would mean dragging the mast through the water. I didn't think I'd get very far using that strategy. I scanned around me. There was no sign of a boat. It must have been my imagination. The sun had begun to rise, casting a halo on the cliffs in front of me.

The cliffs in front of me.

My heart thumped. *The cliffs in front of me.*

*Oh. My. God.* The cliffs were right in front of me.

I was almost to the Washington side of the river and about to crash into the rough and rocky shoreline. There weren't any beaches on this stretch, just a jagged jetty.

I tried screaming for help. I'm not sure why. I knew that no one could hear me, but at least I was doing something. That's when I spotted another windsurfer only a few feet away.

*Thank goodness.*

I paddled hard in the direction of the windsurfer, yelling "Help!" until my lungs burned. As I inched closer something about the board seemed off. By the time I was a few feet away I realized what it was. There was no one standing on the board. The person on the board was missing.

When I finally reached the board, I let out another scream. This one for a totally different reason. I recognized the board. It belonged to Justin Cruise. I also realized the person on the board wasn't missing. His body was a short distance away, dragging along the harsh rocks.

# Chapter 6

*This can't be happening, can it?* My brain tried to process what I was seeing in front of me while my hands kept a death grip on my board. *A death grip.* Here I was in the grip of death again.

I gulped down my fear along with a healthy dose of spray and tried to paddle closer to the body. Maybe I'd made a mistake. My eyes were probably playing tricks on me. Right?

The choppy water pushed the body closer to the shore. Normally the sturdy Washington cliffs reminded me of towering protectors, as if it were their job to contain the river. But now they looked wicked and ominous, like they were pulling me in to be devoured by their jagged rocks.

*Meg, you have to keep moving.*

Somehow my body obeyed my command. I plunged my arms back into the water. My hands were numb and raw. I couldn't feel my feet. Time blurred as I paddled as hard as I could up the river.

I tried to grab the board, but it slipped through

my hands. Without anyone riding it to weigh it down, it washed downriver.

"Justin!" I shouted, stretching every muscle in my neck. "Are you okay?" Internally I knew why Justin wasn't responding, but for some reason I couldn't stop trying to help him. Maybe it's always that way in an emergency, even if there's no hope you have to try, right? I'd learned that from the Crag Rats, my friends and volunteer mountain rescuers. Regardless of how bleak a situation appeared to be, they forged ahead, fully focused on their mission of rescue. Some of their dedication must have rubbed off on me.

Justin's body banged into the rocks again. How was it staying in one place in this surf?

As I got closer, I realized why he wasn't floating down the river. His wetsuit was stuck on a rock.

Had he crashed? What was he doing this far out? Nothing made sense.

*Meg, you don't have time to think about it now.*

I had a decision to make and fast. With the Washington cliffs looming precariously close, I had one shot—and only one—at grabbing Justin. While he wasn't responding, and I was pretty certain I knew why, I had to try and see if there was something I could do. I couldn't just leave him to get swept downriver.

I clutched my board with my right hand and curled my toes around the bottom. I stretched my left hand out as far as it would reach.

*Damn, why do you have to be so short, Meg?* The board was too far.

A wave hit the front of the board. I nearly lost my grip.

*This is stupid. Why am I risking my life for someone who is such a jerk?*

Because you're not a jerk, Maggie. Pops' voice gave me an instant surge of adrenaline. Sucking in my breath, I reached out again. The tips of my fingers grazed Justin's wetsuit. I held on with my pinky. *You can do this, Meg.*

The veins in my arms bulged as I tried to keep my grip on Justin's wetsuit. I gave a hard tug and his body freed itself from the rocks.

*Now what?*

My heart pounded so hard I thought it might leap from my chest. My throat tightened. I had to roll Justin over. The Crag Rats had trained me well. I focused on their mission of always going for the rescue no matter what.

*Don't panic, Meg.* I used all my strength to roll Justin over.

I didn't want to look at his face, but I knew I had to.

*You can do this, Meg.* I blew air out of my mouth in a long exhale and then examined his face. There was a nasty gash on his forehead. Had he fallen on the rocks?

The river slammed straight into the side of the cliff, waves pounded rhythmically over and over again. I scanned the hillside for any patch of land. The sun had risen, offering a welcoming glow on the river.

I couldn't be sure, but it looked like there was a

break in the rocks about twenty feet ahead. It could be an illusion, a bend in the river, but it was my only hope.

There was one major problem. How to get there? If I let go of Justin, he'd get sucked down the river. My only option was to kick.

*Kick, kick, kick. Kick, kick, kick.* I reverted back to my childhood mantra.


Mother made me join a swim team when I was in the fourth grade. Swimming came naturally to me. Probably in part because Pops started taking me to the pool when I was still in diapers. I'd never had any formal lessons. He taught me with his gentle nudging.

"That's right, Maggie. One big breath. Let it out slowly."

I remember feeling so independent when Pops would bring me to the pool and let me splash around on my own while he swam laps. I loved the musty smell of bleach and chlorine, and how the light from above cut through the clear water. Swimming was an integral part of his writing ritual. He used to say that the water helped the words flow.

Mother, as usual, didn't approve. "Charlie, she can't play in the pool while you swim laps. It's not safe."

Pops chuckled and waved her off. "It's fine, darling. I'm right there."

"You're not there. You're off in your own head, like usual. You wouldn't even notice if she slipped under the water. No! She needs supervision. I signed her up for swim team."

I remember the feeling of panic that invaded my body, even at the age of ten. The swim team kids looked like animated robots from the cover of one of Pops' sci-fi novels. I'd watched them with their matching black Speedos and skintight swim caps, while I floated on a kickboard. It didn't look like they were having much fun. They dove off starting blocks and swam lap after lap with their coach pacing beside them, shouting commands from the deck. Nope, that was not for me.

But Mother insisted. The next week I stood on the humid pool deck in my black Speedo, feeling sick to my stomach as Pops introduced me to the coach.

"Don't worry, Maggie." He patted my swim cap. "You'll be a swimming star in no time."

I didn't believe him, and for good reason. The first day of swim practice I couldn't even keep up. The other kids flew across the pool, as if they were skimming the surface. My body seemed to drag along the bottom. My lungs burned. I gasped for air. My face burst with color. I hated every minute of it.

On the drive home, I sulked. Pops stopped at our favorite drive-through for banana milkshakes.

"Why the long face, Maggie?"

"I hated it, Pops. I was terrible. I was the worst one there."

He took a long sip of his shake and met my eye in the rearview mirror. "That could be true." He paused and took another drink. "Or maybe it was your first day and you were finding your legs."

"I don't want to go back. It was too hard. Please don't make me. Please."

"Your mother knows best." He gave me a knowing smile. "You know, Maggie, one of the things that I've learned in life is that it's usually the things that are the hardest that teach us the most."

"What does that mean?" I sucked icy chunks of bananas through my straw.

Pops tried to explain his philosophy, but my ten-year-old brain couldn't comprehend why anyone would *intentionally* want to do something hard. I drank my shake in the backseat and blamed Mother for forcing me to do yet another activity that I had no interest in.

It turned out that he was right. I ended up loving swim team, not that I'd ever admit that to Mother. After that first day I slowly and steadily improved. I came to love the smell of chlorine on my skin, the fact that my hair was always tinted green, and that I was part of a team of kids who all felt as comfortable in the water as they did on land. I loved the sound of the starting gun, the feeling of flying off the blocks and the thrill of winning my first race. Swim team boosted my confidence. The pool became a place of respite and my second home.

As I kicked toward the cutout in the river I said a silent prayer of thanks to those years on swim team.

Kicking drills were part of our everyday routine. I'd grab a blue foam kickboard and warm-up with 200 yards of power kicking. *That's what you're doing now, Meg. Just like practice—kick, kick, kick.*

But my legs felt like butter. I hadn't made much progress. This wasn't working.

Suddenly the helicopter flew above me. Was someone looking for me? How long had I been gone?

I desperately wanted to let go of my board and wave frantically, but I had to settle on stretching my face to the sky and yelling as loud as I could. I knew there was no chance the helicopter could hear me, but maybe if they were close enough they'd see that I was in trouble. What was the universal sign for help in the water?

The helicopter made a giant circle around me. *Have they noticed?* I held my breath. *Please stop.*

Then it turned and flew back toward the opposite side of the river.

So much for that.

I continued to kick. I knew I wasn't getting anywhere, but I didn't care. It was as if I'd slipped into some kind of kicking trance. As long as my feet kept hitting the water, I was doing something.

Exhaustion swept over me like the waves. I wasn't sure how much longer I could hold on. Justin's body was heavy, and the surf was unrelenting.

Just as I was about to give up and let go, I heard the sound of a motor nearby. Out of the corner of my eye I caught a glimpse of a speedboat zooming toward me.

*Thank God.* I exhaled.

Everything happened in a flash. The boat sped to a stop. A random wave sent a new batch of waves over me, as I stopped swimming at the sight of the boat. I lost my grip on Justin.

I couldn't see through the wall of water. Was I going under? I held my breath.

The next thing I knew, a burly hand reached out and scooped me from the river in one move. The boat rocked on the water as another rescuer jumped into the river and swam over to my board. He climbed on, lifted the mast, and surfed into the wind.

*How did he make it look so easy?*

One of the members of the rescue team in a bright orange Coast Guard jacket handed me a blanket. "Wrap up in this. You're shivering." Then he unbuckled my helmet. My head felt instantly lighter.

I took the blanket and wrapped it around my shoulders. What was happening? I felt disoriented. An American flag secured to the cabin whipped in the wind. The words COAST GUARD were printed across the sides of the inflatable orange raft.

The Coast Guard rescuer stood with his legs spread wide for balance and gave me a look over. "How'd you get out this far?"

I glanced at the cliffs as the rescuer whistled and motioned for the pilot to turn the boat back to Oregon.

The boat did a one-eighty and bounced over the

chop. I dug my hands into the heavy rubber seat and held on.

Every cell in my body fired in slow motion as I tried to grasp what was happening. "Wait!" I shouted, and held out my hand.

The rescuer turned to the pilot and cut his hand across his throat. The boat's engine hummed to a stop. He came and sat next to me. "What's up? You forget something out there?"

"No, Justin's out there."

"Who's Justin?"

"Justin Cruise. The windsurfer."

"What about him?"

"He had an accident! He must have fallen. I think he's dead. He wasn't moving."

The rescuer shot me a look like I was crazy. He held up three fingers and scooted closer. "How many fingers am I holding up?"

"Three."

He held his index finger in front of my face. "Can you follow my finger?" He moved his finger from side to side and up and down. Did he think I had a concussion?

I followed it for a moment and then pushed it away. "Listen, I didn't hit my head or anything. I'm totally fine. I mean—no—I'm not fine. I'm wet, cold and freaked out. But you have to turn the boat around. Justin Cruise is dead and he's floating down the river."

The rescuer took another look at my face and

scowled. He grabbed my wrist to check my pulse. "You're going to have to start from the beginning."

"Listen. I'm telling you. He's dead. I found him on the rocks. I held on as long as I could, but I lost him in this wind and when you showed up the waves were just too strong."

"Did you say Justin Cruise?"

"Yes!" I could feel my pulse quickening as he held my wrist. The shock was wearing off. I was becoming surer of myself with every word.

"Please. You have to turn the boat around. He's that way." I pointed behind me with my free hand.

"You're sure?" He looked skeptical.

"Positive."

He shrugged and stood.

I watched him balance his way to the front. He leaned down and whispered something in the pilot's ear. They both looked at me and then huddled together again. After what seemed like a brief debate, the pilot steered the boat to where they'd just recovered me.

We cruised along the cliffs for a few minutes. I wasn't sure if they believed me. But the pilot slowed the motor and they both scanned the rocks.

After a few minutes the rescuer came over to me. "No sign of anything here. We're going to go ahead and get you back to shore. I think you're probably in shock."

I started to protest, but the pilot jumped to his feet. "Look!" he shouted as Justin's board floated past us.

# Chapter 7

In a flash of bright orange, the rescuer dove into the water. The pilot motioned for me to stay where I was. I watched in a daze as the rescue swimmer reached Justin's board. He shook his head and stuck one thumb down.

The pilot sped over and helped hoist the rescue swimmer and Justin's battered board onto the boat.

"No sign of a body." The swimmer held on to the side of the boat and continued to scan the choppy surf. "You better call the dive team."

"We have a witness reporting an adult male swimmer who's gone under," the pilot reported on a radio.

The rocking motion of the boat made my stomach queasy. I wrapped my arms around myself tighter.

"You okay?" the pilot asked.

I nodded. "I'm fine."

Within minutes another boat arrived. The sound of the helicopter's blades buzzed above us. It circled as low as possible. I guessed they were trying to get a tight shot. In some ways I couldn't blame them. The pressure for getting exclusive, breaking news had led journalists to do much worse, but I instinctively wanted to somehow shield Justin from such a blatant attempt to capitalize on his misfortune.

The Coast Guard pilot must have felt the same way. He motioned to the chopper, trying to get them to stop filming. The helicopter rose about ten feet higher and continued to circle. The pilot scowled. "Vultures."

"Yeah," I agreed. Orange life vests dotted the water. The diver was already in the water.

The pilot killed the motor. He stood and navigated the rocking boat with ease. Sitting next to me, he patted my knee. "I need to give the team some direction. Can you tell me exactly where you spotted the body?"

I pointed to the cliff. "Over there. I think." I wasn't sure. The rocks all looked the same.

He asked me when I'd first noticed Justin's body and how long I'd been on the water. I couldn't remember. Everything blurred together. So much for being a reliable witness.

After the pilot finished trying to jog my short-term memory, he returned to the helm. "You ready?" He had to shout over the sound of the chopper and the motor of the second rescue boat.

"For what?"

"I'm taking you back to the beach. Hold on."

"What about Justin?"

"We've got a team in the water. If there's a body out there, they'll find it. Ready?"

I nodded.

He didn't waste any time. The boat throttled to life and zoomed over the cresting waves. Good thing he told me to hold on. I dug my fingers into the rubber seat, afraid that if I didn't hold on I'd get launched back out to the river.

It only took a few minutes to get back to the other side. The pilot helped me out of the boat and pointed to the police cars with lights flashing in the parking lot. "Don't go too far. They're going to want to take your statement."

"Okay." I handed him the blanket.

He wrapped it back around my shoulders. "Keep it. It looks like you still need it."

I was glad for the warmth of the blanket on my shoulders. It felt like I'd been out on the river for hours. The beach had completely transformed since I took off for my ill-fated adventure.

Onshore it was total chaos. Rescue divers and swimmers raced off in another boat. Five police cars, an ambulance and two fire trucks were parked on the beach with their lights flashing. It looked like some kind of laser light show. Who knew that Hood River had so many rescue vehicles?

Kyle stood near a group of windsurfers, his wetsuit hung halfway down on his body. He shouted orders and pointed to the Washington cliffs. Media and vendors had swarmed around the banks of the river with cameras and cell phones directed toward the activity on the other side of the river. Word had spread fast, and everyone was jockeying for position.

I pushed my way through the crowd. On the beach a few feet away from the throng of bystanders, a woman sat sobbing and staring at the river. Another woman towered over her. She yelled at the sobbing woman, who ignored her and continued to gaze at the water.

*What is going on with those two?* I tried to look away but couldn't. The woman sitting on the beach threw her hands over her face and rocked back and forth on her knees. The screaming woman finally gave up and stormed away. I almost stopped to console the sobbing woman, but at that moment I bumped into Matt.

"Megs! Where have you been? I've been looking everywhere for you." He grabbed my shoulders and then took a step back. "What happened? Are you okay?"

I swallowed hard as tears welled in my eyes and a lump formed in the back of my throat.

"Megs?" Matt scooped me into his arms. I couldn't hold it together. Tears flooded my eyes. He held me tighter. I collapsed in his embrace. He smelled like he just stepped out of the shower and of fresh wintergreen gum.

I knew that my tears were my body's response to stress. Gam would say, "Let them flow. Your body is naturally cleansing the negative energy." It felt like a cleanse. I wiped my nose on the back of my wetsuit and freed myself from Matt's hug. "Sorry. I didn't mean to do that. I just kind of lost it."

Matt repositioned the blanket around my shoulders and left his hand on my arm. It felt solid and warm. "It's okay. What's going on?"

"Did you hear the news?" I bent my head in the direction of the frenzy of activity on the beach.

"Only that someone had an accident." Matt shoved his hands in his short pockets and looked at the ground. "I knew you were on the river. It freaked me out when I couldn't find you." He paused and met my eyes. "I was worried about you."

"Sorry."

Matt's expression softened. "Come on. Let's go sit down." He guided me to a nearby bench.

I took a seat and shrugged off the blanket. Sitting felt good. I hadn't realized how shaky my legs were.

As if reading my mind, Matt reached into the messenger bag slung over his shoulder. "Hungry?" He handed me a granola bar.

"Starving." I took the bar, but my fingers shook too hard for me to open it.

Matt gently took it from my hands and ripped it open in one quick move. He crumbled up the wrapper, shoved it in his pocket, and handed the bar to me. "Eat. And breathe. In that order."

I grinned and saluted him. "Yes, sir."

"Megs. Don't mess with me."

"Sorry." I ate a hunk of the bar. Chocolate almond. My favorite.

"So are you going to tell me what happened out

there?" Matt leaned back on the bench and crossed one leg over his knee. He wore a T-shirt with the silhouette of an alien. It read: WATCH OUT. THEY'RE COMING. His Keen sandals were coated in a dusting of sand.

"Don't you want to take that off?" he asked.

"What?"

He tugged on my wetsuit. "This. It doesn't look very comfortable."

"Good idea." I set the granola bar on the bench and tried yanking my arms free from the tight suit. It didn't budge.

Matt laughed. "Here." He straightened my arms and rolled the wetsuit down to my waist.

"Thanks." I polished off the granola bar and let out a long sigh. Matt listened intently while I replayed everything that had happened from getting stuck on the river to finding Justin.

"Geez, Megs. How do you keep getting yourself into situations like this?"

My nerves were already frayed and Matt's tone set them off. "I didn't get myself into any situation. It's not like I asked to get stuck out in the river, or to find Justin."

"I'm sorry." He put his arm around my shoulder. "I know you didn't mean to, but for some reason danger seems to find you no matter where you go." He removed his arm and looked me in the eye.

My heart thumped. Had his eyes always been that blue?

"It's *Northwest Extreme*. You have to quit. You can't keep doing this."

Matt and I had been having this same discussion—or debate, depending on your perspective—for the past few months. He was convinced that Greg was involved in Pops' death. I wasn't sure who to believe.

Getting the job at *Northwest Extreme* had seemed like a happy accident—a chance encounter with a pink umbrella had led to my first official writing gig. Only I came to learn that there was nothing "chance" about meeting Greg. He'd been tracking me for months before "accidentally" running into me at my favorite coffee shop last winter. I found a file with notes about me, clips of my collegiate writing and tons of notes and clippings on Pops' Meth Madness story, an exposé on Oregon's drug epidemic that ultimately got him killed.

At first I agreed with Matt. Why had Greg been watching me? And why lie about needing to hire a junior reporter? But when I'd confronted Greg, he didn't even flinch. I expected him to try to pretend like he hadn't done any of those things, but instead he came clean. He apologized for lying but said that he'd done it to protect me. He swore that he'd been asked to keep me under his wing in order to keep me safe.

I know I still have a lot to learn, but reading people has always been an innate skill set of mine. I believed Greg, despite the fact that I didn't fully trust him. Matt, on the other hand, had been begging me to leave *Northwest Extreme* ever since. I didn't want to leave, but I was worried that my decision to stay was going to drive a wedge between us. I couldn't let that happen. Matt was my best friend.

Matt's voice stirred me from my thoughts. "Megs? Are you even listening?"

"What?" I returned my attention to the present moment.

"I said, 'Are you listening?' When are you going to give Greg your notice? You have enough clips and legit experience to get a job somewhere else now."

"Let's not do this again." I sighed. "I thought we made a deal to table this for a while. I really can't do this right now."

"I know. Sorry." Matt brushed a stray strand of hair from my face. His voice was thick with emotion. "Megs, you know the only reason I keep asking is because I don't want to see you hurt, right?"

"Yeah, but I'm not going to get hurt."

"Ha!" Matt's hands flew in the air. "What just happened out there?"

"Stop. Please?" I gave him a pleading look. "Can we talk about this later?"

Matt frowned. "Yeah, but we're not done with this. I'm not just going to let this go."

"I know." The sun baked my wetsuit. It was dry and starting to feel hot against my legs.

He pulled me to my feet. "Let's get you back to

the house. You need a hot shower and some new clothes."

"That sounds great." I smiled.

As we started to walk toward town, a voice hollered behind us.

"Ms. Reed?"

I turned around to see a police officer flagging us down.

He caught up to us in three long steps. "Are you Ms. Reed?"

"Yeah?" I glanced at Matt.

"I need you to come with me, please."

Matt stepped forward. "What's this about, Officer?"

The police officer gave Matt a funny look. I could feel him thinking "stupid kids," but he gave us both a fake smile, and said, "I need to take the little lady's statement if that's okay with you?"

Matt looked at me and rolled his eyes.

"I'll meet you back at the house," I said.

"You want me to wait for you?"

"No, it's fine. I'll see you later." I walked off with the officer, wondering if anything was fine these days.

# Chapter 8

The officer steered me to the parking lot where the emergency vehicles waited, their lights still flashing. Shouldn't someone turn those off? It was hardly as if Justin was going to need to be whisked off to the hospital in an ambulance.

"Wait here, Ms. Reed." The officer pointed to two folding chairs propped open on the asphalt. I hadn't even noticed how quickly the temperature had risen since I'd been rescued. The sun fell like a laser on the pavement, baking the ground. Heat radiated on my feet as I sat in one of the empty chairs. I tugged the wetsuit the rest of the way off and hung it over the back of the chair. Much better.

I waited for at least fifteen minutes, watching as firefighters and police officers roped off certain areas of the beach and buzzed around barking orders on walkie-talkies. Why were they limiting access to the beach?

An officer on a bullhorn directed people gathered with their cameras to clear the area. Another officer pushed them away from the shore with his hands, like a dog herding sheep.

"Ms. Reed?" A tall, thin police officer cleared his throat and looked down at me.

"Yep, that's me."

He sat in the chair next to me and flipped through a yellow legal pad to a blank sheet of paper. "I have a few questions for you."

"Right." I sighed. "Go for it."

"Are you okay?" He tilted his head to the side and studied me.

"I'm fine. I'm sorry. I'm just a little on edge." To showcase this, I extended my hands, which were still shaky. I could use a zap of Gam's Reiki to help calm and center me right about now.

"Understandable." He clicked a pen. "I'm going to need to ask you a few questions. Are you okay to proceed?"

I let out a little laugh. "Yep, I know the drill."

"Excuse me?"

*Meg, you're an idiot.* "I just meant that this isn't my first dead body. That's all."

"Not your first?" The police officer scribbled something on the legal pad and appraised me with new interest. "Care to elaborate?"

I explained how I'd stumbled upon not one but two bodies in the past year. He didn't look pleased when I assured him that it was purely by accident.

"Are you telling me that you've had previous experiences with two suspicious deaths?"

"When you put it like that it sounds bad."

"In my line of work that is bad, especially since we haven't even recovered a body. Are you suggesting murder? Is there something else you need to tell me?"

I shook my head.

Our conversation didn't improve from there. It just got worse. The police officer let me go, but not before warning me—repeatedly—that he would be in touch and I was not to leave town while the investigation was active.

I left the wetsuit in a pile on the beach and started back to the house in a fog.

"Megs! Wait up!" Matt called from behind me.

"Where'd you come from?" I asked, slowing my pace. "I thought you were going back to the house."

"I decided to wait for you."

"You didn't have to do that."

"I know I didn't *have to*. I wanted to." He offered me his hand. "Are you going to let me walk you home or not?"

"Probably not." I made a funny face and grabbed his hand. The moment our hands touched I felt the familiar tingle of butterflies flopping around in my stomach. I almost let go, but Matt squeezed my hand in a solid, reassuring way.

"Come on, surfer girl." He slung his laptop bag over his shoulder and tightened his grasp on my hand.

We weaved through the morning crowds on the sidewalk. People carried paper coffee cups and noshed on sticky buns and bagels. Lines had queued in front of restaurants for breakfast. I could smell bacon frying as we passed by. My mouth salivated.

"You wanna grab a bite?" Matt stopped in front of a coffeehouse.

"Not with these lines. It's worse than the line for Sunday brunch in Portland."

Portland is notorious for its Sunday brunch rush. Bunch is our version of church. Restaurants in every quadrant of the city cater to large crowds on Sunday mornings, offering artisan coffee and small bites while people wait for hours for a plate of cage-free scrambled eggs and a Bloody Mary. I much prefer to hit my favorite haunts when they're not packed with hipsters.

Matt and I turned off Second Street and started up the hill. We passed Double Mountain Brewery. The brewing team must have gotten an early start. Matt paused to breathe in the scent of grains boiling.

"Aaah. Barley."

Farther up the block, Sherman stood in front of The Quest wearing his signature cape, and a group of teenage boys stood outside his shop, wiping down the windows with wet rags.

"Hey, Sherman," I called out. "What happened?"

Sherman dropped his rag in a bucket of water on the sidewalk. It splashed one of the kids, who proceeded to intentionally dump his rag in the water to create a bigger splash. A water fight broke out between the boys. They flicked each other with their wet rags.

"Knock it off." Sherman tapped on the window. "We can't get back into the game until we clean up this mess."

"What happened?" I asked, stepping closer.

Sherman fumed. "Justin Cruise and his surfer friends egged my store this morning."

"They did?" Upon closer inspection I noticed that the window had been splattered with gooey egg.

"Classic." Sherman grabbed his rag and rang it out over the bucket.

"How do you know it was Justin, though?"

"Who else would it be?"

I gave Matt a questioning look. He shook his head. "Sherman, I don't think you've met my friend Matt."

Matt dropped my hand and extended his other hand to Sherman. "Hey, nice to meet you, man."

"About Justin," I started to say.

Matt shot me a look and cut me off. "Is that an original Millennium Falcon I see on display in there?"

Sherman's dark eyes brightened. "You're a fan?"

"Is there a better movie on the planet?"

"Nope." Sherman paused. "Wait, *New Hope* or the special edition?"

"Duh." Matt scowled. "*New Hope.*"

"Good answer. Good answer."

"What are you two even talking about?" I asked. "You sound like you're speaking a foreign language."

Matt pretended to stab himself in the chest. "Have

I taught you nothing, young Padawan? We're only talking about the best movie of all time."

"*Star Trek?*"

Sherman rolled his eyes. Matt groaned.

"What?"

"*Star Wars!*" They shouted in unison.

I shrugged. "Same difference."

"See what I'm up against?" Matt said to Sherman. "Megs, you're killing me." Matt was always incensed that I didn't agree that *Star Wars* was "the greatest movie ever made." I'm much more inclined to watch 1950s vintage movies. They just don't make them the same way these days. Give me Cary Grant and Grace Kelly any day.

Sherman watched as the kids scrubbed the windowsill. "You want to come check out the Falcon?"

Matt glanced inside and then back at me. "Would you rather head back and take a rest?"

"Actually a distraction might be nice."

"Okay," Matt said to Sherman. "It looks like you've also got a crazy collection of droids. Megs, you're going to have to hold me back, otherwise I might go broke."

"The biggest collection on the west coast." Sherman swelled with pride. He turned to the kids. "Nice work, paladins." He tapped a tall, skinny kid wearing a Batman T-shirt with his sword. "Jordan, you're in charge."

Sherman held the door open for Matt and me. Three steps led down into the underground store. The front section housed shelves with a variety of prank and joke items, like a camera that squirted water and a severed finger with fake blood. Glass cases packed with trading cards lined the far wall. Swords, knives, armor and every weapon imaginable hung from the opposite wall.

"It smells like armpits in here," I whispered to Matt as Sherman directed us toward the *Star Wars* section.

Matt grinned. "Welcome to the world of gaming. Questionable hygiene, pasty skin—it's all part of the fun."

"Here's the Falcon." Sherman waved a flabby arm across the toy with reverence. Matt responded with brevity. I wandered around the store while they geeked out.

The back section of the store had rows of model airplanes, trains and remote-control cars along with a large selection of costumes. Toys and gaming paraphernalia hung from the ceiling with fishing wire.

"Pretty cool, huh?" The tall, skinny kid came up behind me as I studied sci-fi posters tacked to the walls.

"Yeah, cool," I lied.

"We don't get many girls in here." He wiped his eggy hands on his Batman T-shirt.

Shocker.

I suddenly felt exposed in my swimsuit and cover-up. "What's with all the tables?" I said aloud, walking toward a bank of long folding tables at the very back of the store.

"This is where we game." He pointed to a poster board with a schedule of games running throughout the day. "Sherman always has awesome stuff going on. You should play. We're doing D&D today."

"Maybe." I tried to keep my tone noncommittal. "I'm more of a swimmer than a gaming kind of girl."

"Really? You swim? Me too?" He laced his bony fingers together and stretched his arms over his head. "I hold the record for the hundred-meter fly at my high school."

"You fly?" I was impressed. The butterfly is my least favorite stroke. I prefer freestyle or breast-stroke.

He pointed to the other kids outside. "Yeah, they call me king of fly."

"Like King of the Hook?"

He let out a bitter laugh. "No, I don't surf. Those guys are cool, but you know, I'm kind of like king of the nerds."

"Hey, king of anything is good, right?"

He blushed, making his acne look like it was aflame. This was awkward. I felt sorry for the kid.

I noticed a large sheet was draped over one of the tables. It looked like there was something bulky underneath it. Before I could ask what it was, Sherman leaped in front of me. "Don't touch that!" He gave Jordan a funny look. "This is a top-secret project we're working on."

"Top secret." Matt put his arm around my shoulder. "You shouldn't say that around Megs. She's a top-notch investigative reporter, right, Megs?" He winked.

Sherman tucked the sheet around his top-secret project.

"Well, ready to go?" Matt asked me.

I could have kissed him right there. "Yeah, let's hit it."

Matt thanked Sherman for showing him around. Sherman instructed Jordan to stand guard in front of their secret project. He gave him another funny look as he walked us to the front of the shop. "Come back anytime. We're going to be doing some D&D later if you want to join in." He flicked his cape as he opened the front door.

Matt put his arm around my shoulder. "I might have to take you up on that."

"Top-secret project?" I laughed as we walked away.

"They're probably trying to build a hover board."

"Hover board?"

"Megs, come on! *Back to the Future?* You, my friend, need a serious schooling on awesome eighties movies."

Before I could craft a witty comeback, the woman who I'd seen yelling at the sobbing beach babe on the shore came racing up to us. We stopped in front of a flower shop. Huge bunches of fresh-cut lavender were tied with raffia. The smell reminded me of Gam.

"Hey, sorry to bug you, but you're not with the sports network, are you?" she asked Matt.

"Nope, *The O*." Matt removed his arm from my shoulder. "Matt Parker, technology."

I suddenly became very conscious of my appearance. I glanced at my reflection in the flower-shop window. Ugh. My hair had dried flat and was sticking out in all the wrong places. And maybe the rash guard wasn't as flattering as I thought. I tugged it away from my stomach.

The woman grinned at Matt. "I'm Avery Jones."

They shook hands for a moment longer than necessary. Was she flirting? I mean, I know that Matt's cute and everything, but it wasn't like he was drop-dead gorgeous like Greg. I was used to women ogling over my boss, but not my friend. I was a little surprised by how much I didn't like it. Not one bit.

"I'm Meg Reed." I extended my hand and broke their grasp. "*Northwest Extreme*. Maybe I can help you?"

Avery took a step back. She definitely belonged on the water. I could tell by the way she held her athletic body in an easy, balanced stance. Her auburn hair was tied back in a teal bandana, and her matching sculpted rash guard touted a woman's windsurfing competition.

"Are you competing in King of the Hook?" I asked.

Avery put her hand flat to her stomach. "I'm not sure. I might have to bow out of this one. I'm fighting off a touch of something."

*Great. I'm glad you just shook our hands,* I thought

internally. I couldn't tell from Matt's expression whether or not he agreed.

"What do you need the sports network for?" he asked.

Avery's face turned solemn. She opened her mouth and touched the corner of her eyes with her pinkies. "I'm looking for Justin Cruise. I don't know if you heard, but rumors are flying around that he's missing."

"Yeah, we heard." Matt nodded.

"I can't believe it." Avery blinked hard. "He can't be gone. It's not possible. He's the best rider out there."

Matt stepped closer to console her. He reached into his bag and offered her a paper napkin. Where did he get that? Seriously, Matt is always prepared for *every* situation.

"How did you know Justin?" I asked while Avery dabbed phantom tears from her eyes.

"Why are you talking about him in the past tense?" She shot me a hard look.

"Sorry."

She sighed. "This can't be happening. I saw him last night. . . ." She trailed off and buried her face in the napkin. "We had a fight."

I gave Matt a skeptical look. Something about Avery's demeanor seemed forced and felt like a performance.

He shook his head. "Do you need anything?"

Avery balled the napkin in her hands and stuffed it into her pocket. "No, thank you. You've been so nice. Listen, I'm not feeling well." Her hand went back to her stomach. "I need to jet. Hopefully I'll see you later." She directed her last words to Matt.

We both watched her hurry down the sidewalk. I didn't like the look of concern on Matt's face, and I didn't buy Avery's act for one minute. Why had she been screaming at that woman crying on the beach? Could it have to do with the fight? Were she and Justin an item? She made it sound that way. And why was she looking for the sports network?

One thing was for sure, I planned to keep my eye on her.

# Chapter 9

"That was weird," I said to Matt as we continued toward the rental house.

"Huh?" He looked distracted.

"Avery. What do you think that was about?"

Matt didn't take my hand again. He shrugged. "She seemed worried about Justin. That's all."

"I thought she seemed kind of fake." I ran my fingers through my hair, trying to give it some lift.

"You did?" Matt absently reached into his messenger bag and pulled out a pack of watermelon-flavored gum. "Want some?"

"Yuck. No, thanks."

We walked the rest of the way to the house in silence. I wondered if something was bothering him.

"Meg!" Jill raced to the front porch to greet us. Her look was effortless. She wore a pair of knee-length, tailored, crisp white shorts, a coral scoop tank top and matching strappy sandals. Gold bangles adorned her delicate wrists. We'd been besties for over a decade, and I knew she didn't care what I looked like, but I felt very aware of the fact that I probably looked like a drowned rat.

Jill held open the screen door and eyed me with concern. "I heard the news. It's all over Twitter. I can't believe it."

"Me neither."

"Will coffee help?" Jill walked to the kitchen and brought me a steaming mug of French press.

"You made French press?" I planted an exaggerated smooch on her cheek. "You rock."

"I know." She laughed and held the glass press. "I don't go anywhere without this baby. Sit. Fill me in, or do you need to jump in the shower first?"

The coffee tasted of cherries and dark chocolate. I slugged down half the cup, not caring that it was slightly singeing the roof of my mouth. "Shower. Don't ya think?" I pulled my stringy hair so it stood up on end.

"Stop." Jill took my mug. "I'll make more. Go warm up."

This trip was not off to the best start, but at least I had my best friends with me, I thought as I skidded down the hallway to the bathroom. After a quick shower and change of clothes I felt ready to face the firing squad, which I suspected might include another round with the Hood River Police Department. I opted for a green skirt and short-sleeved shirt that brought out the green in my eyes and were made out of the same breathable fabric.

Jill and Matt both sat at the retro dining table in the kitchen when I emerged from the shower with fresh clothes and dry hair. The kitchen was themed like a 1950s diner with prints of milkshakes, soda bottles and root beer floats.

I could go for a chocolate shake right now, I thought.

"Matt's been giving me the lowdown." Jill shook her head. "What are the odds that this would happen to you again?"

"It didn't happen to me." I could hear a slightly defensive tone rise in my voice again, but I couldn't help it. "It happened to *Justin*."

Jill reached across the table and patted my hand. "I'm sure you're fried, but you know what I'm saying." She topped off my coffee. "So is he dead?"

I nodded.

"The news isn't saying much. Just that they're searching for a lost swimmer."

"I hope they find his body."

"What do you think happened?" Jill asked. She offered Matt more coffee. He shook his head.

"I'm not sure. He had a huge gash on his forehead." I put my hand over my mouth. The memory of seeing Justin's bashed face made me gag.

Jill squeezed my hand again. "Did he crash?"

"Probably." I looked at both of them. "But something doesn't add up. Everyone said he's the best surfer. He didn't even wear a helmet. What was he doing all the way on the opposite side of the river?"

Jill tapped her fingers on the table as I spoke.

"He had a big gash in his forehead. It almost looked like he'd been hit by something."

"You mean like he was murdered?" Jill snatched her hand away and sat up taller.

"Wait a minute." Matt held up his index finger and waved it between Jill and me. "Let's not go there yet. *We're* here for work and vacation, right?"

Jill gave Matt her most serious face. "Right." She kicked me under the table. "Of course."

"Look, I know what you're both thinking." Matt gave Jill a challenging stare. "I can't believe you're encouraging her."

"Me?" Jill ran her finger along the top of her coffee mug. "I'm not encouraging her. I'm with you, Matt. Totally." She smirked. "Fine. You know me, you guys. I love getting sucked into a good mystery. Blame Miss Marple. It's all her fault."

Jill's Netflix queue reads like she's a seventy-year-old British matron. She has a serious addiction to British cozy mysteries. The more tea and cardigan sweaters the better in Jill's opinion.

Matt's cell phone buzzed. He checked the screen. "It's my editor. I have to take this."

Once he was out of the room, Jill scooted her chair closer, and whispered, "Dish."

I told her about Avery yelling at the woman crying on the beach and her less-than-stellar attempt at trying to fake being distraught over Justin's death. "Think about it, she's a professional wind-surfer, too. She could have easily killed Justin and then surfed back to shore without anyone noticing."

"Did you see anyone else out there?" Jill leaned back in her chair to check on Matt.

I glanced behind me. He was still on the phone. I knew, well at least I thought I knew, why he was being so protective of me. He didn't want to see me hurt again. Twice in the last year I'd almost been a murder victim, and I hadn't come away from it unscarred. A weak wrist and a permanent scar on my hand were reminders that I'd come precariously close to death. That had to be why Matt was so against my involvement. Right?

"Meg?" Jill touched my knee. "Are you with me?"

"Sorry." I shook my head. "What were we talking about?"

"Other surfers—did you see anyone else on the water?"

"Yeah, that's the problem. There were a bunch of us taking the lesson." I tried to replay the scene in my head. "Then I got separated from the pack. When I was on the other side of the river I couldn't see anyone."

Jill finished her coffee and poured another cup. "Refill?" she asked.

"Yes, please. I have a feeling I'm going to be knocking back coffee all day today." I glanced into the living room where Matt was still on the phone. The house had a comfortable vibe with mismatched furniture and a surfboard hanging on the wall behind the couch.

We both paused and drank the thick, rich brew.

"You know one of the many pieces of critical information that we're missing is if Justin was really killed," Jill said, holding her mug. "How would you kill someone while windsurfing? That's not an easy feat."

I shook my head. "No idea."

Jill twisted the bracelets on her wrist. "Was there blood? Could he have been shot?"

"Honestly, I have no idea. I don't remember seeing blood, except for on his forehead, but the waves and the wind were so strong, I was just trying to hold on." I closed my eyes and tried to visualize what I'd seen: Justin's lifeless body, water and a gash on his forehead. I rubbed my temples. *Think, Meg.* "That's all I remember," I said aloud to Jill. "I feel like I'm missing something, though. Like maybe I did see a clue, but nothing's coming to mind."

"Don't worry about." Jill patted my hand. "It'll come back to you."

"Yeah." I crinkled my nose. "Hopefully you're right."

Jill flashed me the cut sign and motioned toward the living room. Matt was on his way back. "My editor wants me on this story." He held up his phone. "Twitter is on fire. He's got a crew on the way, but in the meantime it's me. Man, I hate breaking news."

"Are you going back to the beach?" I asked, getting up and taking our coffee cups to the sink.

"Looks like it." Matt grabbed a banana from the fruit bowl on the counter.

"I'll tag along. I've got to get started on my feature, and who knows, maybe Greg will want me to do something about Justin. Not breaking news of, course, but a life feature or something."

Jill jumped to her feet. "Wait for me. I'll come, too. I packed a bag full of new beach cozies, some sketching tools and my sunscreen." She hurried to her room to grab her gear.

Matt stepped closer to me. I could feel the heat radiating off his skin. I wanted to touch his tanned forearms, but resisted. He pushed a strand of hair from my face. Normally having hair in my eyes was one of the drawbacks of growing out my hair, but if it meant that Matt was touching my face I couldn't see a downside in that. "Listen, Megs, I'm not trying to be hard on you. I just want you to be safe. You know that, right?" He held my gaze tightly. My body started to sway slightly.

I swallowed, not trusting myself to speak. "I know."

Jill rounded the corner with a blue striped beach towel over her shoulder and a floppy white hat shading her face. "I'm ready!" She stopped and inched backward when she noticed Matt leaning in.

But the moment was lost. Matt fumbled for his phone and stepped away from me. Jill mouthed, "Sorry."

Before I could respond, someone knocked on the door. We all looked at each other.

"Who could that be?" Jill asked.

I shrugged. Matt shook his head. The knock sounded again.

Jill walked over to the door, opened it, and let out a scream of delight.

My first thought was, *Oh no, please don't let it be Will Barrington.* I tried to keep the disappointment from showing on my face as I moved to greet Will at the door. To my surprise I was mistaken. I swung the door wide open. Gam stood on the front porch with a beaming smile.

# Chapter 10

"Gam! What are you doing here?" I practically leaped onto the porch and tackled her in a hug. She returned my embrace.

Once I released her, she laughed. "Well, that's a greeting I could get used to. I'm glad to see you, too, Margaret."

Gam is in her early seventies, but unlike the frumpy British protagonists in Jill's cozy mysteries, she doesn't look it. Her skin was a lovely shade of olive from hours spent on her waterfront deck in the sun. Gam has a firm belief that the skin needs a healthy shot of direct vitamin D every day. It looked like she'd taken that advice to heart. Her bottle-dyed dark hair was cut in a short, modern style, and her expertly applied makeup hid any hints of her true age.

"Come inside." I held open the door with my foot. "What are you doing here?"

Gam paused and pointed to the sidewalk. "I came with Sheriff Daniels."

"Sheriff Daniels is here?" I scanned the sidewalk.

Gam nodded. "He's parking the car. I asked him to drop me off here first. He was called out on business and is needed at the beach." Her voice turned solemn. "I don't know if you've heard, but a windsurfer went missing this morning."

"I heard," I said, trying to keep my tone neutral.

"Margaret?" Gam saw right through me.

"I kind of found the body," I confessed.

Gam put her hands together. "Well, we'll have to give you a zap or two, won't we?"

Sheriff Daniels ambled up the front steps at that moment. "Ms. Reed." He acknowledged me with a nod. He tapped his badge with a cutout of Mount Hood and the words HOOD RIVER COUNTY across the front. "What are you doing in my territory?"

"Um, working," I replied.

When the police officer told me this morning that the sheriff would need to speak with me when he arrived, I never thought about the fact that I would know the sheriff. Sheriff Daniels and I met a year ago when he was investigating a murder at nearby Angel's Rest. I'd sent him to Gam for Reiki healing on his back and they'd been dating ever since. Of course he would be responsible for Justin's case. We were in Hood River after all. I guess I'd just gotten so used to seeing him in Portland and Vancouver with Gam that I'd forgotten this was his territory.

"Not working my case, are you, Ms. Reed?" Sheriff Daniels raised his bushy gray brow.

"No, I'm relieved to see you." That was half true. I was relieved to see a familiar face, but I had a feeling Sheriff Daniels was going to be less than thrilled with me finding Justin's body. I'd wait and let Gam break the news.

Matt squeezed past us. "Nice to see you all, but I've got to get down to the river."

Sheriff Daniels turned to Gam. "Do you want to stay here for a while?"

Gam put her arm around me. "Margaret and I will have a little chat and then I'll bring my book and find a spot in the sun. Does that work for you, Margaret?"

I nodded.

"In that case, I'll give you a lift." Sheriff Daniels said to Matt.

Gam plopped on the couch and directed Jill and me to do the same. Her purple T-shirt had rhinestones around the collar. They caught the light from the bay window and sparkled. Just like her, I thought. Gam always sparkles.

"Gam, I can't believe you're here," I said again.

"When Sheriff Daniels got the call, he offered to let me come along on a little adventure. The Universe lined it up perfectly—aside from this missing surfer, of course—I've been having a bit of an adventure myself."

"What kind of adventure?"

Gam paused for dramatic effect. "Rats."

"Rats?" Jill stuck out her tongue.

"Exactly." Gam clapped her hands together. "You

know me, girls. I love all creatures—they all have something to offer and teach us."

"Even rats?" I mimicked Jill's disgusted face.

"Even rats." Gam smiled. "That is until they invaded my condo."

"In your condo—gross!" I stuck my tongue out, too.

Gam nodded. "In my condo. They got into everything—my flour, sugar, cereal and destroyed my pantry."

The joke in our family has always been that in case of a natural disaster, like the big quake that they've been predicting will hit Portland, or in Matt's mind when the zombie apocalypse hits, we all will run to Gam's house. Gam has lived alone since my grandfather died twenty years ago, but her pantry is stocked for an army. I'm pretty sure she keeps Costco in business. Her pantry shelves sag under the weight of her canned goods. The last time I was at her place she asked me to grab a can of green beans. I counted forty-six cans in her panty. Forty-six!

"At first I offered them a blessing. Then I invited them to leave." Gam continued. "They didn't seem to listen to my invitation, so I decided it was time to get serious. I went to the hardware store and bought rat bait. I said a small prayer for them and helped speed them up to their next incarnation."

Jill burst into laughter. "So you exterminated them."

"I like the idea of speeding up their next incarnation better." Gam winked. "But, yep, I nuked them."

We all cracked up at the image of my sweet spiritual grandmother poisoning rats and blessing them as they continued on to their next journey.

"I had an 'ammonia moment,' as Margaret likes to call them." Gam gave me a sly smile.

Jill looked to me for clarification.

I shook my head. "You don't want to be anywhere near Gam's place when she gets the ammonia out."

Gam keeps her condo neat and tidy all year round. She stocks up on bleach and squeals with delight whenever there's a sale on vacuum cleaners. Her hardwood floors are always perfectly polished, and her kitchen sink gleams so brightly that you'd never believe it even gets used. Although her place would pass a white-gloved inspection, she amps up her cleaning routine at least a couple of times a year.

I've learned that it's best to give Gam some space when she has an ammonia moment. Every cupboard and closet gets emptied, scrubbed, and sorted when Gam goes on a cleaning kick. Usually it coincides with her healing work. She owns a new age bookstore Love and Light, where she offers a variety of classes and private healing sessions. Often when she's introducing something new to her practice, she has to literally and figuratively clear out her space.

Gam grinned. "When Sheriff Daniels mentioned that he had a new case, I decided a trip to the river would be cleansing, and it would give my condo some time to let the rat energy clear out, too."

"I'm glad you're here," I said, squeezing her knee.

"Me too, and it sounds like you could use some work." She brushed her hands together and allowed a calming wave of energy to transform her body. Placing one hand on my knee, she closed her eyes and pointed her other hand, palm out, toward me. I could feel heat pulsing in my knee almost instantly. I closed my eyes. My body started to spiral in small circles. It felt like Gam's free hand was spinning me, up and up, toward the heavens. I didn't want the feeling to end.

"Wow," Jill said when Gam brushed her hands together again and called us back to our bodies. "That was intense."

"Did you feel it?" Gam asked.

Jill nodded. "I did."

Gam clapped. "Oh, yay! I love it when people can feel the energy in the room even when I'm not working directly on them. We're all getting the energy, you know. What did you feel?"

"It's hard to explain," Jill said. "I guess I felt really calm and then I saw this bright white light."

"Yes!" Gam's knees bounced. "That's it. That's the energy you're feeling. Shall I do some work on you?"

"Sure." Jill waited while Gam shifted on the couch and turned her body away from me.

This time I watched as Gam worked on Jill. The energy was so dense it felt like I could touch it. When she finished, Gam checked in with Jill.

"What did you feel?"

Jill let out a long sigh. "A release."

"Mmm-hmm. I felt it, too." Gam reached out and placed her hands on Jill's throat. "You're opening up here."

Jill closed her eyes as Gam held her neck. After a few minutes she let go, and asked Jill in a gentle voice, "Is that better?"

Jill looked at her feet. She wiped a tear from her eye and touched her throat, and said, "It feels so warm."

"Good on you! That's what we want!" Gam patted her knee. She noticed Jill's beach bag and striped towel. "It looks like you girls are ready to hit the beach. Mind if I join you? I could work on bronzing my arms."

"Gam, your arms look like they've been dipped in bronzer." I held my slightly pink forearm next to hers. "You're like five shades darker than me."

"But I can always get even tanner." Gam grinned.

We walked to the beach together. Gam stopped twice to admire and pay reverence to ancient oak trees. Whenever I spend time with her, she reminds me to slow down and really pay attention to my surroundings—not my best quality.

Once we arrived at the beach things were even more frenzied than when I left. Media vans and reporters swarmed in front of the tents lining the riverfront. A row of police officers barricaded the beach. Fans, tourists and locals had taken up residence on the grass. They sat on reclining beach chairs and blankets, trying to get a glimpse of the action on the shore.

Gam and Jill found an empty patch of grass on the far end of the beach, away from the craziness.

"What do you say?" Gam asked Jill. "Does this look good?" She unfolded a patchwork blanket and a bottle of coconut tanning oil. Gam doesn't let the fact that she's in her seventies stop her from doing anything, including wearing a bikini. She striped down to a black two-piece that accentuated her buxom chest. I'd inherited my cleavage from her, and I had to admit she still had it. As the old saying goes, "If you've got it, flaunt it." Gam was flaunting it.

Jill removed a tube of 30 SPF from her bag, her sketchbook, a charcoal pencil and a paperback with a scene of an English village on the front. "This is perfect! I'm going to read my new mystery, do some sketches, and maybe check out one of the kiteboarding clinics. That is, if they're still going on?" she asked me.

I shrugged. "I don't know. That's the first item on my agenda," I said, looping my press pass around my neck. I felt like I looked the part of a professional sport's reporter in my green skirt and causal top.

"Take this." Gam pressed a green and blue iridescent rock with flecks of gold into my hand.

The stone felt cool and instantly calming. "What is it?"

"Labradorite. It will give you strength and help keep you calm and centered." Her eyes traveled to the event tents. She closed her eyes and placed both hands on her heart. A serene look washed over her face as she radiated energy. When she finished, she held the labradorite in my hand. "Margaret, remember you can always call in the light."

"I know, Gam. I will," I promised as I tucked the stone into my skirt pocket and headed toward the crowd, wishing that I felt as confident as I sounded.

My first order of business was to find Kyle and find out whether King of the Hook was even going to continue. That would be important to know for my feature. If the competition was going to be canceled, I'd have to call Greg and break the news.

I pulled a pink polka-dot spiral notebook and matching pen from my bag. Sure, maybe pink isn't what my colleagues would use, but I had to splurge somewhere. Plus, most of my colleagues, and even Matt, use tablets and laptops to conduct interviews these days. I can't do it. I'm old-school. There's something irreplaceable about paper and pen. It allows me to take quick, shorthand notes and maintain eye contact with the person I'm interviewing. Once I gather my notes, I type my features on my laptop. Using my phone to update social media was no problem, but when it came to actually typing, I needed a keyboard. My thumbs just didn't cut it.

Finding Kyle in the mess might prove difficult. I

tucked my notebook under my arm and weaved my way through the crowd. It wasn't even eleven, but the sun burned overhead. The crowd smelled of body heat and sunscreen. I held my breath as I squeezed through the sweaty mob.

I spotted Kyle near the beach talking with a group of surfers. A police officer blockading the area stopped me as I tried to duck under the caution tape. "You can't go in there, miss."

"Oh, sorry. I'm with the press." I flashed my badge.

He shook his head. "Doesn't matter. Press is waiting over there." He motioned to a group of cameras and reporters in heavy makeup waiting to go live.

"I'm not a breaking news reporter," I explained to the officer. "I'm with *Northwest Extreme*. Kyle knows me. I just need to ask him a quick question about the competition."

The officer wrapped his burly arms around his chest and nodded toward the reporters. "You can ask it over there."

Well, so much for that. I hung my head and walked over to the group of reporters.

"Hey, Top Tier! Where'd you disappear to?" Ryan from ESPN stood near the front. He oozed confidence. I could tell that the other reporters were in awe of him. He was definitely top tier.

"I just ran back to the house to get a change of clothes." I pointed to my green flower-patterned skirt and matching shirt.

"Did you hear that someone found Justin's body?"

"Yeah, that someone was *me*."

"Really?"

"Yep."

He looked around and motioned for me to step away from the crowd with him. "Did you see Ian out there?"

"Ian Schoonmaker the surfer?"

"Yeah." He scrolled on his tablet and pulled up a photo of Ian. "I could have sworn that I saw him in the water this morning."

"You did? Where?" My curiosity rose.

"When I was pulling my board out of the water. He was right there. I don't remember seeing him when we took off."

"I didn't see him either. That's kind of weird."

"Interesting, isn't it? Ian's out on the river and his biggest competitor has an accident. Convenient, I'd say."

So I wasn't the only one who thought there was something suspicious about Justin's accident.

He glanced toward the mob of reporters. "Convenient for us, too. News like this sells."

Was that why I was trying to make something more of Justin's accident? I'd always thought of myself as a serious journalist, not someone who just went after sensational headlines. Maybe I wasn't any better than the vultures after all.

I wanted to ask Ryan more, but another reporter interrupted us. I could tell that the reporter was a fanboy, so I decided to make my exit and try to find out if the competition was still on. Giving Ryan a wave and a look of sympathy, I squeezed past the reporters and headed to the organizer's tent to see if any of the volunteers knew the status of the event. Most of the activity was focused on the beach, so I wasn't shocked to find the organizer's tent basically empty when I stepped inside.

"Hey, I'm wondering if anyone knows what the plan is now with the competition?" I asked a volunteer at the long table where I'd picked up my packet and press credentials yesterday.

She typed something into the laptop in front of her and held up a finger. "One sec." She walked over to a printer nearby, plucked a piece of paper from it, and handed it to me. "Updated schedule."

"So the competition is still on?"

"Yep, Kyle just made the announcement to the press. Did you miss it?"

"I must have."

"We're going to be a bit delayed, but he's thinking we should have riders in the water by late this afternoon."

"Really?"

She gave me an irritated look and pointed to the schedule. "It's all right there."

"I just thought maybe the event would have to be canceled."

"Right. Not with Kyle running the show. This is his baby. It would take an act of God to get him to cancel King of the Hook."

Not even learning that his top contender was dead would make him cancel? I thought.

I thanked her for the updated schedule and wandered to the snack table at the other corner of the tent. My skirt stuck to my legs. I could really use some water. The tent felt like an oven. I reviewed the new schedule and made a list of all the events I needed to cover. It was going to be a long afternoon.

I grabbed an orange and sat down on a bench. Could it be that the world's best surfer really had an accident, or did someone have motive to send him into the surf?

In the past few minutes I'd just learned two pieces of information that could be critical in Justin's death. First, that Ian was on the river with us this morning. What was he doing there? Could he have killed Justin and then returned to shore without anyone noticing? Probably. As the surfer in Justin's shadow, he certainly had a motive. King of the Hook was his to lose now. I wondered how much the winner stood to gain in terms of endorsement contracts. I opened my notebook and jotted down a few quick notes.

The second piece of information that I wrote down was to look into Kyle's background. The volunteer had been adamant that Kyle would make sure the competition continued. She'd basically hinted he would do so at any cost. Could any cost mean the death of one of his top competitors?

# Chapter 11

I flipped through my notebook. When I'm preparing for a feature story, I spend hours researching. What makes it into the pages of *Northwest Extreme* was minimal compared to the research and notes I amassed while working on a story. My notebook was packed with clips and photos of windsurfing competitions from all over the world.

While compiling research for my feature, I'd found a story from *The O* from the 2004 presidential election. That was before I could vote. I was in middle school and not really concerned with national politics. Oregon rarely gets a voice in the general election. The winner is usually declared right after the polls close and votes start getting tabulated this far west. But in 2004, Oregon made national headlines. Not because of politics, but because John Kerry, an avid windsurfer, took a break from campaigning in Oregon and showcased his surfing skills in Hood River. He didn't win the election, but he won over the surfing community.

As I skimmed the story, I couldn't believe my eyes. Posing next to John Kerry and his team was Kyle Kaspar. Kyle wasn't kidding about the fact that he'd been part of the surfing scene forever. I'd have to make sure to ask him about meeting the presidential candidate. This little tidbit of local history was definitely going to be woven into my feature.

*Right, Meg, your feature. That's why you're here. Not to play detective.*

The press tent felt like a sauna. Its giant white awnings soaked up the sun and trapped it inside. A wall of TVs blared along the far wall. A group of anchors came in and started rehearsing teaser scripts.

I needed water and to get outside. There was no way I could work in this heat or with so much commotion around me. I also needed to see if any of the vendors or competitors would be willing to tear themselves away from the drama on the beach and let me interview them.

I shut my notebook and grabbed a warm bottle of water from a table near the front with an assortment of melting chocolate-chip cookies and picked-over trays of fruit swarming with fruit flies. Outside had to be better than this.

I decided to start with the line of vendor tents in the parking lot first. I could snap photos of each of them for our social media pages and do a quick post about the innovative products and services on display.

The heat outside was even more unbearable.

There was no escape from the sun's intense rays. I needed to get these interviews done and find some shade—fast.

"Ms. Reed, hold on one moment, please." An angry voice sounded behind me.

I recognized the voice immediately—Sheriff Daniels, and he didn't sound happy. I turned around slowly. He stood with his arms folded across his chest and a toothpick dangling from his pursed lips.

"Hi again." I gave him a half wave.

"Ms. Reed, come with me please." The sheriff pointed toward the area on the beach where all of the emergency workers were gathered.

I let out a sigh and followed him.

A group of police officers linked arms to block the press as a rescue boat sped up to the shore.

"Back up, people. Back up!" one of the police officers shouted on a bullhorn.

The dive team had returned. I knew immediately from their dejected faces that they hadn't returned with good news.

Sheriff Daniels held up his arm to stop me. "Wait right here, Ms. Reed." He ambled over the uneven ground.

It was hard to see through the wall of police officers. I tried to get a better view by standing on my tiptoes. Had the dive team recovered Justin's body? One of them motioned to the ambulance. EMS workers raced to the boat with a stretcher.

I couldn't tell what they were doing, but spotted

Sheriff Daniels' cowboy hat near the boat. After a few minutes the stretcher returned empty.

What did that mean? If only I were taller. Being short is the worst.

Sheriff Daniels shouted out orders as the throng of bystanders tried to press closer. The helicopter circled directly overhead, kicking sand and spray into the air.

One of the police officers made a cut sign across his neck. "Get that thing out of here!"

Kyle ran past me, waving his arms at the copter. When he got closer, he signaled for it to stop. The helicopter obeyed his request and flew farther out over the water.

I watched as one of the officers said something in Kyle's ear. He nodded and hung his head.

They must have found the body, I thought, brushing sand from my face and coughing.

Kyle turned and walked right toward me.

"What's going on down there?" I asked.

He shook his head. "It's not good. They found Justin's body. He's dead."

"Right." I swallowed and looked at my feet.

Kyle massaged his forehead. "This is not good."

"Did you see anything out there this morning? I got separated from the group."

"No, nothing. Why?"

"I thought I saw a boat. I was stuck on the other side, you know. I could have sworn that I heard a motor over the wind. It was out by the sandbar."

He shot his head toward the river. "What kind of boat?"

"No idea. I thought maybe it was a safety boat, but I guess it could have been a fishing boat." I pointed toward the sandbar. "It was out there."

"Couldn't have been a fishing boat. There's no fishing out there. Are you sure you saw a boat?"

"Yeah, I'm positive."

Kyle rubbed his temples. "I don't know, but I've got a ton of work to do with this situation. I've got to go."

So it was true. Justin Cruise was dead.

News spread quickly as the EMS team loaded a body bag into the ambulance. The tension in the crowd was palpable. Soft murmurs and sobs sounded as the ambulance drove off.

All of the competitors removed their bright yellow race bibs and waved them in the air as it passed. I felt tears brimming in my eyes. This couldn't be happening. An eerie silence blanketed the beach. After a few somber moments it was broken by the sound of the helicopter trailing the ambulance. Camera crews raced after it, too, trying to get a shot of the world's best windsurfer making his final appearance.

The crowd dispersed into groups. Sheriff Daniels made eye contact with me. He waved his index finger. Time to face the music.

My skirt caught in the wind. I clutched it to my thighs as I walked toward the sheriff.

He narrowed his eyes. "Ms. Reed, here we are

again. I'd like to know how it is that you were the one to find the deceased."

"Deceased?" I grimaced. "Was it an accident? Or do you think he was murdered?" I couldn't stop the questions from spilling from my lips. What was wrong with me?

Sheriff Daniels chomped his toothpick and gave me a long, hard stare. The brim of his cowboy hat shaded his face, making it appear sharp and angular.

I waited for him to respond. He didn't.

*Not good, Meg. Not good.*

"I mean, I just wondered because I noticed a gash on his forehead."

He cleared his throat and removed a notebook from his breast pocket. "Ms. Reed, start from the beginning, and let's try to keep to the facts—just the facts. Understood?"

I nodded and explained about drifting to the Washington side of the river and my lack of skill controlling the windsurfing board. When I mentioned finding Justin's body stuck on the jetty, Sheriff Daniels stopped me.

"Ms. Reed, think carefully. How was the deceased's body positioned?"

"What do you mean?"

"Was he facedown or on his back?"

"Definitely facedown. I had to turn him over."

He murmured something under his breath and made a note. After a few more questions, he tucked the notebook back into his breast pocket. "That's all I need for the moment. You're free to continue about your business, but let me remind you this is a police matter."

"Understood." I gave him a salute.

He frowned. "Do you, Ms. Reed? This is a serious matter. I hope you're not making light of this investigation."

"No, no. Of course not." I pushed my sunglasses up my nose. "I've got some work to do, but then I'm going to find Gam. Do you have a message for her?"

His demeanor shifted slightly. He glanced toward the rescue boat. "Tell her I might be a while." He tipped his hat and walked away.

I left in the opposite direction. Justin Cruise was dead, and after my conversation with the sheriff, I had a feeling that his death was no accident.

# Chapter 12

I couldn't wait to hash everything out with Jill and Matt, but I needed to focus on my feature for the moment. The vendor area was swarming with people and gossip about Justin. "Do you think he crashed?" I overhead a sunscreen vendor ask one of the competitors.

"Maybe something malfunctioned?" another vendor chimed in.

*Concentrate, Meg.*

My first stop was a vendor selling carbon foil boards. They reminded me of a pogo stick. I interviewed the owner about design and construction. He filled me in on the intricacies of riding a foil board. It was like he was speaking a foreign language.

"The board doubles as a kiteboard. You can carve endless power turns with this baby. Feel it. It's crazy light, man. You'll never want to ride anything else."

I took notes and photos and thanked him for his

time. The next vendor, Big Wind, had a collection
of neon-colored masts. They reminded me of candy
sticks all neatly lined up in a row. I chatted with a
wet and dry suit vendor and a guy selling kneepads
and helmets. Why hadn't I had those this morning?

As I made my way to the next tent, I bumped into
Ian Schoonmaker. He was finishing a live interview
with *Evening Magazine.*

"Hey, Ian." I held up my press badge. "Can I ask
you a couple quick questions for *Northwest Extreme?*"

"*Northwest Extreme,* dude, that's a legit mag. You
bet. Come with me." He walked with a swagger,
flashing hang loose signs and scribbling his signature on the back of fans' T-shirts and surfboards as
we passed.

He led me to a private tent next to a large
warehouse. The tent had individual lockers, a huge
table full of granola bars, Powerade, GU energy gel,
bananas, and bagels. "You hungry?" Ian asked.
"Take anything you want. It's all free."

"I'm fine," I replied, removing my notebook from
under my arm. It was damp with sweat. "Is this tent
just for the competitors?"

"Yep. Dope, huh?" Ian grabbed a banana and
ripped it open.

"Dope." I nodded. I may be young, but I don't
speak surfer.

"Lay it on me. What do you want to know?"

I motioned to a set of faux leather chairs. "Mind
if we sit?"

"If that's your jam, let's do it."

*If that's my jam?* That was going in my feature for
sure. Talk about surfer speak.

Ian flopped on one of the chairs and leaned his
legs off the edge. His well-defined calves flexed as
he kicked off a pair of dusty flip-flops. He wore his
hair shaggy and long. The sun had lightened it. I
snapped a picture of him lounging in the chair,
noshing on a banana. Our followers would love an
insider's view of one of the most famous windsurfers on the circuit.

I rested my notebook on my lap and clicked my
pen. "Can you give me a little background on
you, the event, whatever else you'd like our readers
to know?"

"It's pretty sick, isn't it?"

"You mean what happened to Justin?"

Ian sat up and scowled. "No, the event. Sick. You
know, like killer."

"Oh, right." I made a note: *sick* as in good. Got it.

"It's totally off the chain." Ian tossed his banana
peel in a garbage can. He proceeded to explain, in
his signature surfer speak, that he'd been on tour
for the past three years.

I asked him about his favorite event, stops on the
world tour and his impression of Hood River. Once
I had everything I needed for my story, I decided to
see if I could get him to say anything about Justin.
"How's the vibe around here?"

"Totally chill."

"I mean with Justin." I paused and held my
pencil. "You heard the news, right? How do you

and your fellow competitors feel about going on without him?"

"Bummer, man. A real bummer." He paused and then shrugged. "But it's a dangerous sport. We all know that. You gotta deal. We've got some killer air out there."

My face must have reflected my surprise in his quick shift in tone.

He sat up in the chair. "I mean, we're all bummed, but that's what Cruise Control would have done. Get on the water. Ride, dude." He waved a hang loose sign again.

"Were you out there this morning, when it happened?"

"No, I didn't get in until later."

I thanked him for his time and took a few more pictures of him and the surfer's tent. My interview with Ian left me with more questions about Justin's death. He didn't seem shaken up about Justin. If anything, he seemed excited about how big the waves were and getting back on the water. It would be easy to write him off as insensitive and egotistical, but Ryan told me that he saw Ian in the water, so why did Ian just lie? Ian Schoonmaker was definitely going on my suspect list, assuming I was right about the fact that Justin's death wasn't an accident.

By the time I finished interviewing the remaining vendors and uploading pics to *Northwest Extreme*'s Twitter, Facebook and Tumblr accounts, the river was packed with windsurfers, kiteboarders and paddleboarders. Sheriff Daniels must have given permission for King of the Hook to go on. I was surprised that everyone was in the water so fast, but then again it wasn't like he could maintain a crime scene in the middle of a mile-wide river.

Watching the surfers warm up was truly a jaw-dropping experience. Their colorful sails flew ten to fifteen feet in the air and then came crashing back down on the waves. I found it difficult to tear my eyes away from their stunts. I'm totally compelled by the danger of adrenaline-packed sports, but I much prefer to watch them from the safety of the shore.

I paused in the heat and snapped a few more pictures of the competitors catching huge air. Hot wind assaulted my face. Dust and dry leaves flew through the air. My contacts felt like sandpaper. I blinked hard. That just made them worse.

*You need a sun break, Meg.*

I was about to go seek shade, when I noticed the sobbing woman who Avery had been yelling at, sitting alone on a surfboard near the beach. I headed in her direction.

"Is everything okay?" I paused when I reached her.

She buried her face in her hands and shook her head.

"Want some company?" I bent next to her. The sand was littered with dead seaweed, cigarette butts and driftwood. I caught the smell of fish this close to the river.

Wiping her nose with the back of her tanned

arm, she nodded. I'd pegged her to be about my age with huge eyes and mounds of black curls. She wore a gold bikini with matching gold flip-flops.

I smoothed my skirt, kicked aside a collection of broken shells, and sat on the hot, rocky shore. "I'm Meg." I held out my press badge. "I noticed you earlier. I take it you knew Justin?"

She ran her fingers through her long, wild curls. I'd die for hair like that. Her hair hung below her shoulder in twisty spirals.

"Are you okay?" I reached out and placed my hand on her shoulder. Gam had initiated me in Reiki, using energy from your hands for healing, years ago. I'm not faithful in my practice, or even sure it works when I place my hands on someone, but I had to try. I recognized her grief. After losing Pops I found it easy to recognize and access that dark place.

She sucked air through her nose and wiped her eyes. "I can't believe it. I can't believe he's dead, you know?"

I nodded, keeping my hand on her shoulder and waiting for her to continue. I did know. There were still days I could convince myself that Pops was on an assignment somewhere and that he'd be home soon. It's the little things that hurt the most. Catching a whiff of newsprint or bicycle grease, or seeing the back of a stranger who looked like him in the grocery store. I couldn't even begin to count how many times I'd started to punch his name on my phone, thinking I could give him a quick call to talk through a story or just to hear his voice. Then reality would crash in. I'd probably left him at least a dozen voice mails that I knew he would never answer just to try and let the feeling that he was alive linger a little longer.

Mother suggested that it was time for me to see a counselor. What good would that do? A counselor was only going to tell me what I already knew: Pops was dead and there was nothing I could do to change that.

"I just saw him this morning. How can he be dead?" The woman looked at me. Her eyes were swollen and bloodshot. I blinked mine in empathy.

"I'm really sorry."

"He can't be dead." She put her head in her hand again.

"Is there anything I can do?"

"No." She massaged her curls and rubbed her scalp. "I'm sorry, I didn't even introduce myself. I'm Harriet."

"It's okay. I know how disorientating it can be to learn that someone you know has died."

She wiped her eyes. "You do?" She met my eyes and nodded.

"I do," I said quietly.

We both watched the riders on the river for a moment.

"How did you know Justin?" I asked after she'd calmed down a bit.

She looked wistful. "I've been following him around for years."

"Following him around?" I chuckled, trying to lighten the mood. "It sounds like you're some sort of groupie."

"I kind of am."

"Really? Is that a thing? Surfing groupies."

She shrugged. "Not exactly. I help out, you know. I get gear, wash boards, and help the guys with press. That sort of thing."

"So, like a personal assistant?"

"Kind of, but I help the whole team."

"Huh." I resisted pulling out my notebook. Harriet's story could be a really interesting sidebar for my feature, but I didn't want to lose the moment.

"Justin and I have been hanging out for years." She glanced to a tent nearby where Kyle looked frazzled. He shoved his clipboard at a surfer and held off a camera crew with his other hand. Damage control didn't appear to be working. Avery stood nearby with her back propped against the metal frame of the tent. She looked like she was about to pass out. Harriet glared at her.

"What's up with Avery?" I asked, trying to keep my tone casual. "I saw her yelling at you earlier."

Harriet twisted a curl around her finger and let it go. It sprang back into position. "She's awful. I hate her."

*Don't hold back,* I thought.

"Have you met her?" Harriet asked, keeping her gaze directed at Avery. I watched as Avery put her hand to her stomach and raced to a row of porta potties.

"Yeah, this morning. She said she and Justin had some kind of fight?" I let the question hang.

"Right." Harriet shook her head. "Justin broke it off with her."

"Really. She didn't make it sound like that."

"Ha!" She let out a bitter laugh. "She wouldn't. She likes to play the part of awesome surfer girl. The media eats it up, but we all know the truth."

"Which is?"

"All she cares about is the publicity. She's the first female rider to compete in King of the Hook, and she makes sure everyone knows it. That's the only reason she dated Justin. She knew it would make a great story. She didn't care about him. She's a user."

Tears started again.

I placed my hand back on her arm. She smiled. "Sorry. I never knew I could cry this much."

"Believe me. I know." I frowned. "Do you want a water or something?"

Harriet shook her head. "No, I'm going to go back to my hotel. Sitting here watching everyone else warm up is making it worse. Justin should be out there. He was going to win the whole thing, you know?"

"You really cared about him, didn't you?"

"I loved him. Not like Avery. I really loved him." She wiped her nose and stood. "You want to know something?"

"Of course."

"There's no way Justin crashed. Someone killed him." Her eyes flickered with anger.

Now things were getting interesting. "Really?"

She nodded. "Yeah, and I know who killed him."

"Who?" I asked, rolling onto my knees. The jagged rocks cut into my skin.

Harriet didn't answer. She motioned to the porta potties, where Avery stood, and gave her a death stare. "Guess," she said, adjusting her bikini and walking away.

# Chapter 13

I watched Harriet's curls bounce as she hung her head and walked away. A few windsurfers tried to console her. She brushed them off and stalked toward Second Street. I know it's critical to stay neutral as a journalist, but I had to admit that I tended to agree with her. Avery hadn't appeared to be the least bit shaken up about Justin's death, while Harriet was obviously in a state of total shock. I didn't know whether that meant Avery had killed Justin, but it certainly kept her on my suspect list.

What if Harriet was right? Maybe Avery had been using Justin to promote her own windsurfing career. If he broke things off, could that be motive for killing him? I wondered how motivated Avery was to make sure she maintained her position as the top woman in windsurfing? Could she have killed for that?

Then there was Harriet. She was definitely distraught over Justin's death, but could she be lying? What if Justin didn't return her feelings? Could she have killed him? Wasn't being a groupie one step away from being a stalker? But she doesn't surf, so how would she have been on the water?

I felt like I was reaching, but I knew I had two good pieces of information. A bee buzzed in front of my face as I stepped onto the pavement. At that moment Avery bumped into me. She looked frazzled and paler than the clouds funneling above.

"Sorry." She grabbed my arm to steady herself. "I didn't see you there."

"You don't look so good." I helped hold her up.

She put her hand over her mouth. "I can't believe I'm sick." She nodded toward the competitors in the water. "Now."

"So you're not going to compete, I take it?"

She swallowed—hard.

I took a step back.

"It's okay." She put her fingers back over her mouth. "I kept it down." Her body swayed slightly as she spoke. "No, I can't."

"Do you need to sit down or something?"

"I can't. I have to do an interview. Then I'm going back to my room to lie down."

"Who are you doing an interview with?" I scanned the beach. All of the cameras and trucks were focused on the competitors in the water.

"ESPN. They want to talk about Justin. I can't turn down that kind of coverage."

What had Harriet just said about Avery being desperate for the spotlight? Maybe she was right.

Avery didn't look like she was in any shape to go on TV.

"Is that a good idea? Can't it wait?"

She flinched. "A primetime ESPN feature? You work in media. You should know that's not something you pass on, regardless of what my stomach's doing."

"Fair enough." I nodded in agreement.

"I should be good for a while. I was so sick last night I went to the local health clinic. They hooked me up to an IV all night." She held out her arm, revealing three dime-sized bruises. "They can't ever find my veins."

"Ouch."

"Better than being dehydrated."

"I guess." I wondered if I was dehydrated. The few sips of warm water that I'd taken hadn't helped to cool me. My skirt and shirt were plastered to my skin. I really needed to get out of the sun.

"They gave me something this morning to try to stop the vomiting, so I'm crossing my fingers that it'll work for the next thirty minutes."

My mind clicked. "You were at the clinic this morning?"

"I was there all night. They wouldn't let me go until they were sure I wasn't in danger of dehydration. I had to beg them to take out the IV this morning."

"When did they let you leave?"

"I don't know. Right before I saw you this morning, why?"

"No reason," I lied. "I'm just surprised you're up and doing interviews if you were in the hospital all night. That's impressive."

"That's the job. If you want to make it in this business, you show up. No matter what." She waved to Ryan and his cameraman. "I've got to go. Catch you later."

She looked unsteady on her feet as she walked away. I let out a sigh. So much for Avery being the killer. She couldn't have killed Justin if she was hooked up to an IV.

*That's what you get for trying to insert yourself into an investigation, Meg.* I laughed at my own stupidity. Had I learned nothing from my previous experience? Apparently not.

I'd been wrong twice before, and it looked like I was on track to be wrong again. Time to keep my focus on my job, and leave the rest to Sheriff Daniels and his team.

*Yeah right,* I thought as I caught sight of Gam and Jill. *You are your father's daughter.* I could hear Mother's disapproving voice in my head. It was true. Once I was on a story, it was nearly impossible for me to let it go.

# Chapter 14

I headed over to Gam and Jill, determined to stay focused on my story and put Justin's death out of my mind. The crowd had packed in around them. Any square space of green grass had been taken.

Gam was fast asleep in the sun. Jill flipped her sketchbook shut before I could see what she was working on. I didn't care if she wasn't ready to show me yet. The fact that she was sketching at all—especially on a public beach—was enough for me.

She pointed to Gam and held a finger to her lips. "She said not to wake her." She got to her feet, brushed charcoal from her fingers, and pulled a slinky black cover-up over her bikini. I'd die before wearing a bikini in public. Nothing would stay where it was supposed to if I wore a skimpy top like Jill's.

"Do you want to grab lunch?" Jill asked, adjusting her floppy hat and hiding her eyes behind an oversized pair of expensive sunglasses.

"Come to think of it I am kind of hungry." I glanced at my watch. It was almost one. No wonder. Where had the morning gone?

Jill slung her beach bag over her shoulder. "Me too."

"I'm just going to nudge Gam and let her know we're leaving." I bent down and gently shook Gam. "Gam, we're going to lunch," I whispered.

Gam opened her eyes and smiled. "That's nice, dear. Have fun. I'm going to keep soaking up some of this delightful sun."

Delightful and sun were not two words that I'd choose to pair together. I wiped sweat from under my eyes and followed Jill up the grassy hill. She texted with one hand, barely paying attention to where she was going. I cannot text and walk—or talk for that matter. It's one of the many cons of being a klutz. I was impressed that Jill could maneuver through the crowd without looking up from her phone.

"Matt's going to meet us at Full Sail," she said, unaware that every guy we passed gave her an approving glance. How could they not? Her long, graceful legs seemed to stretch to the sky. She walked with an easy confidence that radiated out around her.

I smoothed my skirt as I dragged behind her, feeling sticky, hot and super unattractive. Jill and I had been friends for long enough that I was used to the attention she received from men, but there was a part of me that would probably always feel slightly jealous that I faded into the background whenever Jill was around—at least when it came to the ogling stares.

*Do you even want that, Meg?* I asked myself as we crossed the street and turned toward Full Sail. *Of course not.* The sound of the emcee announcing the next qualifying event and who was on deck faded as we trudged up the hill.

Full Sail is one of Oregon's oldest and most well-known breweries. Its massive warehouse and taproom are housed in an old cannery that's been transformed into a warm and welcoming pub with amazing views of the Columbia River. Jill and I passed giant stainless-steel fermenters and climbed the stairs to the pub.

Inside, the air-conditioning hummed and the beer flowed. Every table and seat at the bar was taken.

"Outside or inside?" A hostess wearing a blue shirt with a white sail logo on the front asked.

Jill and I answered at the same time.

I said, "In."

"Out." She bumped my hip.

The hostess pointed behind her. "Inside will be about twenty or thirty. I can seat you outside now."

"Is there shade?" I asked.

"Yep." She grabbed menus and we followed her onto the deck.

Full Sail is tucked into the bluff, and the view from its outdoor deck was spectacular. For a moment as I took in the sights, I didn't even care about the blazing temperature. Below us the river was spotted with colorful sails, like someone had thrown strips of confetti into the air. The summit of Mount Adams was dusted with the last remnants of winter snow.

The hostess guided us to a shaded table at the back of the deck and left us with menus to look over.

"Wow. It's beautiful out here." Jill sat next to me so we could both take in the view.

"And hot." I fanned myself with the menu.

"Do you want to wait for inside seating?" She looked concerned. "I'm not that hungry."

"No, no. It's fine in the shade."

"You look a bit red, though."

"Nothing a beer won't remedy." I flipped through the menu for the beer list. I could go for a pitcher of beer right now.

Before we had a chance to order, Matt arrived with three pint glasses and a brimming pitcher of Full Sail's amber ale.

"Anyone fancy a pint?" He grinned as he placed the pitcher on the table and poured us each a glass.

"You are the best!" I took a drink and let the cool, slightly sweet malt refresh my palate. *Ah, perfection.*

We placed our order. I opted for a hummus plate. Jill ordered a beet salad with green onions and dressing on the side. Matt went for his standard lunch fare—a burger and fries.

"How did the interviews go?" he asked, grabbing his iPad from his bag and placing it on the bench.

"Good." I took another sip of beer.

"Good as in you got work done for *Northwest Extreme,* or good as in you were poking around in the investigation?"

"Ouch." I pretended to be hurt by his comment, but then leaned in. "You guys, as far as I can tell this was no accident. Justin Cruise was killed. I'm sure of it, and I'm pretty sure Sheriff Daniels thinks so. He didn't say as much, but it was what he didn't say."

Matt looked to Jill for support.

Jill removed her hat and leaned across the table. "Listen, Matty, you know Meg. What do you say we call a truce and help her do her thing? She's going to do it anyway. We might as well help her."

Matt put his elbows on the table and hit his fists together. "I'm so outnumbered on this."

"Yep." I grinned. "Come on, Matt, you know that five minutes in you'll want to investigate this as much as we do. I promise we'll be careful, right, Jill?"

Jill nodded in agreement.

"I know I'm not going to win this battle, so I guess I might as well join you. Here's the thing, though. If this is really a murder—and from the chatter I heard amongst the breaking news crew this morning, I think you might be right—you go to the police with *anything* we find. Deal? No more wait and see, or trying to interview suspects yourself. If anything comes up that's suspicious, you go straight to the police."

"I can live with that," I agreed. Matt was right. I'd

learned enough to know that taking on a killer by myself was stupid to say the very least.

"Me too." Jill tapped her fingers on the table. "Dish! What did you learn this morning, Meg?"

The waitress arrived with our food. I spread hummus on pita bread and layered on tomatoes, marinated red onions and Kalamata olives. Delish. While I snacked on my lunch, I filled them in on meeting Harriet and learning that Avery had been in the clinic all night and morning.

Matt seemed especially pleased to learn that Avery had dropped on my potential suspect list.

Jill dabbed at her salad. If I ate like she did, then maybe I'd get more ogling looks from men, but there was no way I was ever going to be able to eat like a bird. *Keep dreaming, Meg.*

I polished off my beer. My cheeks, already warm from the heat, burned with color. One pint of beer does it every time.

Matt refreshed our drinks. I paced myself, taking small sips from the fresh pint. Not only because of the heat, but because I don't usually drink during lunch. I knew I had a lengthy list of activities to cover this afternoon and I wanted to make sure I was functional.

We were almost finished with our meal, when a commotion broke out inside at the bar. I glanced in the window to see Sherman, wearing his druid cape and arguing with a surfer at the bar. How could he stand wearing such a heavy cape in this heat?

Jordan, the skinny kid I'd met at The Quest, stood next to him.

Sherman noticed us and seemed to compose himself a bit. He threw his sword over his shoulder, motioned for Jordan to follow, and came outside.

"Hey, Sherman. What's up?" Matt made room for him on the bench. "You want a beer?"

Sherman declined Matt's offer. "No, we've got to get back to the shop. You remember my paladin Jordan?" He stared at Jill.

Jill pinched my knee under the table.

Matt introduced them. Sherman offered her a sweaty hand. She smiled politely and shook his hand while he continued to stare at her. His face reminded me of the beets in Jill's salad.

"What's going on in there?" I asked, trying to rescue Jill. That's when I noticed that Jordan, his face erupting in acne, was giving me the same trance-like look. Just my luck. Some nerdy teen was crushing on me. I gave him a half wave. "How's the super-secret project going?"

He looked at his fingers. "Good." They were coated in grease. "How's swimming?"

"I haven't had a chance to get in the water."

"If you want, I can get you into my high-school pool. I have the key code." He closed one eye. I couldn't tell if he was trying to wink at me or squint.

"Thanks, I might have to take you up on that."

Sherman gazed at Jill as he spoke. "Another surfer. I've warned them all to stay away from the shop. We're done with being harassed by these guys. Right, Jordan?"

Jordan pointed at the Captain America T-shirt he wore. "Right, Sherman. Captain America's on it."

"Did something else happen?" Matt asked.

Still under Jill's spell, Sherman had a hard time focusing on Matt's question. "What?" He finally tore his gaze away. The thick cape made him look even thicker around the middle.

Matt rolled his eyes at me, and asked Sherman again, "Did something else happen?"

"You mean other than the fact that they trashed my store? No." He sounded bitter. "I know Justin and his buddy Ian were responsible, but I told those guys inside that if my store or any of my paladins get touched, I'm turning them in to the police."

"Were Ian and Justin friends?" I chimed in. "I was under the impression they didn't like each other much."

Sherman adjusted his sword. "I don't know. I don't care, but I do know that they were responsible for vandalizing my shop. I saw them."

"You did?" Jill chimed in. "When?"

The fact that Jill was actually speaking to him seemed to fluster Sherman. He turned as red as I felt. "I saw them running down the hill. Like I told Meg and Matt, they've been bullying my paladins all week. I've had enough."

Jordan flexed his nonexistent muscles. "Yeah, we've had enough."

"And you're sure Ian was with Justin?" I asked.

Sherman patted his sword. "Positive. I ran after them with this. I think I scared them off."

"A sword might do that," Jill said.

He puffed up at her words, taking them as a compliment and completely missing the sarcasm in her voice. A group of windsurfers came outside. Sherman hunched his shoulders, swooped his cape, and stalked over to their table. Jordan smiled awkwardly at me and then followed. We watched as Sherman threatened them with his sword and stormed away. The surfers burst into laughter when he left.

"He's creepy," Jill said.

"I think he's harmless," I said, feeling sorry for Sherman.

"And awkward," Jill insisted, giving me a skeptical look. "Can you say pit stains and a neck beard?" She put her hand under her nose. "Looks like you have an admirer, too, Meg. What do you think, Matt?"

Matt frowned. "I'm not sure what to think, but I do feel for the dude."

I clapped my hands together. "Let's get back to Justin's murder for a minute. I think Sherman just gave us another clue."

"What's that?" Jill asked.

"Ian! If Ian really did vandalize Sherman's shop with Justin this morning, that means that Ian was one of the last people to see Justin alive."

Matt grabbed his iPad and clicked it on. "Hang

on one sec. Let me put together a quick timeline. What do we know for sure?"

I explained that Justin was alive when Kyle took us through our training on the beach, and how he was the first one in the water. "We all watched him demonstrate tricks, but then he disappeared. I figured it was because it was dark, and then I was distracted by trying to get up on my board."

"How long was that?" Matt asked as he typed.

"Maybe twenty minutes."

"Then what happened?"

I tried to remember the sequence of events. Who had I seen in the water? Kyle helped me get up, but then had continued on to help the other reporters. Ryan and my fellow reporters. I knew there were other competitors warming up, but I didn't remember seeing Ian. Ryan told me that he saw Ian in the water, though.

Matt waited for me to finish. "So according to Sherman, Ian was with Justin right before he died."

"Yeah, but according to Ian he was at home and in bed. I asked him this morning if he was on the river, and he said his warm-up time was later. He said he didn't arrive at the beach until they'd already recovered Justin's body. Obviously he's lying. Ryan saw him there."

"Maybe." Matt clicked his iPad off. "I don't think we should focus on one person at this point."

"He's right." Jill placed her hat on her head. "And you know what that means?"

"No?" I left cash on the table for my lunch and followed Jill and Matt inside.

Jill weaved her way between the crowded bar tables. Once we were outside and out of earshot she turned to Matt and me and grinned. "We have some investigating to do, you guys."

# Chapter 15

Investigating sounded like fun, but for the moment I had work to do. I told Matt and Jill that they were on their own for dinner. I had an evening banquet to attend and more research for my story to focus on for the afternoon. We agreed to meet back at the house after dinner.

My cell phone dinged like an old-fashioned type-writer as we walked to the beach together. It was the custom ringtone I chose for my text messages. This one was from Greg, my boss. He was coming to the banquet tonight. Great.

Matt tensed when I told them that Greg was in town.

*You're an idiot, Meg. Why did you even need to say anything? This is one of those moments to follow Gam's advice of saying nothing at all.*

"You know I have an invite, too." Matt ran his finger over his press badge. "I wasn't planning on going, but I think it might be wise for me to keep an eye on you."

I started to protest, but Jill pinched my arm.

"Leave it alone," she whispered.

Matt ran into a colleague from a competing paper. We left him in a discussion about what a bummer it was to be stuck covering breaking news.

"Why is he so weird about Greg?" I asked Jill as we walked down the hill.

"Duh." She flicked my shoulder. "He's jealous."

"No, it's not that."

She rolled her eyes. "Trust me. He's jealous. You've got to drop it."

I knew there was more to it than jealousy, but I dropped it for the moment. We passed through the gauntlet of vendors and food carts to Jill's spot on the beach. Gam was awake and reapplying coconut tanning oil. It smelled tropical and good enough to eat. "There you girls are. How was lunch?"

"Great. You should have joined us."

"That's so nice of you, but I have a date." Her eyes twinkled.

"Sheriff Daniels?" I asked.

She laughed. "Who else?"

"You never know, Gam. You've still got it and there are a ton of dreamy surfers around here."

Gam grinned and winked. "I know, I met a couple of lovely young gentlemen who kindly offered me a spot in the shade. But I like my cowboy." She smiled. "He's going to meet me here in about twenty minutes."

Jill placed her bag on her beach towel. "I'm going to go check out the next paddleboard demo. See you both later."

Gam patted the empty towel. "Have a minute to chat, or do you need to get back to work?"

I plopped on the towel. "I always have time to chat with you, Gam."

"They are something, aren't they? I can't seem to tear my eyes away." Gam pointed to the surfers performing gravity-defying stunts on the river. "And they're so easy on the eyes." Gam winked.

"Gam! They're all like my age."

"I know, darling, but that doesn't mean I can't appreciate a nice young body every now and then."

My mouth hung open. "You go, Gam!"

Her face lit up. "Ha!"

We watched the windsurfers skim the surf in silence for a moment, then Gam's tone turned serious. Without making eye contact, she asked, "Is there something more than the death this morning that's bothering you, Margaret?"

Her ability to read my emotions never ceased to amaze me.

"Kind of."

She offered me the oil. I countered with a bottle of sunscreen. "I did NOT inherit your skin, Gam."

"True. You're like your father in so many ways." She twisted the cap on the oil and stuck it back in her bag. "Does this have anything to do with him by chance?"

"Sort of. Yeah, I guess so."

"Care to elaborate?" Gam removed an amethyst pendant from her neck and placed it in my hand.

"Why don't you hold this while we talk? I'll hold the space for you to stay open to whatever message the Universe wants you to receive."

In Gam speak, "holding the space" meant that she'd call in her spiritual guides. Her body shifted slightly as she closed her eyes. I felt an immediate sense of calm wash over me. She spiraled as if the wind were rocking her from side to side. The crowded beach and background chatter became consumed by Gam's serene energy. It was almost like she was sending energy waves and creating a protective bubble around us. The hot wind felt almost cool on my face, as I allowed myself to relax and savor the feeling.

After a few minutes she dusted her hands and opened her eyes. "Is that better?"

"Wow. Yeah. That's so nice. Thank you."

"They're telling me to remind you to keep breathing. It'll help you ground." She modeled this by placing her hand just below her navel—or as she calls it, her solar plexus—and breathing in through her nose. I did the same.

"Now imagine a beautiful red cord wrapping around your stomach and going all the way into the earth. That's your grounding cord. It will keep you tethered and help remind you to stay present in this moment."

Gam's personal philosophy is to be present in the moment. She makes it sound so easy, but I've found it's often profoundly difficult. As she likes to say, "It's simple, but it isn't easy. There's a difference."

Gam appeared to be satisfied with my ability to center. "Good on you, Margaret! Do you feel more centered?"

I did. I told Gam as much and then the words poured out of me. Everything that had been weighing on me from Justin's death, to Matt and Greg, to whatever was going on with Pops' death. I couldn't hold it in.

Gam sat and listened. I thought about the contrast between us—with her dark, olive skin and hair, and my ruby-red cheeks and fair hair. No one would think we were related.

Twice she closed her eyes and sent me energy as I spoke. When I finished with my purge she clasped my hands in hers. "You've been holding a lot in. Let's do a little exercise to release all that negative energy, what do you say?"

I agreed. She started chanting. I became immediately aware that we were on a public beach as throaty vowel sounds escaped her lungs and reverberated to me. For a moment I felt my body tense. What would people around us think? Then as her voice got stronger and stronger the sound enveloped me. It felt like my body detached and everything evaporated around me. I was cradled in the most beautiful white light. Was I having an out-of-body experience? I'd heard people talk about them before—Gam included—but I'd never come close to that myself.

As quickly as the feeling caught me, it disappeared. My focus returned to the beach, the noise of children splashing in the waves, announcements for competitors to get to their starting stations, and the oppressive heat.

I threw my hands onto the towel to try to get my bearings. "What just happened?"

Gam gave me an expectant look. "Did you feel it?"

"Yeah." I breathed out hard to try to center myself again. "I definitely felt something."

"Wahoo! It's a new practice I've been working on. You're my first guinea pig."

"Well, I think it works."

"Did you love it?"

"Uh, I'm not exactly sure."

Gam squeezed the amethyst in my hand. "That's okay. We went way up on that one, take some time to come back down."

I noticed Sheriff Daniels ambling our way. He tipped his cowboy hat to me. "Your date's coming." I nudged Gam and handed her back her pendant.

"He's sure handsome, isn't he?" Gam fluffed her hair. Whenever Sherriff Daniels was near, Gam's flirty side came out. Was that what I acted like around Matt?

"Gam, can I ask you one more thing before you go?"

"You can ask me anything, always, Margaret. You know that."

"What should I do about Matt? I'm so confused."

She pursed her lips and thought for a moment. "Follow your intuition. It will lead you exactly where you need to be."

The sheriff cleared his throat as he walked up behind Gam. A toothpick hung from the corner of his mouth. "Am I interrupting anything?"

Gam kissed me on the top of the head and pushed to her feet. "Not at all. Margaret and I were just having a nice little chat and enjoying watching those amazing athletes on the water."

"I'm sorry to have kept you waiting for so long. Things took longer than I expected." Sheriff Daniels extended his hand to help her up. He didn't let go. "Ms. Reed, do you have a moment?"

I nodded and pushed to my feet.

Gam gathered her things as Sherriff Daniels pulled me aside. "Ms. Reed, I thought you should know that this is now officially a murder investigation, which means I don't want you anywhere near my team, understood?"

"Got it." I felt vindicated that I was right, but I didn't say that to Sherriff Daniels.

"Margaret, would you like to join us?" Gam asked, rolling up her beach towel.

"No, thanks." I shook my head. "I already ate. You two have fun." I gave Gam a knowing look.

"You know we will!" she shot back as they strolled away hand in hand.

Sometimes I wondered how Mother was Gam's daughter, but then I thought about my initial reaction when she starting chanting at me. I loved Gam dearly, but for the first time I could imagine that maybe being her daughter wasn't always easy. I had a moment of empathy for Mother. Clearly the heat was getting to me.

# Chapter 16

I spent the remainder of the afternoon seeking shade, dousing myself with water to stay cool, and working on my feature. One of the things that I like to do when writing a story is observe as much as possible. I might not be the most athletically inclined reporter on the *Northwest Extreme* team, but I was pretty confident that I took the most extensive notes, and spent more time in the library and searching the Net than any of my colleagues.

I kept my notebook on hand as I eavesdropped on surfer conversations. I could weave their lingo into my piece. Whenever something particularly defining struck, I jotted it down. Like a conversation about how "stoked" the surfers were about the "killer" winds. I created a glossary of terms that I'd pepper into my story later, like "sheeting in" (the process of pulling the boom in, back and down) and "gear gazing" (which meant looking at your rig instead of where you were supposed to be going).

By the time the banquet was due to start, I had a

good chunk of my introduction written and a handful of interviews completed. Despite the distraction of Justin's murder, I'd been able to stay on track with my story.

The press banquet was taking place on the riverfront in the parking lot of the Insane Wave warehouse. I walked down the pathway toward the warehouse. There was a hub of activity across the street where fans and spectators waited for a spot at one of the many restaurants. The line looked particularly long at the pizza place where diners sat near a giant wood-fired pizza oven and stacks of chopped apple wood waiting to be burned. Pizza smelled delicious, but who would want to sit next to a fire in this heat?

The Insane Wave parking lot had been roped off and lined with citronella torches. Flames danced in the wind. I breathed in the sharp scent and gave the bouncer my name. He scanned the guest list and pointed me to a table near the buffet.

Fortunately the warehouse shaded the area reserved for the banquet. My table had a view of the river and the waterfront park. I watched as children scampered up a rock-climbing wall and chased each other on the grass, waving plastic bubbles. Votive candles in Mason jars flicked in the wind. Bottles of wine, glass pitchers with ice water and cucumber, and baskets of bread sat on the table. I helped myself to water and a slice of sourdough bread.

I was the first one to arrive at my table. I glanced

at the place cards, all held down with river rocks. It looked like Ryan and Greg would both be joining me, along with five other top-tier reporters. Score. I guess that's why we got the table nearest the water.

I spotted Matt about five or six tables away. With his shaggy blond hair and naturally tanned skinned, he could pass as one of the surfers. He was seated next to Avery and didn't even notice when I waved to him. I wondered why Avery was here for a moment and then remembered that she was a competitor. Being sidelined with the flu wasn't stopping her from flirting with Matt. Ugh.

A waiter circled past me with a tray of appetizers— fresh calamari, Chinook salmon crostini and tuna with wasabi. Obviously Kyle and the other King of the Hook organizers were going for a seafood-inspired theme. I took a crostini and allowed the waiter to pour me a glass of wine. I thanked him as he circulated to the next table.

The wine smelled like blackberries and was a beautiful burgundy color. I swirled it twice and took a sip. Yep. Tastes like wine. Not my favorite. The dry wine tickled my throat. I'd been trying to develop my palate, but wine still isn't my thing. Give me a pint of hoppy ale any day and I'm good to go. But wine, well, that was for adults. Maybe someday I'd develop a taste for it. In the meantime, I planned to stick with beer, and fake it whenever I had to. Like right now.

Greg was a wine connoisseur. He knew everything about the different Oregon varietals and blends. I let the wine linger on my tongue hoping to pick up a hint of oak or cherries, something to impress Greg. Speaking of Greg, he strolled up to the table as I choked down another sip.

"Meg. You okay?" He slapped me on the back.

"Yep." I coughed and waved my hand in front of my face. "I just swallowed wrong." Classic. Every time, and I do mean *every time* I'm around Greg I manage to look like an idiot.

He looked especially sexy tonight with the shadow of the river and the flickering torches behind him. His style was rugged outdoors. He wore a loose pair of khakis, a tight V-neck T-shirt and a blue-checkered long-sleeve shirt over it— unbuttoned. I could see his toned stomach and tight abs from underneath the T-shirt.

*Damn, he's lovely.*

Taking the seat next to mine, he grabbed a bottle of wine, filled his glass, and topped mine off, too. "Nice color. Green looks good on you."

I tried not to fluster at his compliment, quickly taking another sip of wine.

He positioned his chair so that we were inches apart. "I heard the news."

"You mean Justin?" I rested my wineglass on the table.

"Yep." He placed his arm on the back of my chair. I caught a whiff of his aftershave and pinched my knee.

*Stop it, Meg. He's your boss.*

Learning that Greg had some connection to

Pops' meth investigation had helped me get over my crush. But anytime he was near, I could feel my heart rate quicken. It was probably his unsettling good looks that made me blush. Hopefully he wouldn't notice in the dwindling evening light.

"You want to tell me what's going on?"

"What do you mean?"

"I mean the fact that you've been out here for less than twenty-four hours and one of the most famous windsurfers in the world ends up dead."

"That's not my fault."

Greg tapped the back of my chair with his fingers and took a drink of his wine with the other. "I didn't say it was, but you're three for three, Meg. This doesn't look good for the magazine."

"It's not exactly great for me either." I could hear the whiny tone in my voice. I didn't like it, but Greg was being completely unfair. It wasn't like I was trying to find murder cases to involve myself in.

He removed his arm from my chair. "I know, but I can't keep you on this story. I'm not taking a risk like this again."

Why was it that no one thought I could take care of myself? Maybe I'd made some mistakes in the past, but I'd also grown up—a lot. I was tired of no one recognizing that fact, and quite frankly treating me like a child. The voice in my head reminded me that I was acting like a child, but I pushed it aside.

I sat up straight in my chair. "That's not fair. I'm already halfway into the story." I bent down, pulled my notebook from under the table, and handed it to him. "Look." I leafed through the notebook and showed him my notes and interviews. "I've been working. I didn't have anything to do with Justin's death. You can't take me off the story now."

Greg scratched the stubble on his cheeks. "Not bad, Meg. Not bad." He handed me my notebook. "I'm open to listening to your pitch on why you think I should keep you here, but I heard that you found Justin's body. I wouldn't exactly call that not having anything to do with it."

"Yeah, but that was a total fluke. I just happened to be at the wrong place at the wrong time."

"Or the right place at the right time, depending on your perspective." Greg gave me a knowing look.

Before I could protest, other tablemates joined us. The conversation shifted to windsurfing stunts, ad revenue and friendly banter about who had climbed the highest and most dangerous peaks in the past year. Dinner was Oregon trout with fresh greens, basmati rice and a corn, basil and tomato salad. Dinners like these were definitely a perk of working in the magazine business. Since I lived alone, I tended to eat soup from a can and peanut butter sandwiches. Greg emptied the wine bottles and signaled the waiter to bring more.

I felt light-headed from the heat and the wine. Mostly, I sat back and observed the conversation spinning around me. Twice I glanced in Matt's direction. Both times he was completely captivated by whatever Avery was saying. I felt an increasingly familiar sting of jealousy watching him hang on her every word.

After the dinner dishes had been cleared away, Kyle called everyone to attention. He gave everyone an update on the investigation and explained what new safety procedures he'd be putting in place once the competition resumed in the morning. He went on to explain the history of King of the Hook and shared his deep regret over the loss of Justin Cruise—in his words, one of the most revolutionary surfers to ever hit the scene. I couldn't help but wonder about Kyle's sincerity. Then again, I'd been in this position before and knew enough to understand that even a murder wouldn't sideline athletes from competing in something as big as King of the Hook.

Once he finished speaking, waiters brought around trays of marionberry cobbler with vanilla bean ice cream. I didn't even care that Greg was sitting next to me as I dug into mine. The tart berries with the sweet, refreshing ice cream hit the spot on such a balmy evening.

"What's your game plan for tomorrow?" Greg asked as the waiters came by to clear our dessert dishes.

"I was planning to hit the beach early to watch warm-ups. Then, the first round of events starts at ten o'clock. I have a one-on-one interview with Kyle scheduled. I figured I'd be here for the entire day, unless you really want to take me off the story," I said, trying hard not to pout.

Greg considered me for a moment. He tightened his jaw. "Meg, you know you are going to kill me. You can't give me that pathetic look and not make me the bad guy. I'll make you a deal. I'll keep you on the story, but one word—ONE—that you're meddling in the investigation, and you're on the next bus back to Portland. Got it?"

"Actually, I drove." I grinned.

Greg shot his finger at me. "Funny. I'm serious. You're here on assignment."

"I know." I nodded.

"Good." He scowled. "But in case you get any ideas to the contrary, you should know that I'm going to stick around for the next few days."

"Great," I gulped.

Greg winked. "See you tomorrow." He drank the last of his wine and walked over to put his arm around a reporter with *Surfing* magazine.

I felt relieved that Greg was letting me stay on the story, but the fact that he was going to be keeping an eye on me wasn't exactly good news. Trying to figure out who killed Justin had just become infinitely harder.

# Chapter 17

I tried to catch up with Matt on my way out, but he had his arm looped through Avery's and was guiding her up the hill. She didn't look steady on her feet. I hoped that he was just being a gentleman, but I couldn't help but worry that he might actually be interested in her.

As I ducked under the ropes, I bumped into Ian. "Sorry," I said, catching my balance.

"It's cool. Are you trashed?" He had on a pair of khaki board shorts, a T-shirt with a shark eating a surfboard, and a loose tie hanging around his neck.

"Trashed?"

"You know, like, drunk?"

"Yeah, I know what it means, but me? No." I scowled. "Why would you think I was trashed?"

"Dude, everyone is. That wine was wicked intense."

I put my hand to my forehead. Was I tipsy? "Yeah, I agree."

Ian stepped to the side to let me pass.

"Can I ask you a question?" I asked, not moving.

"What's up?"

"Do you know that guy Sherman?"

Ian shook his head. "Sherman? Don't think so."

"The guy who owns the gaming shop."

"Oh yeah, that weird dude who always wears a cape."

"Exactly."

"What about him?"

"He said he thought you were at his store this morning. I don't remember seeing you out on the river, so I was just wondering why he would say that."

Ian shrugged. "Who knows? 'Cause he's a weird dude?"

I waited to see if he would say more and to try to gauge his response.

"What's with all the questions?" Ian sounded defensive.

"I'm considering including some background information about Hood River's response to having King of the Hook in town," I lied. "You know, taking the angle of what businesses and locals think about the competition."

Ian must have bought my lie. "I don't think he likes us much."

"Us?" I asked.

"Surfers."

"Right." I couldn't tell if Ian was including me in his description. If he was, I was flattered to say the least. "So you didn't vandalize his shop?" I pressed on, hoping Ian wouldn't close up.

"Dude, I'm not ten. That's not my style."

Part of me believed him, but then again I had seen him there when Justin was harassing Sherman. He could just be a good liar.

"Have you talked to Harriet?" Ian continued before I had come up with a new question.

"Harriet? No, why?"

Ian shrugged. "I saw her hanging around the shop really early this morning. Maybe she did it."

"Why would Harriet egg Sherman's store? Does she even know him?"

Ian flicked a mosquito from his wrist. "How would I know? I just saw her there and she was acting all trippy. Maybe Justin put her up to it or something."

Harriet doing Justin's dirty work was something I hadn't considered. If she really was in love with him, could she have egged Sherman's shop? Maybe. I wasn't sure how that played into his murder, though.

I wondered why Ian was throwing shade at Harriet. He told me earlier that he didn't come to the river until later. Had I just caught him in a lie?

"When I saw her she ran off," Ian said. "I didn't give it much thought because I was on my way to pick up Avery from the clinic. They wouldn't let her leave without a ride."

Aha! Ian picked up Avery from the clinic, so obviously Avery hadn't lied about that. But then a new thought crossed my mind. If Ian had picked Avery up, that still gave both of them time to get down to the river and murder Justin. Now I knew that Harriet was hanging around the area at the same time. I wasn't sure if what I'd just learned was more or less helpful. All three of them were still viable suspects.

"Dude, I don't get it. Don't you write for *Northwest Extreme?*"

"Yeah." I spoke quickly. It's a bad habit when I get nervous. "It's just that I thought there could be a bigger story about the darker side of the sport. If windsurfers are really doing damage to the towns they visit, that might be something we'd want to cover."

Ian didn't look convinced, but another mosquito landed on his cheek. He smacked it, squashing mosquito guts on his face. Gross. "I'm outta here." He wiped guts from his skin and left me standing in the dark.

He seemed sincere enough, but honestly I had no clue who to trust, and I was breaking my own promise. *Time to call it a night, Meg,* I told myself as I headed toward home.

The King of the Hook party was still thriving on the beach. A metal band played on the stage. Fans jammed on the sand, waving their cell phones in the air. A bonfire roared near the water, where people gathered drinking cheap beer and taking turns tossing each other into the water. The wind had died down a bit. I had a feeling that the party was going to rage long into the night.

I was wiped out from my early-morning start, the stress of discovering Justin's body, and a long day in the sun. I couldn't wait to get back to the house and crawl into bed. As I headed up the sidewalk toward town, the noise from the beach faded away. A handful of late-night diners sat outside, but mostly downtown was closed up for the night.

I passed Sherman's store, The Quest. The windows glinted under the streetlight. I was glad to see that the kids had wiped away any remnants of the egging.

A hazy light glowed inside. I peered in the window. Sherman and his paladins were gaming in the back of the store. Jordan caught my eye and jumped up. Great.

I plastered on a smile as he ran to greet me at the door.

"Hi, Meg." He offered me a plastic dagger. "Did you come to play?"

"Oh, thanks." I took the dagger. "I'm actually on my way home."

"You should come in." His eyes reminded me of a puppy. Did I look like that around Matt? God, I hoped not.

"Uh, maybe for a second."

*You're going to regret this, Meg.*

The Quest felt like a dungeon. That was probably what Sherman was going for. I plastered on a smile as I followed Jordan to the back.

Sherman and his paladins had an elaborate map covering two tables. There were tiny plastic figurines placed strategically around the board, and everyone had stacks of black cards in their hands.

"How's it going, guys?" I asked, trying not to let the stench of teenage body odor mingled with open bags of stale Cheetos make me gag.

"Meg, you here to play?" Sherman stood and swooped his cape in a bow.

"I wish I could, but I've got to head home to work on my story. I was just passing by."

Jordan's voice squeaked as he spoke to an equally gangly kid wearing a knight's helmet. "She'd make a great princess warrior, don't you think?"

"How's the secret project?" I noticed the sheet was gone.

Sherman swooped in front of Jordan and pointed to the ceiling. "Take a look."

I craned my head back. There was a four-foot-long pirate ship hanging from the ceiling, complete with cannons aimed at the floor and a skull flag at the helm.

*That's their big secret?* Classic.

"It looks good, guys." I gave them a thumbs-up. "Listen, I'm going to take off, but good luck with the game."

They're such easy targets, I thought as I left the store. No wonder Justin bullied them. After walking two blocks up Oak, I turned off the main street. The side streets were completely dark. I felt a shiver run up my spine, even though the temperature must have been in the nineties.

I sped up.

Were those footsteps behind me, or was my imagination playing tricks on me?

Either way, it didn't matter. I power-walked for the next block, scanning the historic bungalows facing the river. If necessary I could run up the front steps of one of them and bang on the door for help, right?

I heard the distinct sound of leaves crunching behind me. My heart jumped into my throat. I could feel my pulse pounding in my neck. Was someone following me?

I stopped in mid-stride and spun around. The crunching sound stopped.

"Who's there?" I called, holding up my cell phone like a flashlight.

Silence.

I slowly checked to the right. Then the left.

Nothing.

I still couldn't shake the feeling that I was being watched. The tiny blond hairs on my arms stood at attention. A cold, tingling sensation overcame me. I couldn't explain it, but I knew—or as Gam would say, "had a knowing" that I wasn't alone.

Something snapped behind me. I didn't wait to figure out what it was. I took off in a sprint toward the house.

I ran as fast as my short legs would carry me. The sound of heavy footsteps echoed behind me. I couldn't risk turning around to look, for fear that whoever was chasing me would be able to overtake me if I stopped even for a second.

The rental house was three houses away. Bugs swarmed around the glowing porch light.

*You're almost there, Meg. Keep running.*

Thank goodness Jill had convinced me to take a Pilates class with her. I could feel the difference in the power of my legs.

Unfortunately whoever was chasing me must be even more powerful. Not only were the footsteps getting closer, but it also felt like they would attack me from behind at any second. I could almost feel their hot breath on the back of my neck as they panted in anger.

Why would someone be coming after me? It didn't make any sense. What had I done?

*Think about that later, Meg. Right now you need to run!*

# Chapter 18

The front porch was within arm's reach. I launched my body up the stairs and landed with a thud on the welcome mat.

I gasped for air and pounded on the base of the door with my fist. "HELP!"

Feeling slightly relieved to be back to the safety of the house, I sat up and scanned the dark sidewalk. A figure dressed all in black raced past the front lawn and continued down the sideway.

"Hey!" I called out.

At that moment the door swung open and I fell inside.

"Megs?" Matt bent down and helped me up. "What's going on?"

My face stung with heat. I panted, trying to catch my breath. He guided me to the couch. "Here, sit. What's up? You're a mess."

"Someone was chasing me," I gasped.

"What?" He craned his neck to be able to see out the bay window. "Where?"

"Right there." I pointed behind me with my thumb. "When I made it to the porch he ran off."

"He?" Matt continued to peer out the window.

"I think so, or a really tall woman. Whoever it was almost caught up with me." I wiped salty sweat from my forehead.

Matt took notice. "Hold on. Let me get you some water." He went into the kitchen as I tried to calm my breathing. Who had been chasing me? Was it a man?

I had one guess: Ian. Maybe he got spooked that I'd been asking about his whereabouts this morning. Could he have followed me? But what was he going to do if he caught up with me? Knock me out? Scare me? If that was the case, he had succeeded.

I gulped the water that Matt offered.

"Let's back up a little." Matt paced in front of the couch. "When did you notice someone following you?"

"When I was a few blocks away from the house." I took another drink of water.

"Why did you walk home by yourself in the dark?" Matt folded his arms across his chest. "Not a wise move, Meg."

"I didn't even think about it, honestly. The beach was raging. There was a huge party going on. It wasn't until I turned off the main street that it got dark and deserted."

Matt shook his head. "Megs, you can't keep doing stuff like this. It's going to catch up with you."

"What's that supposed to mean? It's not like I tried to get followed."

"You never know what kinds of crazies are out there. You're an attractive woman." He trailed off as I shot him a death stare.

"I don't like where you're going with this one bit, Matt Parker. I happen to have taken self-defense classes. You know that. I can walk three blocks by myself," I huffed.

Matt threw his hands up in the air. "Easy there, Tex. I'm just concerned about your personal safety."

"Because I'm female, right?" I glared at him.

"Where is this coming from?" Matt looked injured.

To be honest, I wasn't sure. Lately I'd been feeling like everyone was treating me like a child. I guess in fairness, I'd been making some childish mistakes, but the fact that everyone, Matt included, seemed to be taking notice had me on the defensive. Gam would tell me that everyone around me was serving as a mirror for my behavior. The problem was I wasn't ready to see that side of myself reflected back to me.

At twenty-four most of my friends and acquaintances were job-hopping, couch-surfing, and letting their parents bail them out of their problems. Who was I kidding? Most of them were still living at home. I was completely on my own, and for the moment feeling bitter about it. I wanted to curl up on the couch and let someone else take care of me. I wasn't doing a very bang-up job of taking care of myself.

Matt took my water glass to refill it in the kitchen.

*Time to stop the pity party, Meg,* I told myself. Why are you taking this out on Matt? Probably because he was the safest person around.

When he returned with more water, I brushed a tear from my eye. "I'm sorry. I'm an idiot. I don't even know what I'm doing right now, but you don't deserve to get beat up in the process."

Matt sat next to me. I could smell his shaving cream and a hint of mint on his breath. He didn't say anything as he picked up my hand and caressed it in his. I closed my eyes. His gentle touch sent a new kind of shiver up my spine.

We sat without saying anything for a moment. Then he turned and leaned his head toward mine. Our foreheads touched. Our lips were inches apart. My heart pulsed in my chest. I tried not to breath, worried that I might ruin the moment.

He let go of my hand and brought his fingers to my cheek. "Megs." His voice was thick with emotion.

"Yeah?"

"Don't say anything." He placed his finger on my lips.

My breath became shallow.

He moved his mouth closer to mine. I leaned in

to meet his kiss. Just as his lips brushed mine, the door flung open.

"Anyone home?" Jill's voice called from the entryway.

Matt jumped away from me. I put my hand to my heart and felt my cheeks flame with heat.

Jill entered the living room. "Hey, guys, I just . . ." She trailed off, and looked from Matt to me. "Uh, I was just going to fill you in on what I learned tonight."

Matt cleared his throat. "Let me get you some more water." He took my full glass of water into the kitchen.

"Sorry," Jill mouthed. "I keep interrupting you two at the wrong moment. What's that all about?" She'd changed out of her bikini wrap into a pair of skinny jeans and a well-cut black shirt. Her skin glowed with sun.

"The Universe conspiring against me." I shrugged and patted the couch. "Don't worry about it."

"Maybe I should see if one of the hotels has a room. Give you two an opportunity to have some time alone." She gave me a knowing look.

"No." I shook my head. "It's not meant to be right now. I keep messing everything up."

Matt returned with the same water glass. He looked dazed. "You want some water, Jill?"

Jill declined. She tried to break the tension. "I have some news, you guys. You want to hear it?'"

"Of course." I took the water from Matt. He sat in a leather chair that was positioned the farthest away from the couch. He looked like he had his fair share of sun, too. "But first, I have some big news, too. Sherriff Daniels confirmed that Justin was murdered."

"We knew it," Jill said.

Matt's cobalt eyes looked especially bright tonight as he nodded in agreement. No wonder Avery had been cozying up to him. He was super cute.

"I stayed for the beach party." Jill continued. "The first band was amazing. Did you catch any of it?"

"No, we were both at the press banquet."

"I heard them," Matt interjected.

"Yeah, they rocked, but the band that's playing now is terrible. Metal—yuck." Jill shuddered.

"What's that got to do with your news?"

Jill gave me a sly smile. "I'm getting to that. Let me have my Miss Marple moment."

I rolled my eyes.

"It's all in the reveal. That's the best part of Christie's books. She gathers all the suspects into a room like this one for the big reveal."

"Okay, we're ready for your reveal."

Jill frowned. "Come on, you can at least pretend to be more excited than that?"

I scooted forward on the couch and bounced my foot on the floor. "Look, I'm on the edge of my seat."

"Matty?" Jill raised one expertly waxed brow.

Matt played along. He cracked his knuckles. "Do

tell, Miss Pettygrove. What have you uncovered in your investigation?"

"That's more like it!" Jill's face brightened. She rubbed her hands together. "I ran into Harriet at the concert. It was my *jam*—as the surfers like to say—but she didn't look very happy, so I worked my way over to her and struck up a conversation."

She paused to make sure that we were both playing along with her reveal. "Harriet is really distraught over Justin's death."

"Really distraught, like she did it?" I asked.

Jill shook her head. "Really distraught, like devastated. Completely devastated."

"I don't get it. What are you implying?"

"I think they were a thing."

"Justin and Harriet?" I looked at Matt. He shrugged.

"Yes!" Jill's tone was insistent. "I got the impression that they were together last night—you know as in *together.*"

"I got the impression that Harriet was a stalker, and that Justin didn't reciprocate her feelings."

"Maybe that's what he wanted everyone to think. Harriet is totally wrecked by his death, and not just because she had a crush. They were definitely an item."

I agreed with Jill's assessment. Harriet had been a mess when I talked to her earlier in the day. What did that mean in terms of Justin's murder, though? What if Avery learned that Justin and Harriet were having an affair? Could she have killed him because of that? Suddenly Avery was back to my number-one suspect.

Or was it possible that Harriet had killed Justin in a lover's fight? I wasn't sure of anything other than the fact that I needed sleep. Jill and Matt agreed. We parted ways in the living room. I considered bringing my laptop out and setting up shop on the couch. Maybe Matt would take the hint. But he followed Jill down the hall.

Another lost opportunity, I sighed.

Tomorrow I would start fresh. I had a long list of events—watching the final round of stunts, a private interview with Kyle scheduled and the vendor showcase with Greg. I was worried I might not be able to sleep due to the running loop of Justin's murder in my head. Apparently, that wasn't the case. The second my head hit the pillow I was out.

# Chapter 19

There was no reprieve from the blazing sun when I woke the next morning. It was the third day of the King of the Hook competition and the oppressive heat weighed as heavy on me as Justin's murder did.

I lingered in the shower, keeping the temperature lukewarm and trying to wash away the memory of seeing Justin's lifeless body being tossed around in the waves.

*Today's a new day, Meg,* I told myself as I pulled on a ruby-pink sundress made out of equal parts quick dry nylon and spandex. It stretched perfectly and highlighted all the right curves. The lightweight fabric was designed to wick sweat away. I had a feeling that was going to be important today.

Jill offered me a cup of cold brew over ice when I came into the kitchen. Her sketchbook lay open on the kitchen table. She had roughed out a landscape of the Columbia River and Washington cliff side with varying shades of charcoal pencils. The light strokes that she'd used for the clouds hanging above the river made them appear to be floating on the wind.

I gladly took the coffee and poured in a splash of cream. "This is amazing," I said, pointing to her sketch.

She tucked a pencil behind her ear and studied the sketch. "I'm not loving it yet, but it's a work in progress, right?"

"A work in progress?" I laughed. "I'd hang that on my wall today."

Jill shook her head and closed the sketchbook.

"Where's Matt?" I asked, watching the cream sink to the bottom of the glass.

"He had to take off early to cover breaking news. It's all over Twitter." She held up her phone. Her phone case had a Monet painting on the back. "They've officially announced that Justin Cruise was murdered."

"That was fast."

She bit into a plum. "It would have been even faster if they paid attention to us young ones. We know more than they think, huh? Matt said he'd find you at the beach."

"Cool." I stirred the cream into my coffee. The dark brew swirled into a creamy beige color. I felt vindicated. The police had confirmed my suspicion. That meant they were probably going to be even more tight-lipped about their investigation. "What's your plan for the day?"

"More sketching and maybe paddle boarding,

depending on how motivated I am." Jill took another bite of the plum. Juice squirted down her hand. I grabbed a napkin for her. "Thanks," she said, wiping the juicy liquid from her wrist. "These are amazing. Handpicked. Organic. And delish."

"Tempting. But you know me. My morning routine is this liquid gold." I held up the coffee and took a drink. There's nothing like cold brew on a hot summer morning. The cold brew craze had become so prolific in Portland that specialty coffeehouses had installed taps specifically for their cold brew offerings. Not only was cold brew on tap around town, the latest trend was serving it on nitro. Coffee snobs were flocking to artisan shops for a dense glass of the cold brew that was kegged and then infused with nitrogen. The result was a creamier, thicker coffee that looked like it had the consistency of a pint of Guinness stout. Seriously, coffee isn't just for drinking in Portland, it's a lifestyle.

"I hear you." Jill pointed to the almost empty pitcher of cold brew on the table. "I've already had three cups. It's so smooth."

"Do you want to hit the beach with me this morning? Scope out those sexy surfers?" I winked.

She flipped the sketchbook open to a blank page. "That sounds great. I'm hoping that if I hang around Harriet and her groupies, maybe I'll be able to get some more gossip out of her."

"That would be awesome." I finished off the remaining cold brew. "You really think she and Justin were having a fling?"

Jill doodled on the page and didn't meet my eyes. "I know about flings. Trust me."

"Right." I kept my tone neutral. I didn't want to push.

Last winter I had discovered that Will Barrington, Jill's boyfriend, had been cheating on her. I'd never been a fan of Will, but knowing that he had cheated on my best friend intensified my dislike. The only problem was that Jill hadn't exactly been forthcoming about her feelings. She'd said that they were "on a break" and nothing more. I wasn't sure if she hated him, or if she planned to forgive him and take him back. We'd been tiptoeing around the subject for months. For the moment, he was out of the picture. I liked it that way, and hoped Jill did, too.

"So the beach?" She smiled broadly. Obviously she wasn't ready to talk about it yet.

After I lathered every inch of my skin in sunscreen, we walked through town and back to the scene of the crime. No wonder Matt had left early. The beach was more packed with media. News of Justin's death must have spread internationally. There were reporters with thick accents reporting live to Australia and Japan. The national morning shows had sent their top anchors. I recognized one of the national morning hosts in the crowd.

"Wow. This place is *crazy*!" Jill looked at the reporters jockeying for position and feigning serious looks on the grass. "There's no space."

"I guess Justin's murder is big news."

"Makes sense. Everyone already thinks windsurfing is dangerous. This just sensationalized it." She
pointed to a patch of rocky beach. "Let's head down
there."

We pushed through the throng of media. I was
going to have to find Greg as soon as possible. I
wondered if he would want me to come up with a
new angle. We weren't the only ones covering King
of the Hook, but this was a level of press I'd never
seen. If Justin's murder was being covered live by
the national morning talk shows, I had a feeling we
were going to have to strategize *Northwest Extreme*'s
approach.

A group of guys made space for Jill to spread out
her blanket.

"Hey, there's room." One of the surfers elbowed
the guy next to him, who quickly folded his blanket
in half.

She promised to stay in the same vicinity and to
try to learn as much as she could about Harriet and
the other groupies. I left her chatting with four
dreamy men and went to find Greg.

It wasn't even nine, but I could feel sweat beginning to pool on my back. So much for the dress
wicking away moisture. It wasn't working.

Kyle had roped off an area for press, but he
probably hadn't counted on this kind of media coverage. It swelled at the seams. The morning's Big
Air stunt round would take place a few feet away, but
the thought of being packed together like sardines

made me sweat more. There was no way I was going to cram in with the masses.

I decided to see if I could find a different spot farther down the beach. The fact that the beach was a sea of colorful umbrellas, towels and lounge chairs didn't bode well for me finding a less crowded area.

The actual beach where we'd practiced our wind-surfing technique yesterday had been reserved for the competitors and judges. Surfboards were laid out in rows, and the judges sat on a temporary scaf-folding in order to get the best view of the Big Air tricks.

Maybe I could sneak in there.

"Meg!" Greg called. He and Kyle were directing contestants where to go. Why did he always seem to know the organizers of every event we covered? I mean, on one hand it made sense. *Northwest Extreme* is one of the most-read outdoor publications in the United States. Greg made it company policy to sponsor and partner with as many adventure con-tests, races and exhibitions as possible. But I couldn't help but wonder how he knew so many people "in the business."

I smiled and waved to them. Maybe Greg would be my *in*. Better than being crammed with all those sweaty reporters in the press area.

"Are your ears ringing?" Greg asked, clapping me on the back. He didn't know his own strength.

I almost fell on the loose rocks. Catching my arm, he hoisted me up. "Sorry."

"No worries." I'd learned that phrase from an Australian adventure enthusiast and producer, and had adopted it. I like the sentiment. Why worry? People spend too much time worrying about things they can't control. I'd learned that from Pops' death. I never worried about him getting hit on his bike. He was the most safety-conscious rider I'd ever met—except for Matt, of course. It's the random things that sneak up on us. Justin's death was proof of that.

"We were just talking about you," Greg continued. "I was telling Kyle that you might be the most junior reporter on my team, but you are by far one of the most tenacious." He smiled. Kyle didn't.

"That's me. Tenacious." I laughed. "Are you watching the finals here?"

Greg started to speak, but Kyle cut him off. "No, you can't come in here." He pointed at the press area. "This area is reserved for the competitors. All press need to be over there."

Why the sudden shift in his attitude? He'd been so friendly and helpful yesterday, but now he was acting like he wanted to get away from me as soon as he could.

"No worries." *Okay, Meg. Twice is overkill.*

Greg looked a bit taken back by Kyle's direction, but he shrugged it off and looped his arm around me. "What do you say, Meg? Shall we go join the cattle?"

"Sure." I smiled at Kyle. He pursed his lips and pointed to the press area.

"What's his deal?" I asked Greg as we walked back to where I'd just been.

"Who? Kyle?"

"Yeah, didn't it seem weird that he wanted us out of there?"

"Nah, he's probably worried about safety and stressed out with all the pressure he's under. A murder investigation makes for sensational news. He's been up since two a.m. doing the east coast morning shows." Greg stopped and removed his arm from my shoulder. He shook his index finger. "Meg, what are you doing?"

"Nothing. Why?" I tried to keep my tone innocent.

Greg didn't buy it. "I know what you're up to, and it needs to stop right now. Got it? No murder for you."

"I'm not doing anything with the murder," I lied. "I just wondered why Kyle seemed so insistent to get us out of the area, that's all."

"Right. That's all." Greg shook his head. "I love that you don't know how transparent you are." He chuckled.

Before I could protest more, another reporter recognized Greg. "Greg! Dude, come meet the team."

Greg disappeared in the herd. I stuck to the

edges. The area was about thirty feet wide and
enclosed with black mesh netting. Sponsor logos
and banners were attached to the netting. A few of
them caught in the breeze. It felt like I was stepping
into a press mosh pit.

A boisterous radio announcer called our attention to the water where the surfers were mounting
their boards and preparing to take flight. I tried to
make my body as small as possible as the crowd of
reporters pushed forward, trying to get a better
view of the action. This was not going to be fun.

An air gun sounded. I jumped and clutched my
chest. The windsurfers paddled into the surf and
effortlessly raised their masts with one hand. The
competition was on.

Ian was by far the best surfer. I couldn't exactly
pinpoint what it was about his style. Some of the
other competitor's tricks might have caught a bit
more air, but Ian was one with the water. He hung
over the waves. It looked like he was literally being
suspended in midair. I realized I was holding my
breath waiting for him to land. I didn't need to. He
stuck each landing perfectly, barely skimming the
surf and then bouncing back into the air. It was
amazing to watch, especially after being out in the
water yesterday. I knew what a challenge it was just
to get the sail up, let alone catch a giant gust of
wind and control the board twenty feet in the air.

I stood on my tiptoes and leaned over the barri-
cade to try to get some candid shots with my phone.
Greg had hired a professional photographer to

shoot all the glossy pictures for the spread and cover, but I liked to use candid pictures for our social media. There were a ton of photo filter apps that I'd become proficient in using. For this event, I'd use a grainy vignette filter. It should give the pictures a hint of retro—something most of my fellow millennials loved.

The Big Air portion of King of the Hook was where the surfers really had a chance to shine. Other parts of the competition focused on technical skill and maneuvering through a course, but Big Air was exactly that—big air! Even more seasoned members of the press gasped audibly at some of the impressive stunts and winced at some of the killer crashes.

As the morning wore on, the heat continued to rise. I could feel my face and arms starting to burn. Twice I caught myself swaying and had to grab on to the fence to steady myself. This wasn't good. The heat was starting to get to me. A reporter who had to be six and half feet tall jumped over the netting and stood in front of me. There was no chance I could get a shot now. I tucked my phone into my bra and tried to concentrate on the competitors, but waves of dizziness assaulted me.

*Please don't let me pass out,* I prayed silently as bright spots flashed in front of my eyes. That couldn't be a good sign.

Greg, who was on the opposite side of the press area, caught my eye as I swayed from side to side. He frowned. I tried to smile.

My stomach gurgled so loudly that the giant in front of me turned around. Oh no. Was I going to throw up? Maybe Avery had given me the flu.

I was going down. I could feel my legs start to buckle as everything in front of me started going dark. Greg caught my eye. He pushed people out of his way, sprinted to me, and scooped me into his arms just as I blacked out.

"Meg, Meg, are you with me?" Greg's voice sounded fuzzy and far away.

Where was I? What happened?

Greg shook my shoulder. "Meg, are you okay?"

I blinked my eyes. Greg knelt over me. The second I saw the look of concern in his eyes I knew exactly what had happened. I had passed out. Great. Add that to the list of one thousand embarrassing things I'd done in front of my boss.

"Get me some water, and a medic!" Greg yelled to the crowd around us. Someone raced off. I tried to sit up. Not my best idea. Spots exploded in front of my eyes, and my head swirled. I thought I might throw up.

"Easy. Easy, Meg." Greg held out his arm to steady me and keep me from trying to sit up more.

"I can't believe I just passed out. I've never done that before."

Greg scanned the crowd. He held up his palm and forced people to step back. "It's hot out here. You look like a tomato. Have you been drinking water?"

Had I? I guess not.

He didn't wait for me to answer. Someone handed him a water bottle. He twisted off the cap and poured it on my wrists. It felt cool. I didn't realize how hot I'd been. Then he cupped some in his hands and ran it over the back of my neck.

Thrusting it in my hand, he commanded me to drink. "Sips. Small sips."

He watched as I drank from the bottle. "Sip, Meg. If you drink that too fast you'll probably throw it up."

I followed his direction and sipped from the bottle. Even though I was burning up, the water running down my back gave me the shivers.

"Are you shivering, Meg?" Greg rubbed my arm in an attempt to warm me up.

"Yeah," I replied as my teeth started to chatter. "Weird. I'm hot, but all of a sudden I can't stop shaking."

Greg jumped to his feet and lifted me up. "We're not waiting for the medic. I'm taking you to the tent right now."

"Why?" I chattered as Greg scooped me into his arms.

"Because you might have heat stroke. We need to get you medical attention right now." Greg elbowed through the crowd, shouting for people to make room. The medic met us halfway. He and Greg both carried me into the EMS tent.

The medic began misting my face with a squirt bottle. He checked my pulse and stuck a thermometer in my ear. Another medic brought over a cooler filled with ice packs. He placed one on my neck, two under my armpits and one on my back. The thermometer beeped. The medic removed it from my ear and showed me it to me. It read: 103 degrees.

"Is that bad?" I grimaced.

"It could be worse." He fanned me as he spoke. "I want to get your temp below one hundred and one."

He turned to his partner. "I think we should run an IV."

I gulped.

Greg squeezed my hand. "It's okay, Meg. They're just going to give you fluids. Electrolytes."

Have I mentioned that I'm not a fan of needles?

The other medic spritzed my face. "I think we can watch her for a while. Her temp is under one hundred and five."

"A hundred and five?" I think my eyes must have bugged out. I didn't even know temperatures could go that high.

"That's when we classify heat stroke. You're close, but I'd categorize you with having heat exhaustion. It's a good thing your friend here started to administer first aid right away."

I smiled at Greg, feeling completely mortified.

For the next twenty or thirty minutes—I wasn't keeping track of time, but I could hear the announcers broadcasting on the beach—the medics fanned, spritzed, and positioned ice packs all over me. They had me alternate taking sips of water, Gatorade, and orange juice.

One of the medics took my temperature again. "Ninety-nine. Nice. You're going to be okay."

I already felt more like myself. The trembling had subsided. My cheeks stopped burning, and the fluid had restored my energy. Thank God.

Why do you always end up in positions like this, Meg? I asked myself as the EMS workers removed the ice packs and told me I was free to go whenever I felt up to it.

If only by free to go they meant free to go crawl under a rock and escape the embarrassment of having heat exhaustion in front of my boss.

I thanked them for their help and got to my feet. The dizzy feeling was gone, but my stomach gurgled in displeasure. I didn't think I was going to be up for eating anything anytime soon.

Greg followed me outside. "Where do you think you're going?" He put his hand on my shoulder to stop me.

"To work. I have an interview scheduled with Kyle and then we're going to attend the vendor showcase, right?"

"*You're* not going anywhere. *I'm* going to attend the showcase. You are going to get out of this heat."

Passing out and having to receive medical attention wasn't the impression I was trying to make in terms of my improving outdoor skills. I had to finish out the day. Not just for Greg, but for myself. "No, I'm fine. I really want to stay."

Greg scowled. "Meg, you have heat stroke. You can't spend all afternoon in the sun. That's the worst idea I've heard from you yet."

"I'll stay in the shade, and I'll stay ahead of my fluid intake." I held up the Gatorade bottle the medics had sent with me. "You heard what they said. I don't have heat stroke. Just a little touch of heat exhaustion."

"That's a technicality." Greg rolled his eyes.

"I promise, I can do this. I'll take it easy. I feel good."

Greg looked skeptical.

"Really, I do. I feel fine now. It was too much sun, and so hot with all those reporters crammed together. I was stupid not to drink water, or find some shade. I promise, I'll be careful."

"Meg, what is it about you?" Greg sighed and shook his head. "You always find a way to convince me that you're fine, when you're probably not."

I grinned. "It's a skill."

He hardened his eyes. "I'm being serious here. I'm not going to risk your health and safety. I'm almost your father." His voice caught a bit.

"Thanks . . ." What did he mean by that?

"I wasn't done." He cut me off.

"Sorry." I looked at my feet.

"What I was going to say was that I'm keeping an eye on you. If you show even the slightest sign of not feeling well, I will personally deliver you back to your hotel."

"House."

"Huh?"

"House. I'm staying in a house."

He frowned. "Meg, I'm not messing around. Heat stroke can be deadly. I've seen it take out some of the toughest athletes. You need to be very careful."

"I will be." I pointed to the grass. "My grandmother and friend are over there under that huge umbrella. I'll camp out in the shade with them until it's time for Kyle's interview."

Greg agreed, but left with one final warning about staying cool and pushing fluids. I walked toward Gam and Jill, sure that all the eyes staring at me had probably watched me collapse. Awesome.

There was no reason for Greg to worry. Passing out had been one of my most unpleasant experiences to date. I wasn't going to take any chances of having that happen again. Although I did shudder at the thought that heat stroke could be deadly. What was it with the theme of death this weekend?

# Chapter 20

Gam eyed me with concern. "Margaret, what's happened?" She scooted to the side of the blanket to make room for me. "Sit. You look flushed."

I gladly followed her recommendation and lowered myself onto the blanket. Jill moved the umbrella as I sat, and repositioned it so that it completely shaded me. I took a sip from the Gatorade bottle and rested it on the blanket.

"Gam's right. You don't look so good." Jill grabbed a water bottle from her bag and handed it to me.

"I'm okay." I told them, taking the water that Jill offered and holding the cool bottle to my forehead. When I explained what happened, they both insisted that I should head back to the house. I refused, giving them the same pitch I gave Greg.

Gam moved closer to me. She placed one hand on my heart and wrapped the other around my neck. "I'm going to do some work on you." She closed her eyes. Usually when she placed her hands on me they radiated heat. This time they felt cool to the touch, like ice.

"Doing work on you doesn't mean that you're off the hook, though." Gam's doe-like brown eyes widened. "You have personal responsibility when it comes to your self-care."

"I know."

"Do you?" Gam's head tilted to the side. "It seems like some of your choices haven't been aligned with your highest and best."

"You're right." I sighed and twisted the cap off the water bottle. "It's just that I'm really committed to doing a good job for *Northwest Extreme.* You both know that I made some mistakes early on, and I guess I'm pushing too hard because I really like this job and I want to prove to myself and everyone else that I can do it—that I can do it well."

Gam nodded. "I understand, but can I offer one reminder?"

"Please."

She smiled and then she looked past me. Her eyes glazed over for a moment. She held up one finger and bobbed her head. Returning her focus to us, she turned to Jill. "They're telling me this is for you, too."

Jill seemed taken aback.

"They're reminding you to stay open and in the flow. When we try and force an idea or agenda it creates a kink in the energy." To demonstrate this, she held both of her arms in a V-shape over her head. "The energy flows into us like a funnel." She pulled her hands together over her head and ran them down her body.

I could almost see the energy in her graceful, intentional movement.

"When we try to force or push something"—she paused and punched the air with her fist—"we create resistance." Her hands twisted together, like she was ringing out a wet dishtowel. "If we can relax and concentrate on being present in this moment, then the energy can flow."

"That makes sense," Jill said.

"It does, doesn't it?" Gam smiled.

"Yeah, but how do you do it?" I asked. "That's my challenge. I get it. I want to stay *in the flow,* but usually I end up forcing everything."

"It's like what I was saying about the concepts we're working on being simple, but not easy," Gam said. "It takes intention and practice. When those thoughts appear, try to acknowledge them. You don't have to fight them, that's just going to give them more energy. Acknowledge and return to center." She placed her hands in prayer in front of her heart. "Return to center."

Jill and I moved our hands in the same prayer stance.

"Are you girls up for a little experiment?" Gam's face brightened.

"Sure." Jill shrugged. "Meg?"

"You know I'm always up for an experiment."

Gam's eyes twinkled. Her foot bounced on the

blanket. "Great. Here's what I want you to do. Think of an intention. It can be anything you want it to be."

Jill started to speak. Gam put her finger to her lips. "Wait. Don't tell me what it is. This is for you."

"Don't say it out loud?" I asked.

"Don't say it out loud. Think it in your head. Do you both have one?"

We nodded.

"Great!" Gam clapped her hands together. "Now comes the fun part. What I want you to do for the next few days is be open to seeing and receiving your intention wherever you go. Let's say my intention is to see more joy. In setting that intention I'm partnering with the Universe to allow me to experience more joy. Does that make sense?"

Jill pointed to a woman a few feet away from us wearing the same hat. "I bought this hat and now I'm seeing it everywhere I go. Is it kind of like that?"

"Yes!" Gam shouted. "Exactly. I get so excited about this. It's exactly like that. Have you ever noticed that right after you buy a new car you suddenly see that car everywhere? You probably saw that same car a hundred times before and never noticed it, but once you've purchased that car your focus—or we could say intention—is on that car. You start to see it everywhere you go. It's the law of attraction. If you want more joy and light, focus on seeing more joy and light."

"I want more joy and light." Jill chuckled.

"We all do," Gam agreed. "Are you excited to try

our little experiment? Let's report back on how it works."

We agreed. The truth was, I wasn't sure what I wanted to attract. I had so much personal growth to do. Choosing just one intention was difficult. Could I choose three? Four maybe? No. That would defeat the point. I decided on "being in the flow." That's what I needed most. I needed to find a way to let go of trying to be perfect, and just work on doing what I knew. I knew how to write. I knew how to listen. I knew how to observe. If I could work on *staying in the flow* like Gam suggested, then everything—maybe even the truth about Justin's murder—would fall in line. A girl could hope, right?

With the intention of being in the flow, I sat back and watched the surfers flow through the river. Maybe there was something to this exercise.

The shade of Jill's large beach umbrella and Gam constantly forcing water on me had me feeling back to normal, or at least as close as possible given my brush with heat stroke. We all watched in awe as the finalists took to the river for one last time. I knew that Ian was the clear winner. About an hour later that was confirmed when he took to the winner's podium to receive the Big Air trophy.

"I'm going to go see if I can get a couple pictures for social," I said, standing.

Gam searched the beach. "I think I might go see if I can find that hunky cowboy boot–wearing sheriff of mine."

Jill waved to us. "Have fun, you two, I may take a morning nap."

I gave Gam a quick hug and left before she had a chance to suggest that maybe I should get out of the sun.

The area surrounding the podium was clogged with fans and press. Fortunately, it was in the shade of the bridge. At least I would be out of the sun while I fought the masses to get a shot of Ian.

*Or you could stay in the flow, Meg.* I laughed at myself, trying to imagine the crowd flowing away for me.

Harriet and the other groupies had congregated at the front of the podium. She looked weepy. Poor thing.

I grabbed my phone from my bra. It was damp with sweat. I wiped it on my dress and unlocked it. I knew exactly which photo app I wanted to use. As I held it up to take a shot of Ian, something incredible happened. The throng of people in my line of sight actually parted.

*This Gam experiment works,* I thought as I snapped a round of photos and a panorama shot. Then I realized why the crowd had begun to disperse. A line was starting to form in front of one of the vendor tents nearby. The DJ announced that they were giving away free gear to the first hundred fans.

No wonder the crowd had thinned. Freebie gear—everyone was in for that! Whatever the reason, Gam's experiment was two for two so far.

I'd count that as a success. Maybe it was as simple as she said.

I scanned through the photos. They looked great. I was happy with the filter and the fact that I had a wide-open shot of Ian posing with his trophy on the winner's platform. I pulled up our social media pages and uploaded the photos with a quick caption: "Go Big or Go Home. Ian Schoonmaker takes home the King of the Hook Big Air trophy!" Fans would share that like crazy, especially because Ian's sun-kissed skin and hang loose surfer style made him look like a model.

I finished my posts and tucked my phone back in my bra. Harriet stood near the podium alone. Her fellow groupies must have deserted her in hopes of scoring free gear. I decided this was my chance to see if she'd talk to me more about Justin's murder.

"Hey, Harriet!" I waved as I walked up next to her.

She wiped a tear from her eye and gave me a forced smile. "Hey."

"You okay?"

"Not really. It should have been Justin up there." I nodded in agreement.

"He won Big Air every year, you know?"

"That's what I heard."

She put her hand over her mouth and shook her head. "I still can't believe he's dead. I keep searching the river, thinking he's out for a long ride or something."

"I know the feeling."

Harriet let out a sob. I reached out and placed my hand on her arm.

"I'm sorry." She wiped her eyes again. "I'm such a mess."

"You really cared about him, didn't you?" I knew I had already tried this tactic before, but I doubted that Harriet remembered much from our conversation yesterday.

"Yeah, I did."

"Did he love you, too?"

She looked at me in surprise. "How did you know?"

I shrugged. "A good guess."

"That's the problem. He finally told me how he felt, and now he's dead. This is like some cruel twist of fate. I've been waiting forever for him to return my feelings. He did." She put her hand under her nose as more tears spilled from her eyes.

"When did he tell you?"

"The night before he died." She coughed as she sobbed, placing her hand on her heart. "I mean, we'd hooked up a couple times over the years, but he always went back to Avery. This time it was different. He called it off for good. We had the best night. He told me he was serious about us and that he wanted me to come on tour with him. Not as a groupie, but as his girlfriend." She twisted one of her jet-black curls and looked at her feet. "Now he's dead."

"I'm so sorry." That wasn't a lie. Harriet was genuinely consumed by grief. I recognized her raw emotion. There's no way she could have killed him.

Ian jumped off the stage. Kyle escorted him and

his shiny gold trophy past us and over to a group of fans waiting for autographs.

Harriet pursed her lips and glared at them as they walked by. "He's the reason Justin's dead, and I'm going to do everything I can to make sure he pays."

"Who?" I followed Harriet's dark stare in their direction. "I thought you said Avery killed him."

She shook her head. "No, I was wrong. It's Kyle."

"Kyle?"

"Yes, Kyle killed Justin, and I have proof that he did it."

# Chapter 21

"Kyle?" I asked again.

Harriet rolled her eyes. "Yes, *Kyle*."

"I'm surprised. I thought Kyle was Justin's number-one fan. Wasn't Justin the star of this whole competition? Why would Kyle want to kill him?"

"Because he was a star, and Kyle couldn't handle it."

"What do you mean?"

Harriet shifted from sadness to anger in a split second. I was familiar with the erratic nature of grief. Maybe her anger at Kyle was misdirected. Matt, Gam and Jill had all suggested that perhaps some of my anger at Mother was misdirected, too.

Mother and I had always struggled to find common ground. After Pops died, I put up a wall between us. I wasn't sure the wall would ever come down. And honestly, I wasn't sure I even wanted to try to find a way to tear it down. Mother was the nagging voice in my head. "Mary-Margaret Reed, don't slouch. It's terrible for your posture." Or, "Mary-Margaret Reed, do *not* leave this house without an umbrella. You'll look like a drowned rat by the time you get to school."

Pops was the calming voice in my head. "Sweet, Maggie, don't worry. You're perfect just the way you are." With Pops by my side, I felt like I could accomplish anything. With Mother by my side, I felt like a failure.

In some cruel twist, fate had left me with Mother and taken Pops. It wasn't fair. I blamed her for his death, and pretty much everything else that was wrong in my life. I knew that it wasn't her fault—at least not all of it—but I couldn't bring myself to forgive her.

She'd been trying to tear down the wall between us. She called weekly to check in on me, and dropped off gifts like expensive tubes of lipstick and sparkly earrings that I would never wear. It was her way of trying to connect, but I couldn't let her back in. I wasn't entirely sure why. I felt terrible for hurting her, and yet I didn't answer her calls or thank her for the gifts. It wasn't like me. Sooner or later, I was going to have to face my anger and hurt and find a way to heal the thing between us.

"Justin's career really took off last year," Harriet continued, shaking me from my thoughts. "He's always been on the top of the windsurfing circuit—that's how he got the nickname Cruise Control—but last year he won every international competition. Every single one."

"I remember reading that during my research."

"Yeah, well, Kyle has been cashing in on Justin's name and fame. Justin finally had enough. He told Kyle that he wanted more money. If Kyle was raking in the cash from Justin's fame, then Justin deserved a piece of it. Justin didn't even need King of the Hook anymore."

"And you think Kyle killed him because of that?"

"I don't think, I know it. I was so foggy yesterday, I should have thought about it. I heard them fighting the night before Justin was killed. Justin told Kyle to cut him in on some of the cash. Kyle flipped out. He told Justin that he'd see him dead before he gave him an extra dollar. He went off. Said that Justin was giving the sport a bad name. He'd heard rumors that some of the international competitions weren't going to take him back next year."

"Was that true?"

"No, that was a total lie. I bet Kyle has been feeding them with those rumors, trying to ruin Justin's reputation."

I thought about seeing how horrible Justin had been to Sherman and the nerdy crew the other night. I had a feeling Justin had done a fine job of ruining his own reputation, but I didn't say that to Harriet.

"Justin told Kyle that he didn't need him. He had the contacts to start his own competition. That's when Kyle totally lost it." She stifled another sob. "I know he killed him. He's so obsessed with King of the Hook. Without Justin this competition would be nothing."

"Did you tell the police?"

"Of course." She sighed. "I don't think they believed me. They thought I was being hysterical or something."

"Who did you talk to? Did you tell Sheriff Daniels?"

Harriet looked thoughtful. "The old grizzly dude?"

"Yeah, he's really good. He'll follow up. I know he will."

She looked skeptical. "He didn't seem like that to me. He brushed me off."

"That's his style. Don't worry about it."

Harriet's friends returned with their freebie gear. They invited me to join them on the beach for the next round of competition—jumps. I declined. The vendor showcase was starting, and I wanted to get my own jump on the crowds.

"Take it easy." I squeezed Harriet's arm as she walked away.

"I'll try." She gave me a sad smile as her groupie friends surrounded her. At least she had support. I knew from personal experience how invaluable Jill and Matt had been right after Pops was killed.

As I walked to the vendor tent, I was more convinced that there was no way Harriet could have killed Justin. Kyle, on the other hand, was creeping higher on my suspect list. He'd been weird this morning. His chipper personality had shifted dramatically.

Could his feelings have shifted dramatically about Justin? I wasn't sure, but I was definitely going to use my one-on-one interview with him later to see if I could learn anything from him.

The air in the vendor tent felt like it was over 120 degrees. Its thick awning trapped the heat inside. As much as I didn't want to admit it, I might have fudged a bit on how I was feeling. I grabbed a glossy sea kayak brochure from a vendor table and fanned myself.

*Get this done quick, Meg,* I told myself as I clutched the table to steady myself.

There was a main stage inside the tent, where vendors were doing product demos. Rap music blared on the speakers. Even though the press had access to the showcase an hour before everyone else, the place was already packed with people and so loud that I couldn't hear anything over the sound of vendors shouting and waving me toward their tables.

I stopped to chat with a company selling high-end sunglasses and a new style of water shoes made from recycled tires. I snapped pictures and did quick interviews with the owners. Everything from boards to sails to gear and energy products were on display. Many of these same vendors had booths outside, but the showcase was an opportunity to have them feature their products to everyone at once.

The beat of the music pulsed through the room. It was like walking through the rows of carnival games. At every booth a cheerful, athletic model shouted incentives to try to draw people in. Maybe it was because of the heat, but I retreated inward as I pushed through the throng of press.

After half an hour, I had everything I needed. I started to make my escape. On my way to the exit, I spotted Kyle near the stage. He and Ian were in a deep discussion. Only they didn't look like they were swapping stories about the surf. They looked like they were as hot as the temperature inside.

What were they fighting about? I had to know.

I snuck over and positioned myself behind a colorful red, white and blue striped sail. They were definitely fighting. Kyle's jaw was clenched so tightly, I didn't understand how words were escaping from it. But they were. Spit sprayed from his teeth. Ian made a face and wiped his cheek.

Their voices were too low for me to hear over the beat of the music and noise from the crowd. I inched closer, still keeping my body hidden behind the sail, and cupped one hand behind my ear.

"You are an ambassador for this sport. Start acting like you just won the most prestigious award in all of windsurfing."

Ian didn't keep his voice low. "I don't need your approval, dude. This used to be the only show around, but it's not anymore."

People nearby turned to see what the commotion was about. Kyle shot Ian a hard look and motioned for him to quiet down.

Ian blew him off. "I don't need this." He waved the Big Air Trophy in his hand. "I'm not taking this.

Especially from you." Ian stormed off and left Kyle with his mouth gaping.

What did Ian mean that King of the Hook wasn't the only show around? Harriet said that Justin was thinking of starting his own competition. If he and Ian were friends, maybe he was planning to have Ian help him launch something new. I'd have to ask Ian about it.

"Meg?" Kyle's voice interrupted my thoughts. "What are you doing?" He furrowed his brow.

"Me?" I gulped and stepped away from the sail. "I was looking for you. We have an interview slotted."

He glanced to the sail. "So you were looking for me behind that?"

"Well, I . . ." Have I mentioned that I'm a terrible liar? I'm not good at thinking on the spot.

He stuffed his clipboard under his arm and rolled his eyes. "Let's go. Let's get this done. I've got a ton of stuff to do."

I followed after him as he opened the door to the tent and let the flaps hit me as he walked outside. This should go well.

Kyle sprinted to the event tent, where I'd met him on the first day. He didn't even bother to turn around once to see if I was keeping up.

It actually felt a tad bit cooler outside than it had in the vendor tent. I hurried after him, shading my face from the sun.

Inside, the event tent was empty except for two volunteers manning the information table. Kyle sat at a high table near the beach. The plastic windows allowed for a view of the action outside but didn't provide any escape from the heat.

I climbed onto one of the bar stools and pulled out my notebook.

Kyle rested his clipboard on the table and removed his phone from his shorts. He scrolled through it. I got the impression he was checking Facebook and intentionally making me wait, versus doing any real work.

I waited with my pencil ready.

He shook his head and held his phone out for me to see. Yep. Facebook. "Would you look at this? I can't believe the stuff these surfers post."

The picture was of Ian holding up his trophy. The caption read: "Coolest dude in surfing + lamest competition = easy win."

"Did Ian post that?"

Kyle clicked off his phone. "Yes, they don't have any respect in this new generation coming up. None at all. Everything I've worked for in building this sport." He shook his head and glanced out the window where Harriet's groupie friends had surrounded Ian and were pushing up their bikini tops and posing for selfies with hang loose signs.

I kind of had to agree with Kyle.

He sighed and rested his hand on his cheek. "What do you need to know?"

I almost felt sorry for him, but then I reminded myself he could be the killer. "Could you start by giving me a little history on King of the Hook and your vision for the future?"

Kyle tapped his fingers on his face. "What future? This might end up being the last time I do King of the Hook."

"Why? Because of Justin?"

"It's not just Justin." Kyle pointed out the window. "Look at them. This group of surfers doesn't have any attachment to our mission. All they care about is catching big air."

"Isn't that kind of the point?" I held my pencil in the air.

"You're not writing all of this down, are you?"

"Is this off the record?"

Kyle frowned at the group selfie shot taking place outside. "I don't know. I don't want to put negative press out there about these guys. Maybe you can focus your story on how I got started."

I nodded. "I can do that."

"Good. I've spent the last two decades working to legitimize the sport. The vast majority of surfers are connected to the water and land. Sure we like the adrenaline rush of a great ride, but we're also committed to preserving public spaces for future generations. That's the true mission of King of the Hook."

My pencil flew over the paper as Kyle shared the staggering amount of land that he and his crew of volunteers had worked to preserve. "At last count we're over a thousand acres of protected space."

"That's amazing," I said, shaking my hand.

It was. I knew that Kyle was committed to giving surfing a name, and I'd read about the preservation work he'd done, but I didn't realize how committed he was to the land. I had to admit I was impressed. It didn't square with being a murderer.

I continued my interview, trying to strike a delicate balance between staying on topic and sneaking in a few leading questions that might give me better insight into Kyle. "What about Justin? How does his death factor into this year's competition?" I asked.

Kyle shook his head. "I'm not sure. He was worse than Ian. Those two together have single-handedly done more damage than I'm afraid I can repair."

Enough to drive you to kill one of them? I thought.

As if reading my mind, Kyle continued on. "But of course I would never wish any athlete dead. Or anyone else for that matter. Murder isn't great press for a sport that people already think is dangerous."

He had a point.

I finished my questions and thanked him for his time. Speaking of time, it was late. Time for a pint. I texted Jill and Matt and told them to meet me at Double Mountain Brewery up the hill.

A cold beer sounded like perfection. Plus, I wanted to talk through everything I'd learned. I wasn't sure if Kyle was a killer or not, but his comments about Justin definitely made him a suspect.

# Chapter 22

The walk up Second Street was torture. I huffed my way up the hill toward town. My body moved like molasses as I trudged past Naked Winery where a bachelorette party whooped in delight. They all wore matching black miniskirts and shirts that read, LET'S GET NAKED.

"Come get naked with us!" one of them shouted to me, holding up a bottle of wine.

I thanked them and pushed on. A cold pint of Double Mountain's draft was calling my name. Although if I was going to improve my palate when it came to wine, Naked Winery was probably the place for me. Jill had stopped by their tasting room and told me that their wines were delicious and served without any pretension. "Meg, they have chocolate and goldfish crackers to cleanse your palate. You have to come with me next time!"

One of the reasons I'd been intimidated by

wine was because wine enthusiasts tend to be very specific on what you should and should not know about imbibing. And what you should and should not like. I didn't know what I liked, but I was willing to give anything a try.

"Margaret!" Gam's voice called out behind me.

I turned to see her and Sheriff Daniels holding hands and walking toward me. She beamed in the heat. Her head came to the sheriff's shoulder. Despite the difference in their height and style, they fit. The sheriff wore jeans, cowboy boots and a plaid short-sleeved shirt. Gam wore a silk scoop neck tank top and a flirty black skirt. Her eyes were dusted with teal shadow and her lips shimmered with a cranberry gloss.

"What are you two doing?" I asked when they reached me.

Gam looked up at Sheriff Daniels. "We're going to hear some country music."

"That sounds like fun."

It did for Gam. Country music is right up there with wine for me, but I knew Gam loved to "boogie down" in her words to old-school country. I remember when I spent the night at her house as a kid, she'd play Dolly Parton, Loretta Lynn, and Johnny Cash for me. Come to think of it, Sheriff Daniels reminded me a bit of the picture I'd seen on Gam's CD case of Johnny Cash. He was older and a bit more weathered, but the resemblance was there. I wondered if Gam thought so, too.

"You can join us," Gam offered.

"No, thanks. I'm meeting my friends for a beer."

Sheriff Daniels surprised me. He did a little two-step dance. "And miss my moves?"

"Those are some pretty awesome moves." I laughed.

"That's nothing. You should watch him square-dance." Gam swatted him on the hip. "I have to tell the other women to back away from my man." She winked; then her tone turned serious. "How did the rest of the afternoon go?"

"Good." I nodded. "I'm fine. Much better."

Sheriff Daniels frowned. "What happened?"

Gam waved him off. "It's nothing. Margaret got a touch of heat stroke, but I gave her a good zap, and she looks much better, doesn't she?"

The sheriff studied me.

"I'm fine. Really. But I think there are a few things you should know."

"About heat stroke?" He removed a silver tin from his breast pocket, pulled out a wooden tooth-pick, and popped it in his mouth. It was like his grown-up version of a pacifier. I could imagine why he would need to gnaw on something. I couldn't seem to shake the vision of Justin's lifeless body from my head.

"About Justin's murder." My bra vibrated. It startled me. Someone must be texting. I removed my phone from my bra and wiped the moisture on my skirt. Black spots flicked on the screen. That couldn't be good.

Gam laughed. She lifted strands of gemstones circling her neck, reached down her shirt, and pulled her flip phone from her bra. "Good trick." She patted her chest and winked at the sheriff. "Wonder who taught her that one?"

Sheriff Daniels looked slightly uncomfortable. He cleared his throat. "You were saying something about the Justin Cruise investigation."

The text was from Jill. I had to squint to read it. There was something funky going on with the screen. She had scored a table at Double Mountain. I tucked my phone back in my bra. "Yeah, when I was doing interviews for my story, I learned a few things that I think might be helpful in your investigation."

"Emphasis on *my* investigation, Ms. Reed." Sheriff Daniels twisted the toothpick with his tongue.

"I know. I know," I interjected, and quickly followed up with everything I'd learned from Harriet, and about Ian and Kyle's fight.

Sheriff Daniels frowned as I spoke. I knew he wasn't happy that I was "meddling," but he took out his pocket-sized notepad and wrote everything down.

When I finished, he tucked the notepad back into his pocket and patted it into place. "Ms. Reed, do I need to remind you—yet again—that this is a murder investigation?"

I shook my head.

"Good." He extended his arm to Gam. "In that

case, your grandmother and I have a date with the dance floor."

Gam blew me a kiss and they walked up the hill together. Despite Sheriff Daniel's reprimand, I was relieved that he knew everything I did. The first time I'd been involved in murder, I tried to keep everything to myself. Bad idea. I'd learned my lesson—tell the authorities *everything*. Content that I'd done that, I continued on toward the pub.

Double Mountain was located in the heart of downtown. In the summertime its walls open for sidewalk dining. Fortunately they were closed tight this afternoon, and the air-conditioning was humming. As I stepped inside a blast of cool air sent goose bumps up my arms. I rubbed them in delight. Ah, cool air. I breathed it in.

A woman at the front counter gave me a strange look. "Can I help you?"

I scanned the bar. Jill was sitting at a table near the back. "I'm meeting a friend," I said to the hostess. "She's over there."

The hostess handed me a menu and sent me on my way.

"What's up?" I tapped Jill on the head with the menu.

She startled. Her hair was tied in a ponytail high on her head. It made her long, thin neck appear even more gazelle-like.

"Oh, sorry. I didn't mean to scare you." I sat next to her.

"I guess I was daydreaming." Jill smiled, but there was a sadness to her face.

"Is everything okay?" I leaned closer.

She ran her finger around the rim of her pint glass. "I've been thinking a lot about what Gam said to me earlier."

"What did she say?"

"She said that I'm in charge of my own destiny."

"That sounds like something Gam would say."

"I've probably heard her say it before, but for some reason today I really get it, you know?" She met my eyes. I could tell that something had shifted in her. Spending some quality time with Gam was probably the best thing for Jill.

"That's good." I reached my hand out and touched her arm.

She sighed. "It's also hard."

"How so?" I pulled my hand away.

Jill took a sip of her beer. "Do you know that I'm often envious of you, Meg?"

"What? Me? Why would you be envious of me?" I scrunched up my face. "You're beautiful. You're in law school. You have a swanky condo in the Pearl. I barely scrape by month after month and I look like this." I crossed my eyes and snarled.

She laughed. "Meg, I'm serious."

I rested my chin in my hands. "I am, too. Why would you possibly be envious of *me*? I'm a mess. You know that better than anyone."

"Exactly. You're a mess—a beautiful mess—and you own that. That's why people love you."

"People love you, too." I made a heart with my index fingers and thumbs.

"Not the messy me. They love what they see. They don't really know me."

"I know you. Matt knows you."

Jill looked out the window. "True, but that's two people. What about everyone else?"

"What about them?" I shoved my menu to the side of the table. "Who cares what anyone else thinks?"

She adjusted her ponytail. "I do. That's the problem."

"Do you really?" I tilted my head to the side. I wasn't sure that was true. Sure, Jill had made some decisions in the past to please her parents, but the Jill I knew had so much more depth to her than that.

"I think I do. That's what I realized when I was talking to Gam. I'm the one holding myself back. No one else is. I'm responsible for my choices, and I'm choosing to hide. How lame is that?"

"It's not lame."

Jill rolled her eyes.

"It's not. We're in our early twenties. None of us has anything figured out yet. Isn't that the way it's supposed to be?"

She looked down. "Not in my world."

"Well, it is in my world. Name one person you know who has it all figured out."

"Will thinks he has it figured out."

"Will's an ass." I threw my hand over my mouth. "I'm sorry. I didn't mean that."

"Meg, I know you don't like him. I'm not that dense."

"It's not that I don't like him." I tried to backpedal.

"You don't like him. Admit it." She held my gaze.

I swallowed. How was I supposed to answer that? Jill and I were having the conversation I'd been hoping to have with her for months, but I didn't want to offend her. "I don't like him for you, that's all."

She shook her head. "Meg, you can't stand him."

"Okay, fine." I threw my hands up. "Maybe he's not my favorite person on the planet, but I love *you* and if you love him, then I'll deal with it."

The bartender came over to take my drink order. I opted for an India Red Ale. In the beer world it's called an IRA.

"Do you love him?" I asked as the bartender left.

Jill took a sip of her drink. "I don't know. Part of me does. But part of me knows that's only because he's easy. He doesn't push me out of my comfort zone."

I thought about Matt. Was he easy? Did he push me out of my comfort zone? What did that even mean? No wonder Jill looked lost. These were deep questions.

"Did I tell you that I sold a painting?" She studied her nails. Jill's addiction to fingernail polish is equal to my addiction to vintage fashion. Her nails were painted in a matte coral, making her hands look especially tan.

"No!" I almost fell out of my chair. "Are you kidding me? Why do you look so casual about that? How? To who?"

"A gallery owner from San Francisco. My art teacher introduced us."

"Jill, that's awesome! How long have I been telling you that your stuff is amazing?"

"I appreciate the vote of confidence, but I'm not sure I can keep doing classes. Law school is going to be intense fall term."

"Why not?" The bartender delivered my beer. It was a beautiful ruby color. I took a long sip and waited for Jill to answer.

"Well, for starters there's the whole problem of cash."

I nodded. Jill's parents thought that art was a nice hobby. "Do you think they'll cut you off?"

She sighed. "They'll kill me."

I understood why Jill felt such internal pressure. Her doctor parents had been grooming her for her professional career since we were kids. While I was tagging along with Pops on a story or spending a lazy Saturday morning watching cartoons in my pajamas, Jill was attending piano, ballet and Spanish classes. Her weekends and after-school hours were packed with lectures and trips to museums. Free time wasn't in her vocabulary. I remember when she'd spend the night at our family farmhouse she couldn't believe we didn't have to set an alarm to wake up early and do math worksheets.

Jill was at a crossroads. She'd been my steadfast supporter after Pops died. Now it was my turn. I didn't know how I was going to convince her to follow her dream, but I knew I had to find a way.

# Chapter 23

Jill and I talked a bit more. Mainly I tried to listen and gently nudge her wherever I could. Matt showed up about a half hour later. My cheeks warmed with heat when he strolled into the pub. This time I didn't think it had anything to do with the beer.

We ordered another round of beers and food. As always, I was starving. It's hard to want to dine anywhere other than a pub in the Pacific Northwest. Pub fare has been elevated to fine dining, with breweries going far beyond a greasy burger. Most pubs offer organic, free-range meats, artisanal small plates, and rich, beer-inspired desserts. Double Mountain was no exception. We decided to share a salami and arugula wood-fired pizza.

A group of gorgeous surfers took an empty table a few feet away from us. The waiter arrived with a fresh pint of Hop Lava and handed it to Jill. "This is for you. Compliments of that table." He nodded to the surfers.

Jill blushed, but raised the glass in a toast to the surfers.

They cheered in response and motioned for her to join them.

"Should I?" Jill whispered.

"Uh, yeah." I shot a look at the table. "They're all dreamy and they bought you a drink. It's the least you can do to go thank them."

Matt rolled his eyes.

"Why not?" Jill grabbed her beer and walked to the table.

I winked at Matt. "This is a good sign. Maybe she's finally getting over Will."

"Or maybe she just wants a free drink." He shot me a challenging look. I gulped as I stared into his eyes for a moment too long.

"Whatever." I punched him in the arm, trying to break the tension.

The waiter delivered our steaming pizza. Maybe we should have opted for a cold salad instead.

Matt removed a slice from the pan. The cheese stretched and oozed. He dropped it on my plate and blew on his hand. "That is literally hot out of the oven."

Laughter erupted from the surfers. Jill held them completely captivated with whatever story she was telling.

"That's going well," I whispered to Matt.

He served himself a slice of the gooey pie. "Speaking of going well. How did the rest of your afternoon go? Did you get more work on your story done?"

"I did. In fact, I have a great start." I took a bite of the pizza. It burned my tongue, but I didn't care. The tangy tomato sauce with the spicy salami was a perfect pairing.

"What about Justin's murder? Did you learn anything new?" Matt leaned his arm on the table. I couldn't help but notice his well-defined muscles.

*Stop, Meg. Focus.*

"A lot actually." I scooted my stool closer and filled him on Ian and Kyle. "What about you? How was your afternoon?"

Matt's face lit up as he told me about the helicopter drone he got to pilot over the river. He's like a kid when it comes to new technology toys. Somehow he always has the latest and greatest phone. He also seems to know the new trends weeks before they're released to the public. I know he scores most of his tech toys from his job, but I think he must have some other secret source. "You won't believe how smooth the flight is, and the photos we took turned out incredible. I need one."

"How much do they cost?"

"About five hundred dollars."

"Yikes!"

"Yeah." Matt took a bite of his pizza. "Not in the budget."

"Somehow I have a feeling you'll find a way to get one."

He shrugged. "I might have a guy."

"A guy?"

Matt feigned hurt. "Yeah, I've got a guy for everything."

"Do you have a guy who can wrap up Justin's murder investigation?"

"Maybe, but I think you already know him. He's older. Gray hair. Wears cowboy boots. Dating your grandmother."

"Haha." I finished my slice of pizza. "Did you learn anything new about Justin's murder?"

Matt shook his head and put a finger to his lips. Avery and Greg appeared at the doorway. Greg ushered her inside. He caught my eye. I thought they might come join us, but then he looked at Matt and walked the other direction to the bar.

Avery did just the opposite. When she spotted Matt, her face broke into a flirtatious smile and she made her way toward us. Great.

Her face had more color than it did this morning, but something was off. I noticed her catch herself twice as she weaved through packed tables toward us. She looked like she was having trouble staying upright.

"Mind if I join you two?" She grabbed the table and steadied herself.

Matt jumped to his feet and pulled out the stool Jill had been sitting in for her. "No, please sit." He looked at her with concern.

"Thanks. I'm feeling better, but I can't seem to shake these waves of dizziness."

"Are you hungry?" Matt offered her a slice of pizza.

Avery put her hand in front of her mouth. "No. No, I'm not ready for food yet."

"You must have had a nasty flu." I scooted my plate away from her.

"I'm not contagious," she insisted.

How would she know? From everything I'd ever heard, the flu is highly contagious. I didn't want her germs contaminating my pizza.

"You looked great out on the water today," she said to Matt. "You're quite a natural you know. When I'm feeling better, you should come out with me."

"Thanks." Color rose slightly in Matt's cheeks. "That would be fun."

Was she flirting with him? Matt hadn't mentioned anything to me about being on the water.

"When were you on the water?" I dabbed my chin with my napkin.

Matt shrugged. "The drone vendors took me out for a spin. That's all."

"That's all?" I couldn't keep the snarky tone out of my voice. *You sound jealous, Meg. Knock it off.*

Avery jumped in. "He was awesome. Knew instinctively how to ride the waves."

I had a feeling that if I stayed at the table much longer, I might say something I would regret. For some reason Avery put me on the defensive. I finished off my beer and made up a lame excuse about needing to check in with Greg.

Matt almost started to say something, but he stopped himself. He didn't stop me, though. Was he interested in Avery, or just flattered that she was flirting with him? I knew I was being childish, but I wanted him to stop me, not get sucked into Avery's praise for his natural surfing talent. Matt had a natural inclination for everything he tried. Avery's interest had triggered my insecurities.

I blame Mother. She always hinted in not-so-subtle ways that she wanted me to be something I wasn't growing up. If only I could have been more athletic or graceful or interested in what she was interested in. I think I've always disappointed her. She's never said that outright, but I sense it.

*Get out of your own head, Meg.* I walked to the bar where Greg sat with a group of surfers.

"Hey, Meg. Pull up a seat." He pointed to an empty bar stool.

I placed my beer on the counter. It sloshed and splattered on my arm. Classic.

He handed me a bar napkin and pulled the stool out for me.

"Thanks." I wiped beer from my arm and took a seat.

"Guys, this is Meg Reed. She's a junior reporter on my team, and the kid can write some killer copy." He winked at me. "She's the reason our Facebook page is 'lighting up,' right, Meg?"

I think I blushed.

Greg's friends greeted me by clinking their pint glasses to mine. I listened while they tried to outdo each other with tales of their escapades on the water. They egged each other on, and stopped to show me who had the gnarliest bruise. One guy whose elbow looked like it had been shoved through a shredder took the prize.

I must admit that I might have played up how much fun I was having listening to their stories. I threw my head back in laughter when one of them told me how his wetsuit had a wardrobe malfunction when it got stuck on the sail. It was a funny story, but maybe not that funny.

Sneaking a glance Matt's way, I realized my effort to make him jealous was futile. He didn't even notice the little solo production I was putting on. Avery had one of his arms and seemed to be demonstrating some sort of balance technique with it. A lousy ploy to touch him if you ask me.

Greg pulled me back into the conversation. "Don't let our little Meg's love of pink fool you, boys. She's the most tenacious reporter on my team. Isn't that right, Meg?"

"I don't know if I'd say that."

"You don't have to. I just did."

His surfer friends left to hit another beach party. I got the impression that surfing was synonymous with bonfires on the beach. Why not? It made sense to me. Finish off a long day on the water by watching the flames dance in the fire and drinking a cool beer. I could get used to that lifestyle.

Once we were alone, Greg asked if I wanted another beer. I declined. Even though I'd only had two, the room was fuzzy and slightly off-kilter. I could hear myself stumble to find the right word. What was wrong with me?

"How's the feature coming?" Greg asked.

"Great. Really great." I explained how I'd shot video at the vendor showcase and had a ton of interview material to compile. "Social media's been blowing up all day. Our readers are really loving the action shots I posted earlier." I found my phone and scrolled through Facebook to show him how many people had liked our posts.

"A few vendors approached me about doing an exclusive giveaway for our social users. What do you think?"

Greg signaled the bartender to refill his beer. "I like it. Good stuff, Meg. You never fail to surprise me on what you come up with."

"So should I go for it, or do you want me to loop them in with you?"

"It's all yours. I trust your judgment."

I appreciated his vote of confidence. It was exactly what I needed at the moment.

"How are you feeling? You look better, but you're taking it easy, right?"

"I feel good," I assured him. "Much better." Without thinking I glanced in Matt's direction.

Greg noticed. "I didn't know your friend was going to be here."

"He's on assignment for *The O.*"

"So I heard."

I wondered how Greg heard. It shouldn't have

surprised me. Greg had an uncanny way of being in the know.

"Is everything okay, Meg?"

"Yeah, I'm cool. Really cool." There it was. My Greg speak, also known as total idiot speak.

Greg massaged his chin. "You sure?"

Was I that obvious? Maybe.

"I think it's Justin's murder." I sighed. "It has me on edge, you know."

Greg nodded and waited for me to say more.

"What do you know about Kyle?"

"Kyle? Why?"

"Didn't you think he was acting kind of cagey earlier?"

"Cagey?" Greg raised his brow.

I told him my suspicion and about the fight I'd witnessed.

He stretched his arms together. His knuckles popped. "I thought we were over this, Meg."

"Over what?"

"You getting sucked in to murder investigations."

"I know, but this is different."

"Really?" Greg looped his hands behind his head and leaned back. "This ought to be interesting. How is this different?"

*Now you've done it, Meg.*

"Stuff has come out while I've been interviewing everyone for the feature."

"Mmm-hmm. And you haven't prodded that at all?"

I flashed to hiding behind the sail to spy on Kyle and Ian earlier, and could feel my cheeks redden. "Well, not really."

Greg sat up. "Meg, you are too much. Always. I don't know what to do with you."

"Can you blame me? Have you ever found a dead body?"

He didn't answer. His jaw twitched. Before he responded he carefully considered his words. "Meg, you're here to do a job. Nothing more. Nothing less. I suggest you do it." He stood, knocked back his beer, and walked away without another word.

Great. Add my boss to the growing list of people not thrilled with me.

# Chapter 24

I finished my beer alone. Jill and one of the surfers were deep in conversation. She flipped her hair and tilted her head back in a laugh. Oh my God! She was flirting. Go Jill!

On my way out, I stopped by her table. "Looks like you're having fun," I whispered.

She squeezed my hand. "I am. Come sit."

"No, thanks. I'm beat. I'm going to head to the house, but have fun. I'll see back at home."

"You're sure?"

"Are you sure? Do you need me to stay?" Jill and I had a deal in college that we never left the other alone with a guy we didn't know without checking.

"I'm good." She grinned.

"Catch ya later." I blew her a kiss and said good night to the other surfers.

Matt had his iPad on the table and was showing Avery photos when I passed them. He didn't even look up.

Awesome. Jill had warned me not to drag things

out with him. Had I lost my chance? Was he really interested in Avery? Ugh.

I ducked out of the pub. The air was heavy with heat. Wispy clouds stretched across the moon. It illuminated the street, casting an eerie glow.

"Meg!" I heard a voice call. "Is that you?"

I turned to see Sherman and his posse of role-play kids walking down the sidewalk. They were dressed in a variety of medieval costumes—knights, a king, an ogre, and a wizard. Each of them held flashlights and wooden swords.

"Hey, Sherman." I stopped and waited for them to catch up. "What's going on?"

"We're going to the beach for some late-night larping."

"What's larping?"

"Live-Action Role-Playing."

"Right."

"The moon's full, you know." He extended his cape like vampire wings. The motion exposed his armpits and sent an unpleasant waft of body odor in my direction.

I pursed my lips and held my breath, waiting for the scent to dissipate. "Does that matter?" The moon, eclipsed by thin clouds, gave off a mysterious iridescent glow.

"It makes the experience more authentic." Sherman held his sword up to the veiled sky.

I guess he had a point. "But won't the beach be packed with surfers? I think there's a bonfire and a band down there tonight."

Sherman flicked his sword. "They don't own the beach. We can be down there, too." He sounded angry.

"Yeah, absolutely. I just meant it might take away a bit of the authenticity."

He frowned. "I cannot wait for them to get out of town."

The paladins raised their weapons in response. Metal swords and daggers clanked together as they let out a collective roar. I felt like I was watching the Lost Boys from *Peter Pan*.

He stuck the sword back in the leather sheath tied around his waist. "Come on, guys, let's go."

"Have fun!" I waved.

Sherman perked up. "Do you want come with us? It might be a good story. Larping is really popular, you know."

"That's what you said. Thanks for the invite, but I'm super tired from being in the sun all day. Maybe I can take a rain check?" I knew there was no way Greg would be interested in a feature story about larping, but I didn't want to hurt Sherman's feelings.

"We'll be on the beach every night this week. Come anytime." He led his geeky group down the sidewalk.

A thought occurred to me as I watched them go, I wondered if Sherman had been on the beach the night before Justin died. Maybe he'd seen something. I'd have to ask him about that tomorrow.

I didn't get very far before I heard my name again. This time the voice sounded weak and pleading.

"Meg?"

It was Avery. She was clutching the side of a building. I hurried over to her.

"Are you okay?"

She shook her head. "I'm going to be sick."

I took a step back just as she threw up all over the cement foundation.

Gross.

"Sorry." She wiped the back of her hand across her mouth and stood up. I noticed she didn't let go of the brick wall.

"Do you need help getting home?"

"That would be great. I'm right over there." She pointed to a boutique hotel across the street.

I helped her stand and looped my arm through hers. If nothing else, maybe I'd have some good karma. Getting this close to someone who'd just thrown up pretty much assured that I'd get Avery's flu.

"What happened to Matt?" I asked as we started to walk toward the hotel. Avery wasn't steady on her feet.

"I left him at the pub. I thought I could make it to the hotel, but obviously I couldn't."

"You're still not feeling any better?"

Avery sighed. "I'm not going to be for a while."

"Don't say that." I tightened my grip on her elbow as we stepped off the six-inch curb. "My grandmother is a Reiki healer, and she says the best thing you can do for yourself when you're sick is to encourage your body to heal. That will give its natural healing system a boost."

"What if I can't *heal* this?"

"Of course you can heal. You just have a bad case of the flu."

Avery laughed uncomfortably. "Yeah, like the nine-month kind of flu."

"Huh?"

I stopped in mid-stride and caught a glimpse of her face in the moonlight. I'm such an idiot. Duh. Why didn't I think of it before? "You're pregnant?" I couldn't keep the disbelief from my voice.

"Knocked up. That's what I've been saying to myself. Somehow it seems less scary than pregnant."

"That's why you said I couldn't catch what you had?"

Avery nodded.

We started walking again. Lights glowed inside crowded restaurants and shops. The evening air was thick with the scent of wood-fired grills and the sounds of happy diners.

"How far along are you?" I asked, focusing on my footing as we crossed the street.

"Not that far. A couple of months. The doctors keep telling me the morning sickness will get better when I'm out of the first trimester. I don't know why they call it morning sickness, though. I've been sick morning and night. It's terrible."

"I remember reading somewhere that that can happen."

"Well, it sucks." Avery almost tripped stepping

back onto the curb. I grabbed the small of her back to steady her. "Thanks."

We made it to the hotel. Twinkle lights adorned the front doors. A chalkboard sign read: WELCOME TO BIG AIR COUNTRY. Avery waited for a moment before going inside. "I'd appreciate it if you didn't tell anyone. I'm kind of trying to figure out when the best time is going to be to break the news."

"Because of your surfing career?"

"Because of Justin."

"Justin?"

She put her hand over her stomach. "It's his."

"Oh, wow. I'm sorry."

"Don't be. I'm not."

Her snippy response surprised me. My reaction must have given that away.

"I didn't kill him, but I did break it off with him once I found out I was preggers. I couldn't imagine trying to raise a kid with him." She looked wistful for a moment, but then squared her shoulders and continued. "I was over him constantly hooking up with those groupies."

She rubbed her stomach. "I don't want my kid to grow up without a dad, but in some ways maybe it's better. They can watch the superstar surfer and won't ever have to know that he wasn't a superstar in real life."

I wasn't sure how to respond. I knew how tough it was to be fatherless at twenty-four. Maybe if I'd grown up never knowing Pops I would have felt differently. Having a father around, even a crummy father like Justin Cruise, would be better than not having one at all.

"Is that why you've been flirting with Matt?"

"What?" Avery gave me a confused look.

"My friend Matt. You know, the guy you were just having beers with at the pub."

"I know who he *is*. Why would you think that I've been flirting with him? He's kind of a geek. Not my type."

Her words put me on the defensive. Matt might be a geek, but he was my geek. "You've been acting like you're interested in him."

"I am interested in him. I'm hoping that he'll connect me with his editor."

"Why?"

"His newspaper is supposedly looking to hire someone with outdoor experience for a new vlog they're launching."

"A vlog?"

"Yeah, like a video blog."

"I know what a vlog is," I snapped. Why wouldn't Matt have told me about the job? I was perfect for it, and I'd been dreaming about working for *The O* since I was a kid.

"You want to write?"

"No, Matt said it's not writing as much as it is having a personality for the vlog. It's kind of perfect." She placed her hand on her stomach again. "I'm not going to be surfing anytime soon, and it would be steady income."

"Won't you get money from Justin?"

Avery shrugged. "I might, but we weren't married or anything. It might be a crazy fight in court. That's why I'm not sure when I should let people know that I'm carrying his baby. He made a ton of cash in the last couple of years, and that money should go to his kid."

I agreed.

An elderly couple came out the double glass doors from the hotel lobby. We stepped to the side to let them pass.

"I better head in. I think I might get sick again." She smiled. "Thanks for helping me and listening. You won't say anything, will you?"

"No, your secret is safe with me," I promised. It was. I wouldn't tell anyone about Avery's pregnancy unless she wanted me to.

I turned to walk back up the hill toward the house. Avery was pregnant with Justin's baby. Things continued to get more complicated. Her illness made sense, but learning that she was pregnant didn't make her any less of a suspect in my mind.

If anything, she was even more suspicious. She'd made it clear that she was fine—eager actually—to raise a child on her own. And then there was the matter of Justin's money. She and her unborn child stood to receive a "big chunk of cash" with Justin dead. Avery had just put herself back in my number-one position.

# Chapter 25

I crossed the street and walked back to where I'd started at Double Mountain Brewery. I peered in the window. Jill was still chatting with the cute surfer. Maybe her Will Barrington days were behind her for good.

"Looking for someone?" Matt's voice startled me and made me jump.

"Just checking on my bestie." I turned around.

He reached into his cargo shorts and pulled out a pack of spearmint gum. "Want some?" He offered me a stick of the silver-wrapped gum.

"No, thanks."

"Suit yourself. This is my good stuff. I don't hand it out to just anyone."

Matt unwrapped a piece of gum and proceeded to devour it as if he were eating caviar.

"Funny, because you seem to be able to hand out insider job tips for *The O* with no problem. I'm surprised the same isn't true for your gum." I could hear the jealous tone in my voice, but I didn't care.

I couldn't believe that Matt hadn't told me *The O* was hiring an outdoor vlogger.

"Insider tips? What are you talking about, Megs?"

I wrapped my arms around my chest and gave him a hard look. "The outdoor vlog position that you told Avery about, but somehow managed to never mention to me?"

"Oh, that." Matt waved his pack of gum in the air. "You're mad about that?"

"Yeah, I'm mad. Why didn't you tell me?"

Matt squinted. "Are you serious? Do you want to do an outdoor vlog?"

"Well, I don't know, but I could."

"You could, but come on, Megs, do you really want to do that?"

I wrinkled my nose and stared at him.

"A vlog? You're a traditionalist. You're one of a kind. A true reporter. You love to write. Why would you want to do a gimmicky vlog? That's not you."

He was right, but I wasn't ready to let him off the hook yet. I gave him an expectant look. "And?"

"And what? Avery's a surfer. She's the kind of personality they're looking for. They don't want a serious journalist for the vlogs. They want on-air talent. The concept is quick two-minute snap shots of the Pacific Northwest. Honestly I'm not even sure the gig is paying. If it is, it's pennies."

"Really?"

"Really. It's just an attempt by management to try to engage people online, but none of us on the writing side want anything to do with it."

"Huh." This made me feel even surer that Avery must have had something to do with Justin's death. She made it sound like the vlog was going to be a full-time job. She must have some other source of money. I had one guess what that was—Justin's bank account.

"Megs, it's not a job. It's just fluff filler." He stared down at me. The moonlight illuminated his face. "Trust me, if there was any chance of getting you out of *Northwest Extreme*, I'd jump on it."

The intensity of his gaze made me suck in a breath. "About that. We made a deal, remember?"

"Before you say anything, there's something you need to see." He held a finger in the air and reached into his laptop bag. Matt's laptop bag is never far from his body. Technology is like an extra appendage for him. I'm not sure how Matt would survive in a technology-free environment, and according to him it's a real possibly when—not if—the zombie apocalypse hits. He's obsessed with the zombie apocalypse—he's read every book on the subject, watches zombie flicks, and is constantly reminding Jill and me that it's never too early to prepare for a zombie attack.

He clicked on his iPad and scrolled through his photos. "I know we agreed to take a break from the investigation into your dad's death, but I found this, and you have to take a look." He positioned the iPad for me to see.

There was a photo of Greg, the editor in chief of *The O*, and Pops. Pops? I blinked and grabbed the iPad from Matt's hands. I expanded the photo with my fingers. Pops. What was Pops doing in a photo with Greg? The three men were posed in front of a desk. It looked like desks at *The O*.

"What is this?" I asked Matt.

"I found this in *The O*'s archives when I was doing research for another story last week. Zoom in. See the caption?"

As I zoomed in closer on the photo, I realized Matt was right. The caption read: "Behind the scenes in the newsroom. Editor in Chief Mike Huddley, lead investigative reporter, Charlie Reed, and intern Greg Dixon collaborate on a breaking story."

"Greg worked at *The O* with Pops?"

Matt nodded. "Yeah, about ten years ago. He was probably about our age."

"He knew Pops? Why hasn't he said anything?"

"I'm not sure." Matt took the iPad from my hands. His voice became softer. "Do you understand why I don't trust him?"

My mind felt like it was churning like the current on the river. Nothing made sense. Greg knew Pops? Why hadn't he told me? Or had he? I thought back to our first meeting at the coffee shop. What had he said? Something about me being Charlie Reed's daughter. I remember him acknowledging that he knew Pops was dead, but that was it. All this time and he never mentioned that he worked with Pops. Why?

"I wonder if I ever met him," I said aloud.

Mother and I used to have lunch at Pops' desk at *The O* once a week when I was growing up. This was

before the rift between them became too wide.
Mother would help Pops organize his files, and I
would chat with the newsroom staff. I loved how
they all looked up to and respected Pops. His im-
portance to the paper was palpable.

Young reporters would drop off a story they were
working on. "Hey, Charlie, would you mind giving
this a look?"

Pops always said yes. It didn't matter how busy he
was. He'd carefully review his younger colleague's
work and offer a thoughtful critique. "Have you
considered opening with this?" he'd ask, taking his
red pen and circling a paragraph halfway down the
page. "I think your story really starts here. Packs a
better punch, you know?"

Had Greg been one of those young reporters? I
would have been twelve or thirteen when he was
working at *The O,* too young to care about some
twenty-year-old reporter when I was obsessed with
the hot soccer player who sat next to me in
math class.

"Megs, are you okay?" Matt put his hand on my
shoulder.

"No." I gave him a look of disbelief. "Why would
Greg lie to me all this time?" Maybe he hadn't lied
outright, but it was a lie of omission to be sure. And
a big one.

"I wish I knew." Matt frowned. "I think it might
be related to the Meth Madness case. I just haven't
figured out how."

"You think Greg had something to do with his
death?" I thought about all the points of connec-

tion between Greg and me. He had to be lying. I just didn't want to believe that he could be involved in Pops' death.

Matt reached for his pack of gum and stuffed another piece into his mouth. Whenever he's nervous, his gum chewing increases. "I'm not sure, but we can't rule it out as a possibility."

"Right." I sighed.

"Megs, the thing is, if Greg had something to do with your dad's death, we have to be very, very careful."

"What do you mean?"

"I mean if—if—he killed Charlie, or he knows who did, and he thinks that we're on to him, you could be in danger."

"No way. Greg wouldn't hurt me."

"How do you know?" Matt crumpled the silver wrapper in his hands.

"I don't know. I just do. I mean, it's really unsettling to think that Greg knew Pops. But I can't believe he would hurt me. He's had plenty of opportunities, and he's always protected me."

"Megs, listen, I know you have a crush on him, but you've got to take your blinders off and wake up to the truth. He might be dangerous."

"I don't have a crush on him."

Matt rolled his eyes.

"I don't. Really. I don't. Yes, he's dreamy, but that's it. We don't have anything in common."

"Except for Pops." Matt folded his arms across his chest.

I felt my lip curl. "Hey, that's not fair."

"Sorry. It's just that sometimes you can be a bit naïve, Megs."

"I know that. I sort of like that side of myself."

"I like it, too, just not when you're putting yourself in a potentially dangerous situation."

"Greg's not dangerous, though."

"How do you know?"

"I can't explain it. I just know it. Like in a Gam way. I don't know why he lied about knowing Pops, and I don't like it, but I know he would never hurt me."

"Well, then I guess we're going to have to agree to disagree for the moment."

"Don't be mad at me," I pleaded.

"I'm not mad." Matt held my gaze. "I'm worried."

"Thanks for being worried. I appreciate it. I really do, but I can take care of myself when it comes to Greg." I touched his arm. I wanted to fall into his body and forget this entire conversation.

Matt's expression softened. "What are you going to do?"

"Nothing."

"Nothing?"

"No, I promise. Not for the moment. I need to think on this for a while."

"And you're not going to go to Greg with this, right?"

"Right." I nodded.

Matt gave me a hard look, like he didn't trust me.

"I promise. I'm not going to talk to Greg, at least not yet."

"Will you promise me that if you change your mind, you'll tell me first?"

"I promise."

Matt held out his hand and shook mine. "It's a deal."

The gesture broke the tension. I laughed. "Deal."

"In the meantime, I'm going to keep on the story, as your dad would have said. I'll keep you posted on what I learn, but this is just between us."

"Just between us," I repeated.

Matt adjusted his laptop bag on his shoulder. "Do you want to walk back to the house with me?"

"I think I need to be alone for a little while."

"I thought you might say that. I'll go grab another pint. You can have the house to yourself." Matt pointed at the busy brewery.

"That's okay. I think I'll go walk on the beach. You know what they say about water being healing for the soul? I could use a dose of healing right now."

Matt looked unsure. "By yourself?"

I could hear the sound of the band in the distance and pointed to a group of people walking toward the beach across the street. "It's not that late and there are people everywhere. I'll be fine."

"If you're sure?"

"I'm sure. I'll see you back at the house later." I turned and crossed the street before he could stop me. I knew that Matt meant well, but the more I learned about Pops and Greg's potential involvement the more confused I became. Disappearing into the crowd sounded like the escape I needed.

# Chapter 26

I stumbled along the sidewalk to the beach. Happy partygoers buzzed with excitement around me. The warm night air held a hint of smoke from the bonfires down on the beach.

Every step I took toward learning more about Pops' murder and the Meth Madness investigation led me somewhere I didn't want to be. Was I being naïve about Greg? Did I have blinders on? Maybe Matt was right. There was no escaping the fact that Greg had lied to me more than once, but I couldn't believe he would try to hurt me.

When I arrived on the beach, the mood was much lighter than mine. People gathered in front of the stage and were jumping up and down—pulsing with the beat of the music. I stopped to listen for a moment. The band was fine, and I appreciated how animated they were, but rock music isn't really my scene. I continued past the bonfire where surfers and groupies were slamming cans of cheap beer and rehashing the day's epic stunts.

One of them shouted to me and offered up a can. I declined and kicked off my flip-flops. The sand had cooled in the moonlight. It felt like a foot massage as I walked over the warm rocks toward the water. I plopped down near the shoreline and stuck my feet in the water.

*Breathe, Meg.*

The river lapped at my feet. I watched the waves glide onto the shore in a steady rhythm. It was mesmerizing. Moonlight danced on the water, casting a silver glow. Behind me flames blazed on the beach. I got lost in the moment, allowing my head to clear.

Taking deep, centering breaths, I focused on the water, letting everything else go. I didn't have to figure out Greg, or Justin's murder tonight. Tonight I just needed to *be*. I thought of my intention of being in the flow. *Flow like the river, Meg.*

I'm not sure how long I sat there. The sound of the party faded away as I meditated.

After a while, my head felt heavy. I removed my feet from the water and scooted away from the shore. *I'll just rest my eyes for a minute,* I thought as I propped my bag behind my head, using it as a pillow. The next thing I knew, I woke up shivering.

It took a minute to figure out where I was. I sat up and rubbed my eyes. I must have fallen asleep.

I turned to check on the party behind me. The flames from the bonfire had been tamped down and the band had packed up all their equipment and exited the stage. Where was everyone? The beach was deserted. How long had I been asleep?

What time was it? I pulled my phone from my bra to check. The screen flickered. I could barely make out the numbers—it was after one.

*Time to get home, Meg.* I brushed sand from my feet and grabbed my flip-flops.

I stood and stretched. The wind had picked up. I rubbed my hands together for friction. It was chilly.

As I started for the grass, I noticed movement out of the corner of my eye. Was someone walking farther down the beach?

*Why does it matter, Meg? Get moving.*

I quickened my pace. My flip-flops sunk into the sand. I kicked them off and walked through the grainy sand with bare feet. Once I made it to the grass, I put them back on.

Again something flashed in my peripheral vision. I turned my head toward the movement.

Nothing.

*Meg, you're freaking yourself out.*

The distance to town suddenly seemed much longer than it had in broad daylight. I hurried through the damp grass toward Second Street.

I could hear my heartbeat pounding in my head as I power-walked up the hill. My active imagination has always been a strength and weakness. Tonight it fell into the latter category. Someone was following me. I was sure of it.

All the tiny blond hairs on my forearm stood at attention as I stopped and turned around.

Clouds blocked the moon. The sidewalk plunged into darkness.

*This is stupid, Meg. Really stupid.*

I ignored my body's warning signals and kept walking. As I was almost to the overpass, someone jumped to my side, and shouted, "Halt! Who goes there?"

I screamed.

"Meg? Is that you?" Sherman flipped on his flashlight and shone it my eyes.

I shielded my eyes from the light and took a step backward. "Sherman? What are you doing?"

"Larping. Remember?" He held up his wooden sword. "Jordan was really hoping you were going to come join us. We needed a princess."

I let out a long breath. "Right. Larping. You scared me to death."

"Sorry. The paladins had to go home. I'm on my way to deliver this to the store." He removed a canvas bag from his shoulder. A variety of wooden swords and spears protruded from the top.

"How was your game?"

His brow furrowed. "It's not a game. It's much, much more than a game. It's a lifestyle. Without this outlet many of my paladins wouldn't have a single friend."

I could tell that he had personal experience with that feeling. "That must be hard."

"You wouldn't understand. You're cute and popular. Being on the outside and constantly being teased and bullied by the cool kids takes a toll. I wish I'd had a larping group when I was growing up." His voice was laced with bitterness as he continued. "I do anything—*anything*—to make sure that my paladins don't have to go through what I did."

I felt sorry for him. "Listen, Sherman, I know something about being on the outside."

He shook his head. "No, you don't."

"Trust me, I do. I'm not athletically inclined at all!" I pointed to my skirt. "I like pink dresses and yet I'm writing for *Northwest Extreme.* I'm constantly out of my element, and feeling like an outsider."

"That's different. You're not a kid. You have no idea what these kids go through." A streetlight reflected on his face. His eyes were dark and furrowed.

"No, but I understand wanting to fit in." I tried to keep my voice calm. I could tell talking about this was triggering deep-seated feelings in Sherman.

We walked across the overpass. A semi breezed by below us. Otherwise the freeway was devoid of cars at this late hour.

I touched the side of his cape. "You really care about the kids, don't you?"

Sherman flinched. He tightened the bag of weapons on his shoulder. "I'd do anything to protect them from what I had to go through. *Anything.*"

I believed him, and I admired his resolve. Obviously, whatever experiences he'd been through as a kid had left a lasting scar. I appreciated that he wanted to make sure the same thing didn't happen to the group of kids who had found a safe haven at his shop. Maybe there was a story for me after all. I wasn't sure how it would tie into *Northwest Extreme,* but bullying was a hot topic these days. Greg might be interested in a feel-good story about Sherman taking a group of misfits under his wing.

His voice was thick with disdain as he continued. "Justin and the other surfers don't even give a single thought to the damage they do. They think it's some kind of funny joke to pick on us. And the worst part is, no one stops them. In fact, they praise them. They're superstars with their groupies and endorsement contracts. I can't believe no one sees them for what they really are."

"What are they?"

"Bullies." Sherman jerked his head toward me. "Bullies who need to be stopped."

There was something unsettling about his tone. "Not all of them," I replied, taking a long, slow breath in hopes that he would do the same. "Most of the surfers who I've met have been wonderful."

He scoffed. "Not Justin Cruise. He's the worst person I've ever met."

"You really didn't like him, did you?"

Sherman looked at me like I was crazy. "I hated him. I've hated him for as long as I can remember. I've hated him since we were kids and every day of my life since."

His words made me shiver. As long as he could remember? How long had Sherman known Justin?

I started to ask him what he meant, but he stopped in mid-stride. "I didn't mean that. Never mind."

Every day of his life and since they were kids. Sherman had known Justin since they were kids. Had he just revealed too much? Suddenly his concern and caring about his paladins had a different meaning.

I picked up the pace. We quickly reached the turnoff to his shop. Sherman gave me a little bow. "My lady, do you need an escort home?"

"No, thanks. I've got it from here." A gnawing fear rose in my stomach. Sherman's entire demeanor had shifted when he spoke about Justin. Why hadn't I thought about it before? Sherman could be the killer. It made sense. If Justin had been harassing and bullying Sherman and his paladins, had Sherman finally had enough? Had he snapped? But how would he have gotten out on the water? Sherman made me look like an expert surfer. I couldn't imagine him taking Justin down in the heavy surf.

I didn't need to figure it out now, but I did need to get away from him.

"Maybe I'll come by your shop tomorrow," I said, starting to walk up the hill. "I think it's great what you're doing for these kids. I think my boss might, too."

Sherman scowled. "Why are you acting so weird?"

"Me? I'm not acting weird. I'm just wiped out.

Ready to call it a night, you know?" I could hear my words running together, but I couldn't stop myself.

He didn't look convinced. "Yeah, well, I'm at the shop all day. Come by anytime."

"You got it!" I gave him a thumbs-up. Was Sherman picking up on my nervous energy? I didn't wait to find out. Giving him a quick wave, I spun around and started power-walking up the hill.

# Chapter 27

*Subtle, Meg. Real subtle.*

If Sherman suspected that I was on to him, hurrying up the hill was probably not my wisest choice. I couldn't believe I'd been so blinded by Kyle and Avery when Sherman had been right in front of me the entire time. What had he said? Bullying took its toll. Of course it had. If Justin had been harassing Sherman, I couldn't exactly blame him for snapping.

Bullying had been making headlines all over the nation with tragic stories of teens committing suicide over the pressure of being bullied. Sherman didn't want to see his "paladins" go through the same struggles he had. He'd created a gathering place for them, but Justin's return to town threated that, too. I could feel my brain cells firing. I just wished it wasn't so late.

I fumbled to grab my phone from my bra. No matter the time, I had to call Sheriff Daniels.

Were those footsteps behind me?

I didn't dare turn around. I kept walking at a brisk pace up the hill, using one hand to navigate my phone.

Something was wrong with it. The screen kept pulsing with flashing white dots. I had a sinking feeling I knew why—sweat. Water and mobile phones aren't a good pairing. How stupid of me to leave my phone in my bra all day.

I punched buttons at random, hoping that something would work.

The sound of the phone ringing came over the speaker. I must have dialed someone's number.

"Stop right there." Sherman's voice sounded behind me.

I dropped the phone.

"Don't move." He was behind me before I had time to react. I was surprised at how agile he was.

He shoved a wooden sword into my neck. "Leave the phone and come with me."

I turned around, holding my hands in the air in surrender. "Sherman, listen. You don't want to hurt me."

His eyes didn't even seem to register that he was speaking to me. It was like he was in some sort of trance. I wondered if this was a self-protection strategy that he'd learned from being bullied.

"Turn around. Walk down the hill." He nudged me with the sword. It jabbed my neck.

"Ouch." I winced and followed his order.

My cell phone rang on the sidewalk. I stopped and glanced toward it. The sound of jingling typewriter keys buzzed as it vibrated on the ground. Had someone heard us?

Sherman jabbed the sword deeper into my skin. "Leave it. Get moving."

I moved forward with him breathing down the back of my neck. His breathing sounded erratic and disturbed, just like him.

*What are your options, Maggie?* I heard Pops' voice in my head.

Good question. What were my options? Sherman was prodding me down the hill with a wooden sword. How much harm could he do with a fake sword? Probably not much. My neck felt bruised, but he couldn't kill me with a wooden sword, could he?

*You could run.* I heard Pops again.

I could, but Sherman seemed surprisingly spry all of a sudden. Those hours spent larping had him in better shape than I expected. I could try to make a run for Double Mountain, but he was twice my size and could probably easily outrun me. Plus, everyone was probably long gone from the pub by now.

What I needed to do was to stall Sherman. Sherman wasn't a killer. He was disturbed, and lonely. If I could meet him where he was, maybe he would relax a little.

"Why are you walking so slowly?" Sherman poked my shoulder with the sword.

"I'm not. I'm just walking."

"Keep moving. We're going that way." Sherman pointed the sword toward his shop, which was three stores away. It was completely dark, and there was no sign of any movement on the streets.

*You're on your own for the moment, Meg.*

"Sherman, I want to understand what you've been through. I really do."

He exhaled through his nose. "Yeah right."

"I do. Justin was horrible. I don't blame you."'

He paused in mid-stride. I thought maybe I'd gotten through to him, but he pulled his keys from his pocket and pushed me closer to the front door of his shop.

With one hand pressing the sword onto my neck, he used his free hand to unlock the door. "Get in."

I almost tripped on the indoor/outdoor carpet. I caught myself.

Sherman clicked on his flashlight, illuminating our feet. Mine were coated in a fine layer of sand and needed a good scrubbing.

*Why are you worrying about your feet right now, Meg?* I wasn't sure why. Maybe it was my way of dealing with stress.

Sherman shoved me toward the back of the store. We passed by racks of air guns and walls of mediae-val swords and weaponry. When I'd first visited the shop, it seemed like a nerd mecca. Tonight it felt like I was reliving some sort of ancient torture chamber.

How crazy was Sherman? He had probably killed Justin after all.

"Over there." He shined the flashlight on a metal

folding chair next to one of the gaming tables. The light caught on a poster of a zombie video game.

I let out a little scream and jumped backward.

Sherman chuckled. "Not a fan of the *Walking Dead*?"

I gulped and shook my head.

He flashed the light on the chair again. "Sit. I have to figure out what I'm going to do with you."

"Why do you have to do anything with me? Why don't you let me leave? I'll go home and forget all about this."

"Right. I know you tried to tell someone about me." He pounded the sword on the chair next to me.

I flinched in response.

"Who was it? Who did you call?"

"No one." I shook my head. "My phone isn't working."

He tapped the sword to my forehead. "You want to tell me who you called, or should I knock you out?"

"I swear. I had it in my bra all day. It got wet."

"Wet?"

"Yeah, it was too hot."

Sherman held the sword in one hand and stabbed it into his other hand in a rhythmic motion. I wondered if he was trying to decide if he believed me or not.

"Let me call my friend Matt." I tried a new tactic. "He'll help us."

"Help? I don't need help. I know how to take care of myself. You should know that by now. Justin should have figured that out, too, otherwise I might have spared him." He paused and laughed. "What am I saying? No, I wouldn't have. He needed to die."

Sherman was definitely not operating in reality.

"Can you tell me about it? What did he do?" I already basically knew the answer to my question, but I was counting on the fact that Sherman was still in such a blind rage about Justin that he'd keep talking.

"What didn't he do?" Sherman kept stabbing the palm of his hand. It made my hand hurt to watch. Was he trying to stab away at his memories?

"Justin has been terrorizing me since kindergarten."

"Kindergarten?"

"That's right, kindergarten. It started with stealing my lunch and chasing me on the playground. It escalated in middle school. He used to egg my house, corner me in the boy's bathroom at school and give me atomic wedgies."

"Ouch." I crinkled my nose.

Sherman paid no attention to my response. He was talking to himself more than to me.

*That's fine, Meg, let him talk.*

"In high school he and his buddies would follow me home from school and beat me up in the alley-way behind my house. No one paid any attention. My mom tried to talk to my teachers, the principal, but no one cared. No one wanted to hear that superstar Justin had a nasty side. They thought I was antisocial and jealous of Justin. Jealous! Hardly. I hated him."

There was that word—hate—again. I knew without a doubt that Sherman meant it when he said he hated Justin. I just didn't know how I was going to get myself out of this situation alive.

# Chapter 28

"It sounds like he was awful."

"He was a monster. He deserved to die."

I agreed that Justin did some terrible things, but I couldn't agree that he deserved to die. Probably best to keep that thought to myself.

"How did you do it?" I asked.

"Do what?"

"Kill him. I didn't know you surfed."

"I don't."

"Then how did you get out to the other side of the river? And how did you even know that Justin would be there?"

"A boat."

"You own a boat?"

"My paladins and I have been working on a special project to restore an old boat. I knew that Justin would want to show off for the cameras and press that morning, so I took the boat out for an early ride."

The image of Sherman throwing the sheet over

whatever "special project" he'd been working on the day I met him flashed in my mind. I remembered seeing grease on Jordan's hands. "Is that what you were working on here?" I pointed to the table against the back wall. "You weren't really building a pirate ship, were you?"

"I might not be athletic, but I have something even more powerful than Justin—my brain." He tapped the sword to his head. "I've been teaching the paladins how to build model airplanes, boats, and cars for years. I figured it wouldn't be too hard to build a real motor. I found one at the salvage yard. I've been fixing it up for Joe—the guy who runs the fishing and outdoor store. He was paying me to get it up and running. I thought it would be a good test project, but then when Justin showed up in town again, I realized it might come in handy."

"But you didn't have a boat."

"Sure I did. I took an old dingy of Joe's out. I told him the motor was ready, but I needed to test it in the water before I handed it over." He gave me a smug smile. "It worked perfectly. Perfectly."

"Weren't you worried that Joe would turn you in?"

"Why would he turn me in? He didn't know. Like I said, I told him I was testing the motor. I thought you were smarter than that."

"I know, but I'm sure that Sheriff Daniels has been interviewing everyone in town. What if Joe told him that you were out on a boat that morning?"

Sherman scowled. "And what? They'd think the

nerd did it? Hardly. It's the same as growing up. No one even notices me."

The more Sherman spoke, the more empathy I felt for him. He and his paladins really only had each other. It made me feel guilty about taking my friendships and support for granted. As soon as I got myself out of this mess, I was going to make sure that Jill, Matt, Gam and everyone else in my circle of friends knew how much I appreciated them. Sherman even made me feel slightly nostalgic for Mother.

Mother and I hadn't spoken after Pops died. Well, that's not entirely true. She tried to speak to me, I opted to ignore her. I couldn't forgive her for walking out on him. His entire world fell apart when his editor at *The O* put him on mandatory leave.

He'd been working the Meth Madness story for months. Pops had a tendency to get sucked in to whatever story he was on, but Meth Madness took that to a new level. He went undercover—deep undercover. We didn't hear from him for weeks.

I don't know whether Mother worried about him or not. When I'd call from school to check in, she didn't sound upset. She'd usually launch into the latest gossip that she'd learned from her girlfriends at the club.

Then news broke that he'd inflated statistics and used false sources. When he was officially placed on leave, Mother walked out. She couldn't handle the social hit she might take. Being married to *The O*'s somewhat quirky, but Pulitzer prize–winning reporter was one thing, but being married to *The O*'s most disgraced journalist was another.

Pops called to tell me the news.

"Maggie, how's my favorite editor doing?"

Pops told everyone who would listen that his daughter was the editor of her student newspaper. He couldn't contain his pride.

"I'm great, Pops. We just finished a piece on access to the student union. It turned out really well. I'll send you a copy."

"Please do. I can't wait to read it. Only a few more months and you'll be moving on to greener pastures. I've already put in a word for you, but I'm not sure if that'll help or hurt your chances right now." He cleared his throat.

"Pops, about that. Mother told me what happened. I can't believe it. I can't believe they'd take you off a story, and believe that you of all people would ever lie about a source. You're the most ethical journalist I know."

He chuckled. "Oh, sweet Maggie. What I wouldn't give for the exuberance of youth. Don't lose that fight." His voice caught. "Don't you worry about your old Pops either. I'm fine. I want you to focus on school. No matter what happens I'll be there on graduation day. I can't wait to see you flip your cap into the air. So many good things lay ahead, sweet one. So many good things. Maggie, there's something I need you to know." His voice caught.

"What's that, Pops?"

He paused. I heard Crosby, Stills & Nash playing in the background. "It's about your mother."

"What about her?"

"She's leaving."

"Leaving? Where?"

"Not where, me. She's leaving me."

"What? Why?"

Pops started to respond.

I cut him off. "Is it because of the stupid *O*? Is she worried what her friends will think or something?"

"Now, Maggie, give your mother a little more credit than that."

"Why? It's true. All she cares about is that stupid club and her fancy lunches."

Pops laughed. That only made me angrier.

"Sweet one, your mother and I have had challenges for many years, it's time. That's all. It's no one's fault."

"But you love her. You would never leave *her.*"

"I do love her, Maggie. Indeed, I do." His phone buzzed. He sounded flustered. I should have clued in then that something was terribly wrong. "I have to take this. Keep writing and I'll see you at graduation."

Only he was wrong. He didn't make it to graduation day. The first weeks of my adult life were spent grieving, not throwing my graduation cap in the air and celebrating with my classmates. That was our last conversation. I never heard from him again. I'd played our final conversation over and over in my head about a thousand times since his death. What else could I have said? Why didn't I tell him that I loved him, or ask him more about the Meth Madness story?

He loved Mother and she'd deserted him at his lowest point. How could I ever forgive her for that?

Only Mother insisted that she didn't leave Pops. She swore he left her. I didn't know what to believe. Every time I replayed his last words to me, I knew she must be lying. He clearly told me that she was leaving, not the other way around. I had a feeling I knew why she was lying. She probably figured it was the only way I'd let her back in. The thing is, I wasn't sure I wanted to let her in whether she was telling the truth or not.

But lately a small part of me had begun to wonder if maybe she was telling the truth. She said that Pops wanted her to tell everyone that to keep her safe. What if she was right? I didn't know if I could forgive her, or if I even wanted to. I'd spent so much time being angry with her, I didn't know if I could find a way to let go.

There was one thing I did know, and that was that she wasn't going to give up without a fight. She'd been trying to make amends all through the spring and into the summer. I'd come home from work to find a box wrapped with Tiffany's blue ribbon waiting on my front porch. When I opened it there was a vintage typewriter charm necklace and a note from her that read:

*Mary-Margaret,*
   *I found this and thought you'd love it. Let's do
lunch soon.*

*Love,*
*Mother*

I hadn't called her for lunch. It was easier to shove her to the back of my mind. She was like a nagging toothache that wouldn't go away but wasn't painful enough to go to the dentist. I was dreading the day that the pain became too much to bear.

If only Pops could have left the Meth Madness story alone. Maybe we'd all be laughing at the farmhouse right now. I guess I couldn't blame Pops for staying on the story. I had apparently inherited the same tendency. Look where it got me.

"Hey!" Sherman's voice jolted me from my memory. "Why aren't you answering me?"

I pulled my mind back to the present. "I'm sorry, what did you say?"

Sherman pounded the table with the sword. I jumped in my chair, banging my knee on the table. "Who else did you tell?"

"Tell?"

"About me!" he yelled. "Who else knows about me?"

"No one. Really, I swear. Sherman, you don't have to do this alone. Let's call Sheriff Daniels. He's a really good guy. I know that he'll understand your motives. He'll find you a good lawyer. Maybe it can be self-defense."

"I was defending myself, and protecting my paladins."

"Exactly! That's what I mean. Sheriff Daniels will understand. You don't want to get yourself in more trouble, do you?"

He frowned and stared at me. "I'm not in trouble."

"But you will be, if you hurt me." I wasn't sure it was worth trying to rationalize with someone who was so clearly irrational, but Sherman considered my words.

"Damn." He threw the sword at the wall behind me.

I ducked just in time. The sword sailed over my head and crashed on the floor.

He started pacing. "What am I going to do?"

"Sherman, you're a good guy. You're going to do the right thing. Let's call the sheriff together, okay?"

"The right thing was making sure that Justin can never, ever do what he did to me to anyone else. You're right, it was the right thing, and I'm not going to pay for his mistakes."

I didn't like the sound of that. So much for getting through to him. Sherman reached for a real sword hanging on the wall.

*You need a new plan, Meg. Like now!*

# Chapter 29

Everything happened in a blur. Sherman yanked the sword free from the wall. I took the opportunity to jump to my feet and grab the wooden sword he tossed on the floor. Sure, it was no match for the real thing, but at least it was something.

I made a break for the front door.

Sherman must have been having trouble getting the sword down. I heard him grunting and muttering.

*Get out of here now, Meg!*

I sprinted to the door. I twisted the handle. It was locked. Damn.

*Unlock it, Meg.*

The lock stuck as I tried to twist it open.

I glanced to the back of the store. Sherman had the sword and was coming my way. I gave the lock another twist and bumped the door with my hip.

It swung open. I caught myself and ran outside smack into Sheriff Daniels.

I'd never been so happy to see the sheriff's unsmiling face. "Good evening, Ms. Reed."

"Sheriff, I-I."

At that moment Sherman lunged for the door.

The sheriff pushed me to the side, stepped forward, and removed his gun from his holster. "I'll take it from here, Ms. Reed."

How was he always so calm?

"Put the weapon down, son." Sheriff Daniels stepped closer.

Sherman's hands shook violently. The sword slipped and clattered on the ground. He collapsed with it, falling to his knees and sobbing.

Sheriff Daniels returned his gun to his holster, picked up the sword, and knelt down next to Sherman. "You want to tell me what happened, son?"

I was impressed with Sheriff Daniels' kindness. He obviously had picked up on the fact that Sherman was disturbed. Maybe Gam's intuition was rubbing off on him.

"Justin was belittling my paladins. I caught him making fun of them and pushing them around. Someone had to stand up for those kids. And that someone was me." Sherman stood taller as he confessed. "It took me years to recover from the things Justin and his surfer friends did to me. I couldn't let that happen to my paladins. I couldn't."

The sheriff didn't respond.

There was a long pause. I thought maybe he'd lost Sherman. So much so that I almost started to say something. Sheriff Daniels shot me a look.

I waited, wrapping my arms around my body to warm up. This time I knew my chills were from the emotional roller coaster I'd been on the last few days, and not the night—or was it morning—air.

Sure enough, Sherman continued. "I waited for Justin that morning. I knew he was the one who had vandalized my store, and I knew just like at school that he'd come back to do it again."

He sat on the sidewalk and stretched his T-shirt away from his stomach. I recognized that move. He was uncomfortable with the weight around his middle, even in the middle of the night and in the middle of confessing to murder. Justin probably teased him about his weight, too.

"I did my own stakeout that night," Sherman said. Sheriff Daniels crouched down next to him on the sidewalk. I knew his back bothered him, and wondered how long he could hold the uncomfortable position.

"Justin showed up with an armful of egg cartons. He nailed the shop, one egg after another. I was ready for him this time, though. I had my strobe lights and gaming gear all set up in the front of the shop. I let him hit the windows a few times before I flipped the switch. The entire store lit up like the Death Star had just exploded."

"Death Star?" Sheriff Daniels wrinkled his brow.

"You know, from *Star Wars*, when they blow up the Death Star?"

"Hmm." The sheriff nodded. I knew he was clueless about what Sherman was talking about.

Sherman's face twisted in a grin. "I scared the crap out him. He jumped so high, shattered all the eggs on the sidewalk and took off running. I knew I had him. I waited and gave him time to get out on the water and then I headed for the boat. I already had it all ready to go. It was so easy. He didn't even see me coming. He was out on the far side of the river showing off as usual. I sped out that way. My motor worked perfectly. When I reached him, I waved him over, pretending I was having trouble with the boat. I wasn't.

"I nailed him on the head. I was just going to give him a scare—a taste of his own medicine, but one hit and he was out."

"One hit?" I couldn't contain my surprise.

Sheriff Daniels shot me another look to say keep out of it. "Ms. Reed." Sheriff Daniels cleared his throat.

"Sorry."

"No one ever gives us nerds any credit. He went down hard with just one hit."

I wanted to say more, but Sheriff Daniel's warning face made me stop.

Sheriff Daniels shifted his weight on his knees. A look of pain flashed across his face. "And you were alone?"

Sherman tugged at his shirt. "Yeah, I was alone. Completely alone. No one helped me. I killed Justin Cruise. This is my confession. Shouldn't you be writing this down or something? Shouldn't I call a lawyer?"

Sheriff Daniels stood. As I watched him try and stretch, I could almost feel the tightness in his bones. The poor guy. I wondered if he was still letting Gam do Reiki on him. "How about we head into the station and we can chat more there." He extended his hand to Sherman.

"Okay. Let's go. I want to make an official statement." Sherman took his hand and let the sheriff assist him to his feet.

Why the sudden shift in tone from Sherman? I mean, he hadn't tried to hide the fact that he'd killed Justin, but why was he insisting that he confess?

Sheriff Daniels turned to me. "Ms. Reed, I'm going to call my deputy to give you a ride home."

I shook my head. "No, I'm fine. It's just a couple blocks away."

He kept a tight grasp on Sherman's forearm. "You and I will need to talk in the morning."

"Got it." I headed up the hill as Sheriff Daniels led Sherman the opposite direction.

Hopefully my cell phone was where I'd dropped it. I retraced my steps. A pulsing bright light illuminated the sidewalk. Yep, it was there, but it was definitely not working. As I bent down to grab it I wondered how Sheriff Daniels knew to come to the shop.

The screen was toast. Waves of electronic bars flickered in horizontal stripes. I could make out a few letters between the flashing. Someone had tried to call me. Matt and Jill were probably worried.

Maybe they called Sheriff Daniels and sent him out in search of me.

*You're lucky to have such good friends, Meg.*

Friends. *What Sherman did to protect his friends.* I turned back and watched him get into the squad car. Could that be why Sherman was so eager to confess to Justin's murder? Could he be covering for someone else? What if one of Sherman's paladins snapped and killed Justin?

# Chapter 30

That had to be it. Sherman was confessing to protect one of his paladins. What should I do? I didn't want to see a teenage kid go to jail, but at the same time if he was really involved in Justin's murder, how could I not say anything?

I considered following after Sheriff Daniels, but I was shaky and wanted to see my friends. It could wait until morning.

Matt sprinted around the corner at that moment. He raced down the hill and scooped me into his arms. I fell into him, letting his embrace warm my body.

"Megs! I've been looking everywhere for you." He kissed the top of my head. Then he pulled away and placed both hands on my face. He leaned in and touched my forehead with his. I could feel the heat building between us. His voice turned husky. "Megs."

His lips were inches from mine. My body moved toward him in response. We stood there on the empty sidewalk with the moon above us and our bodies frozen in anticipation for what felt like an eternity.

I tried to control my heartbeat and steady my breathing. It was impossible with Matt's bright blue eyes locked on to mine. Was he going to do it? Was he going to kiss me—finally?

As if he read my mind he dropped his hands from my face.

Oh no. Not again.

Then he moved them to the back of my head. He gently ran them through my hair. He leaned closer. I could almost taste the minty smell on his breath.

He paused. I closed my eyes as our lips met. The kiss was soft.

I couldn't believe this was actually happening. *Stay in the moment, Meg.*

Matt's kiss became more searching. I allowed myself to get lost in the moment and his strong arms. It felt familiar and exhilarating.

When he finally pulled away, he brushed a strand of hair from my forehead. "Sorry. I guess I got caught up in the moment."

"I'm glad you did." I stood on my tiptoes and kissed him on the cheek.

"Megs, when we didn't hear from you I assumed the worst. I thought . . ." He trailed off.

"I know." I squeezed his hand. He clasped mine back. "I'm sorry. I didn't mean to scare you. I realized it was Sherman. I tried to call you, but my phone is broken. And then Sherman cornered me.

I don't think he would have hurt me, but I didn't want to do anything to test that theory out either."

"Sherman? He killed Justin?"

"Can you believe it?"

"Not really." Matt shook his head. "What happened?"

I told him about Sheriff Daniels arriving at exactly the right time and how Sherman confessed to Justin's murder.

Matt let go of my hand and wrapped his arm around me. "I didn't see that coming." He led up the street.

"I feel sorry for him, you know?" I leaned into Matt's shoulder. It felt like things had always been like this between us.

"Yeah, constantly being bullied has to take a toll."

Was this actually happening? Had Matt and I finally taken our relationship to the next level, or had we both become caught up in the stress of discovering that Sherman had murdered Justin?

I wanted to pinch myself, but I was afraid if I did, I might wake up. My stomach fluttered with happy nerves as Matt and I continued home. I tried to walk as slow as I possibly could. I didn't want to get back to the house and have this evening end. Quite a change from the way I was feeling just a few minutes ago.

Alas, when we walked up the front path, Jill was pacing on the porch. She took the steps two at a time and almost tackled me.

"Meg! You terrified us!" She loosened her grasp on me and patted Matt's arm. "Good job, Matty."

A nostalgic look flashed across Matt's face. He waited for Jill and me to walk inside and followed us up the steps. Was he feeling the same way? Was he worried that we wouldn't be able to get the moment back?

Jill pushed me into the living room. "Sit."

"Gladly." I kicked off my flip-flops. Tiny grains of sand coated the bottom of my feet. My toes ached.

*Poor footwear choice, Meg.*

"So what happened?" She stood in the doorway. Her cheeks had a glow to them that I hadn't seen in a long time. Was she just worked up about me, or had her date with the surfer gone well?

"It was Sherman." I rubbed my foot.

"The nerdy dude?"

"Yep."

Matt poured himself a glass of water. "Anyone want one?" he asked from the kitchen.

Both Jill and I declined.

"He killed Justin? How?" Jill sat next to me.

"Honestly, I'm not sure." I sighed. Then I filled them both in on everything Sherman had told me.

Matt placed his water glass on an old issue of *Windsurfing* magazine on the coffee table and leaned back in the recliner. "Sherman took a boat out in the water, hit Justin in the head in heavy surf, and made it back to the shore without anyone seeing him? That's his story? Something doesn't add up."

I sat up and clapped my hands together. "Exactly! Thank you!"

Jill jumped up. "Hang on. I need chocolate to think." She ran into the kitchen and returned with a bag of dark chocolate candy. "I found these at one of the shops downtown. There's plain chocolate, chocolate and hazelnuts, and chocolate and cherries. What do you guys want?" She reached into the bag and pulled out a handful.

"How about all three?" Matt held out his hand.

"I'll take a chocolate and cherry," I replied.

Jill tossed us chocolates and unwrapped one for herself. She popped it in her mouth and took a moment to savor it. Once she swallowed it, she smiled. "Okay, better. Now I can focus. Do either of you have a theory?"

Matt shook his head.

I bit off a piece of the candy. It was a nice balance with the tang of the cherries blending with the rich dark chocolate. "Here's what I think." I held the rest of the chocolate in my hand. "I think Sherman had help."

"Who?" Matt reached for his water.

"What if one of Sherman's paladins was in the boat with him? I mean, I was out there, you guys. The waves were huge. I just can't figure out how Sherman could have done it alone."

Matt tapped his fingers to his chin. "And you think one of the kids was his accomplice?"

"It makes sense. You know Jordan—the tall kid who is always tagging after Sherman?"

"The swimmer with a crush on you?"

"Exactly. He's a swimmer, and a strong one if he competes in the fly. It all makes sense. He had to be the one in the water. That's why Sherman confessed so quickly. He's trying to protect Jordan."

"But why would Jordan help him?" Jill asked, offering up the candy bag.

"No, thanks," I declined. "All those kids totally look up to Sherman. They idolize him. Maybe he didn't know what he was getting into. Sherman said he was just going to mess with Justin. He said something like, 'Give him a taste of his own medicine.' Maybe when they got out there things went wrong. Sherman didn't intend to kill Justin, just scare him off, but then with Jordan with him, he felt terrible and knew he had to protect him."

"It does make sense," Matt agreed.

"What do we do, though?" Jill munched on another piece of chocolate. "That's so sad, and kind of sweet that Sherman is trying to protect the kid. I mean, I get that he killed Justin, but at the same time, if it really was an accident . . ."

"I totally agree. Do I tell Sheriff Daniels?"

Jill scrunched her face. "I don't know. What do you think, Matty?"

Matt frowned. "It sucks. It really does, but you have to tell the sheriff. It's something the authorities are going to have to sort out. The sheriff's a smart guy. He probably has already worked out that Sherman couldn't have pulled something like that off on his own."

"You're right." I tucked my hair behind my ears. "It's so late. I'll find Sheriff Daniels first thing in the morning, but right now I need to go to bed."

"Good plan." Jill gathered up the foil chocolate wrappers and bag.

Matt looked like he wanted to say something, but he picked up his glass and gave me funny a look. "Good night, Megs."

"Good night." I took my flip-flops and headed down the hall. It suddenly didn't feel like a good night. Did Matt regret kissing me? And why did I have to be the one to break the bad news to the sheriff?

# Chapter 31

I woke the next morning feeling slightly sick to my stomach. It would have been nice to blame last night's events for the churning, fluttering feeling assaulting me, but I knew there was only one reason for my nerves, and he was sleeping in the bedroom right down the hall.

I lay in bed for at least an hour staring at the textured ceiling and willing my stomach to stop flopping. It didn't. How was I going to get through the rest of this trip? Matt's kiss had shifted something in me. I couldn't stop replaying it my head. It ran on a recurring loop. I could almost feel his warm breath on my neck and taste his minty kiss.

Our moment of passion had me hungry for more. I felt like a twelve-year-old girl. Did he really like me, or had he been caught up in the moment?

*Stop it, Meg.* I stretched and kicked the covers off. The sun had risen and filtered light streamed through the old glass panes of the window and danced on the hardwood floors.

I needed to put Matt's kiss aside and focus on the rest of the day. My first order of business was to call Sheriff Daniels. Then I needed to wrap up interviews for *Northwest Extreme* and finish my story.

Only before I did any of that, I needed a shower. I dug through my suitcase and found another sundress. The house was quiet as I tiptoed down the hall. I paused in front of Matt's door and leaned my head against it. I could hear the steady rhythm of his snores. It took every ounce of resolve not to twist the doorknob and sneak in. I could imagine curling up next to him and having his strong, sturdy arms wrapped around me.

*God, Meg, you have it bad.* I chided myself and continued on to the bathroom.

Maybe a hot shower would rinse away some of my infatuation.

Nope.

Ten minutes under the water and my stomach still felt like I was out on the choppy water. This was going to be a long day. How should I act when I saw Matt? Like nothing happened? Greet him with a good morning kiss?

I gave my hair a quick blow-dry, and have to admit that I spent a few extra minutes dusting my lids with a light coat of gold powder. It made my eyes glimmer. Of course that could have also been from my growing crush.

The sundress I'd chosen was lemon yellow with teal trim around the waist and halter straps. It flattered my figure perfectly and accentuated the slight tan I'd developed over the past few days.

Satisfied with my appearance, I ran lip gloss over my lips, returned my towel to the rack on the wall, and cracked the window to let the steam that had amassed from my shower escape.

As I opened the door, I bumped straight into Matt's chest. His face looked groggy. When our eyes met he smiled. My stomach flopped.

"Morning." He rubbed his temples.

"Good morning to you." I felt my throat tighten. "I'm up early. I'm going to go find Sheriff Daniels and fill him on our theory." Why was I talking so fast?

"Okay."

"Okay. See you later, then?"

"Sure." He stepped to the side to let me exit. Our hands brushed. I felt my stomach lurch. Matt smiled again.

I hurried down the hall.

*Gawd, Meg, you're an idiot.*

How had I gone from hanging out with Matt, kicking back with pints, to this? And the bigger question was how was I going to get over it?

I couldn't stop myself from trying to analyze his response in the bathroom doorway as I grabbed my gear and headed for town. It was much too early to find the sheriff. What was I going to do for the next hour?

What had Matt's smile meant? Did he feel the energy between us, too?

Sure, I'd had a few work crushes like Greg and the Crag Rats, Oregon's original mountain men and the first high-altitude rescue team in the United States, but this was different. For the first time, I understood why people said falling in love with your best friend was a bad idea. Matt might wreck me. *Tread carefully, Meg.*

The closing ceremonies for King of the Hook wouldn't start for another two hours. I decided to find a secluded table at the coffee shop and work on my feature. Maybe writing would distract me from my emotional roller coaster.

Hood River has several coffee shops, which might be unusual for a small town in some other part of the country, but in Oregon our insatiable lust for fresh-roasted beans makes it easy for multiple shops to succeed in the same market.

I ordered an iced mocha and chatted with the friendly barista while he expertly pulled shots. That was definitely different. In Portland, baristas are known for their less-than-cordial demeanor when it comes to customers.

"Can I grab one of those cherry scones?" I pointed to the glass pastry case when the barista handed me my drink.

"Sure. They're baked fresh across the street." He removed one with tongs. "In fact, I think this one might still be warm."

"Perfection. Thanks!" I stuffed a dollar bill in the tip jar and scanned the room. It wasn't very crowded at this early hour, but I needed seclusion to focus on my work. Some of my writer friends thrive writing in public. Not me. I need a space where I can tune out. And quite frankly I often talk to myself when I'm working on a story. That tends to lead to funny looks from strangers.

I spotted a small table at the very back of the shop near a bookcase. *This should do the trick,* I thought as I carefully balanced my coffee, scone and laptop bag.

The bookcase was crammed with outdoor guidebooks and pictorial historical books on the Oregon Trail. I could spend hours leafing through the musty pages.

*Focus, Meg. Focus.*

Right. I turned on my laptop and took a sip of the coffee while I waited for it to boot up. The cold, creamy mixture settled my stomach. Thank goodness.

I logged on to *Northwest Extreme*'s social media pages and blinked twice. Were my eyes playing tricks on me? The comments on the pictures I'd posted had blown up. I'd been working on building a steady following since I'd taken over social media. I explained to Greg that one of the keys was consistency. We had to update our pages on a consistent basis, otherwise our stuff would just get lost in the slew of information spinning on the web. The other key was interaction. Getting our followers to interact was much harder than it sounds.

For the past few months I'd been tracking when our engagement was the highest, and what sort of posts were pulling people in. The action shots and commentary I'd been uploading this week were working. Our numbers had tripled overnight and there were so many comments, I couldn't even begin to respond to all of them.

This was tangible data to share with Greg. Ugh. Greg. That reminded me that I was going to have to have a conversation with Greg about Pops.

I wasn't ready to dive into that pit yet, so instead I thanked our followers for their feedback, posted some new pictures, and then plugged in my headphones. If I was going to write, I was going to need some tunes.

Bobby Darin's "Somewhere Beyond the Sea" blared in my ears. The lyrics made me pine even more for Matt. "My lover stands on golden sands and watches the ships that go sailing."

Too distracting. I clicked it off and opted for classical instead. Much better.

The words spilled onto the screen as my fingers clicked away. I lost track of time. That tends to happen when I'm in the zone. The coffee shop hummed to life around me. People gathered at the counter and packed into tables. I was oblivious to the bustle. My story was coming together and my headline was nothing short of genius, if I do say so myself.

### FROM HELL TO HIGH WATER: THREE DAYS ON THE MIGHTY COLUMBIA.

I grinned as I typed it at the top of the page and took a bite of the cherry scone. The vanilla flavor mingled with the tangy cherries. It crumbled in my hands. Yum. I savored every morsel of the flaky scone and sipped my iced mocha.

What did I want to say about these past few days on high water? I thumbed through my notes. Despite my brush with heat stroke and distraction over Justin's murder, I was happy with the details and quotes that I had captured.

I began typing again.

*My journey on the river carried me to unexpected jetties this week.*

Most of my features are written in third person as a distant or omnipotent observer, but this felt different. I wanted to give our readers a deeper look into what I'd experienced, and I had to start with Justin's death.

*SILENCED IN THE SURF: REMEMBERING THE LEGENDARY JUSTIN CRUISE*

That would be my tagline.

The story unfolded quickly. I knew it would need time to sit, and a good round of edits, but as I typed the last lines a sense of closure came over me. I needed to write this for myself, as much as I needed to write it for anyone else. Justin's death had rattled me. Sharing his story without glossing over his weaknesses helped sort out some of my muddled feelings.

*We're all flawed, aren't we?*

I wrote in conclusion.

*Maybe it's our flaws that define us. For Justin
Cruise, his bravado made him a superior surfer,
but ultimately led to his demise. Perhaps that's
something for all of us to reflect upon.*

I clicked save and shut my laptop. One feature
done. Three to go. But hey, it was a start. I wasn't
sure what Greg would say about the tone of the
story, but I knew it was the story I wanted to tell.

The ice had melted in my coffee, giving it a thin,
watered-down taste. I drank it anyway and finished
my scone. As I was about to pack up, someone
tapped me on the shoulder.

"Morning, Ms. Reed." Sheriff Daniels tipped his
hat to me. "Is this seat taken?" He nodded at the
empty chair.

"No, sit." I tucked my laptop and notebook into
my bag and placed it on the floor.

Sheriff Daniels brushed crumbs from the table
and cleared his throat. "You're up early."

"I couldn't really sleep. Not after last night. Plus,
I had work to do."

"Let me guess. You're behind because you've
spent this week meddling in my murder investigation, as always." He frowned, but his eyes twinkled
ever so slightly.

"I didn't—"

He cut me off. "That'll be enough, Ms. Reed."

Pausing, he removed his toothpick canister from his breast pocket and twisted off the cap. "Toothpick?" He offered me a wooden pick as he stuck one into the corner of his mouth.

I wondered what his dentist thought of his toothpick addiction. The man must go through a case of toothpicks a week. His teeth had to be worn down from years of gnawing on wood. No judgment. His job had to be horrific at times.

He waited for my response, holding the canister out for me.

"No, thanks." I shook my head.

Returning the canister to his pocket, he surveyed the room and positioned his chair so he had a clear view of the front door. "Now, back to business. I believe you need to fill me in on the rest of the details from last night." He chewed on the toothpick and opened his notebook.

For a moment I was struck at how similar our interviewing process was. I was old-school like Sheriff Daniels. I smiled to myself as he waited with his pen.

"What do you want to know?"

He twisted the toothpick in his teeth. "Start with the timeline. When did you confront Sherman?"

"I didn't confront him. He and I were talking on the way back from the beach. When I realized it had to be him, I tried to call for help."

"Hmm. And what time was that?"

I shrugged. "I don't remember. I can see if my phone is working."

"Please do that." He waited.

My phone was tucked in the bottom of my bag. I had to remove sunscreen, lip gloss, a melted chocolate granola bar, mints, pencils and two notebooks to find it.

"You have quite a collection of items in there." Sheriff Daniels looked amused as I rifled through my bag.

When I finally found my phone, I tried to power it on. It was completely dead.

I held it up for the sheriff to see. "I had a bit of a mishap with it."

"Mishap?"

"Yeah, it got wet."

"Ah."

"Can't you pull cell phone records or something?"

"We can. Although that probably won't be necessary." He scratched something on the notebook and looked up at me. "Continue."

I replayed the details of last night, explaining how Sherman confessed, and how sad I was for him. "He'd been bullied his entire life. Can you imagine? I get why he finally snapped."

Sheriff Daniels didn't comment.

"Do you think he really did it alone?" I asked.

"I'm not clear on what you mean, Ms. Reed."

"I mean, how could pudgy Sherman have physically managed to kill Justin? Don't you think he had to have help?"

"Let me guess." He held up his index finger. "You have a theory who this 'help' might be?"

"Well . . ." I bit my bottom lip.

"Ms. Reed, you are one sharp young lady. I don't understand how you never seem to grasp that you are not a member of my investigative team."

"I know, but don't you want to hear what I think?"

"If I say no is that going to stop you?"

I gave him a sheepish grin.

"Go ahead, then. Proceed." He leaned back in his chair, intentionally placing his pen on his notebook.

"There's this kid who hangs around the shop with Sherman. He's one of the paladins."

"Paladins?"

"That's what Sherman calls his nerd posse."

"Hmm." Sheriff Daniels picked up his pencil. "How do you spell that?"

I laughed. "Anyway, one of them, Jordan, has been taking a beating all week. For some reason Justin and his friends seemed to single him out."

"In what way?"

I explained everything I'd witnessed.

Something must have made an impression, because Sheriff Daniels sat at attention and began jotting down everything I said.

When I finished he removed the toothpick from his mouth and broke it in half. "Paladins, you say?"

"Paladins." I nodded. "Yeah, and Jordan is a great swimmer. He's by far the most athletically inclined in that group. Most of them don't see much of the sun, if you know what I mean. I think Sherman confessed to protect Jordan. Which, if you think about it, is pretty sweet actually."

"Ms. Reed, there's nothing sweet about murder."

I blushed. "I know. I just mean that it shows that Sherman isn't some dangerous psychopath. He just didn't want to see any of those kids go through what he had. I mean, we can't entirely blame him for that, right? Doesn't Justin deserve some of the blame?"

"I don't have much tolerance for bullies either, Ms. Reed, but murder is murder. There are many other avenues that Sherman could have taken. He chose the wrong one. Had he come to us for help, we would have been able to provide protection."

"How?" I noticed a couple sipping lattes at a table nearby turn their heads. "Sorry." I lowered my voice. "But really, how could you have provided them protection? The surfers are superstars. Everyone in town worships them."

"Perhaps. Or perhaps the town would have rallied around the paladins, as you call them. I'd give the people here more credit than that. No one likes a bully."

He was right. I didn't want to admit it, but his words rang true.

"If there's nothing else, I'll be on my way." He closed the notebook and tucked it into his pocket.

I don't know what came over me, and I knew that Matt would kill me for asking this, but it just sort of came out. "Sheriff Daniels." I reached for his hand. "Can I ask you something else?"

He folded the broken toothpick in his hand and nodded.

"It's about my dad."

Sheriff Daniels flinched. It only lasted for a split second before he recovered and returned his face to his normal, almost skeptical gaze. "What about your father?"

I stopped myself from asking the question I really wanted to ask. Why had he flinched? Was Matt right? Did Sheriff Daniels know something?

"Ms. Reed, what about your father did you want to ask me?"

"Have there been any new leads?"

He shook his head. "I'm afraid not. The tip line has gone cold. It's been a while. That tends to happen. Unless someone comes forward with new information, my sense is that this case will remain open for a long, long time."

I sighed.

"If I could offer a small piece of advice?"

"Sure. Anything."

"Go on with your life, Ms. Reed. Leave the past in the past. That's where it belongs." He glanced at his wrist. "I best be on my way. Duty calls." He tipped his hat again and walked away.

I didn't feel comforted by his advice. Leave the past in the past? No way. Even if I wanted to, I had no idea how to make that happen. And something else felt unsettled. Had Sheriff Daniels been offering me wise advice or some kind of warning?

# Chapter 32

I bussed my dishes and headed for the beach. The air felt slightly cooler. Maybe the heat wave was finally starting to loosen its hold. A girl could hope.

Downtown Hood River, drenched in morning sunlight, looked cheery and hopeful. In stark contrast to last night.

*Last night.* I shook my head. It was hard to believe that I had been walking this very route a few short hours ago with Sherman on my heels.

Closing ceremonies were due to start in thirty minutes. I wanted to get a prime spot in the front. As I walked toward the beach, I found myself glancing over my shoulder and checking behind me. Not because I was worried about Sherman or someone else stalking me on the sunny streets, but because I was dying to see Matt.

What was I feeling? Was I in love with him? How had one kiss completely changed everything? Even thinking about him made my heart race and sent my stomach flip-flopping. This was bad. Really bad.

*You have to shake it off, Meg,* I told myself as I made it to the viewing area.

Closing ceremonies were an opportunity for the competitors to demonstrate their tricks and stunts without the pressure of being judged. I was looking forward to the freestyle display and gathering any last-minute photos and information for my feature. This was it. One more event and I was done with this story.

It had been a whirlwind few days filled with some wonderful and equally horrific events. I wasn't sure how to process it all. I had a feeling it was going to take some time, but I was actually starting to feel ready to get back to Portland and my normal routine. Maybe that would be a start.

"Top Tier, I've been looking for you." Ryan tapped my shoulder.

"Hey, how's it going this morning?"

"Not too bad. Should be crazy out there." He motioned to the beach where the surfers were warming up.

"I know. It's hard to believe it's over. I feel like we just got here, you know."

"Yep, that's how these things go. Fast and furious. You'll get used to it."

"Will I? Have you?"

He moved his head from side to side. "I get tired of being on the road sometimes, but I don't have a family, and the perks are pretty sweet."

I'd never thought of that. Could I do a job like

this and have a family? A vision of Matt and I getting married flashed through my head.

*Knock it off, Meg. What are you doing?*

There wasn't any part of me that was interested in getting married right now, let alone thinking about starting a family.

"Hey, I got a call from my boss this morning." Ryan was talking to me. I shook off my daydream and focused my attention on him.

"Oh yeah?"

"Yeah, he wanted to know why *Northwest Extreme*— some regional magazine—his words not mine, was crushing us on social media."

I grinned. "We are?"

"You are." He showed me his phone. Sure enough, *Northwest Extreme* was trending higher on Twitter than ESPN. I couldn't believe it.

"Awesome."

"Well, my boss doesn't think so. He's not very pleased."

"Are you in trouble?"

"No, I don't do social media. I do this." He pointed to the river already alive with colorful kite-boards. "We have a new team dedicated to social in our New York office."

"Oh."

"My boss wanted to know what *Northwest Extreme* is doing to generate the kind of traffic you're getting. I told him I had a pretty good idea it had something to do with a junior reporter who was covering the event with me."

"Thanks." I grinned.

He shook his head. "No need to thank me, you're doing the work."

"Well, I appreciate the compliment."

"That's good because there's more."

"More?"

He handed me a business card. "My boss wants you to e-mail him. He's interested in hiring you."

"ESPN wants to hire me? Are you kidding?"

"Not at all. I told you he was impressed. He's looking for someone to come head the social media team. This might be your big break, kid."

"Head the social media team?" I could feel my jaw drop. "As in head the social media team for ESPN?"

"Yep, I get the sense that the job is yours if you want it. Send him an e-mail. He'll probably want you to fly out."

"To New York?"

"Well, we're headquartered in Connecticut." He gave me a look that made me wonder if he regretted telling his boss about me. "The job is in New York, though."

"Right." I stared at the business card. "ESPN. Wow."

He pointed to one of the surfers nearby. "Listen, I've got to run. I want to see if I can get a quick interview. Good to meet you, Meg. Maybe I'll see you in New York soon." He shook my hand and left.

I kept staring at the business card. ESPN wanted

to hire me? ESPN! How had that happened? What an opportunity. How could I pass it up? But then again, did I want to leave the Pacific Northwest— my friends, my family, Matt? Did I want to live in New York? But, oh my God, ESPN!

There wasn't much time to think about it. Kyle stepped onto the platform and announced that the King of the Hook closing ceremonies were about to commence. I stuffed the ESPN card in my bag. I'd have plenty to think about on the drive home later.

For the next hour the surfers put on an incredible show. The wind felt warm on the back of my neck as I watched the surfers take flight. For the first time in weeks, the rising sun felt good.

I became lost in the display of athleticism. Kites and sails bobbed in the air above the water, chasing the wind. The crowd oohed and aahed as surfers flipped in the air and launched themselves over a giant plywood ramp constructed in the river.

How did they make their bodies contort in such seemingly painful ways? And manage to land without breaking their necks? Thank goodness I didn't have to get out there again.

The stunts wound down, and the surfers took turns on the podium. Kyle awarded the first-, second-, and third-place winners, along with a number of hilarious awards like best crash and worst flop. He had the crowd rolling with laughter as he played film of some of the craziest crashes on an inflatable movie screen.

Fireworks erupted over the water as Kyle finally declared King of the Hook closed. A band took the stage for the after party. I shot a few more pictures and reviewed my notes. I had everything I needed to finish my story. This was a wrap.

Another assignment in the books, and shockingly I had survived. Time to pack up and head home.

"Meg!" Jill called out as I weaved through the boisterous crowd jamming in front of the stage.

She was dancing with the cute surfer from Double Mountain. He had one arm around her waist and kept bumping her hip in a playful, yet sexy way. Yes!

"Hey!" I waved, but didn't push through the throng of bodies to join them.

Jill whispered something to the surfer and motioned for me to wait. I watched the surfer follow her graceful moves. Our eyes met. He winked. I winked back and gave him a thumbs-up.

"Where are you going? The party is just getting started." Jill's cheeks were flushed and her voice was breathless.

"I see, and I see you've met up with your dreamy surfer again."

Jill turned redder. "He's a good dancer."

"And pretty easy on the eyes, too."

She grinned. "Yeah, he's not too shabby. Come dance."

"I can't." I held up my laptop bag. "I've got to

finish a few things and pack. We're supposed to check out by noon."

"Already done. Matt and I gave the house a quick cleaning this morning, too. My stuff's in my car. You just need to grab your stuff and leave the key on the counter." She paused and looked around the beach. "Where is Matt? He said he was going to be down here."

Now it was my turn to blush. "I don't know. I haven't seen him."

Jill didn't notice. "You sure you don't want to stay for a while? You've got some time."

"Nah, I'm good. Thanks, but please, I beg you— go have fun. If I don't see you today, I'll see you back in Portland later, okay."

"Cool." Jill planted a kiss on my cheek. "Smooches, Meg. Catch you later." She danced back through the crowd, her arms in the air, her hips swinging to the beat of the music. I'd never seen her look so free. Maybe spending the past few days with Gam had worked magic on my friend.

I smiled at the thought. Life was funny, so much goodness mixed with so much sorrow. I couldn't wait to see where Jill's new-found sense of freedom was going to take her. I'd have to ask her what her intention had been.

Lost in thought, I bumped into someone.

Kyle towered over me. "Hey, Meg."

"Sorry about that. I didn't see you."

"No problem." He had a rolled-up King of the

Hook program in his hands. "What did you think of the show?"

"Amazing. Really amazing."

"Yeah, I like to save the crazy stunts for the last day. It's always fun to see what new energy the competitors bring." He tapped the program on my shoulder. "I hear you have been the media darling this week."

"What?"

He nodded. "That's the word on the beach. The social media star. I think you may have made a name for yourself."

I chuckled. "That's better than the kind of name I've made for myself in the past."

"I'm not sure I understand?"

"Let's just say my tendency toward being a klutz hasn't exactly scored me many points within the extreme outdoor culture."

Kyle rolled the program tighter. "I don't know about that, but you've definitely made your mark here. Well done. I'll be eager to read your feature in a few weeks."

He started to leave, but I stopped him. "Hey, can I ask you something?"

"Sure. Hit me.'"

"It's about Justin Cruise."

Kyle's lips pursed. "Yeah?"

"I sort of got the impression that you were irritated with me the last couple days, and I couldn't help but wonder if maybe it had something to do with Justin."

"What do you mean?"

"Like maybe you thought I was asking too many questions about Justin."

Kyle shrugged and pointed to the revelry on the beach with his rolled-up program. "I've been focused on this. Maybe that's what you were picking up on."

"Yeah, but what about your conversation with Ian. Were Ian and Justin really going to start their own competition?"

"No." Kyle gave me a dismissive look. "That was all talk on Justin's part, and Ian came to his senses once he cooled down."

"So he's not starting his own thing?"

"Not a chance. I made it clear that he's my go-to guy from here on out. Ian might have a bit of swagger. It comes with the territory if you're willing to put your body through everything these guys do, but he's no Justin Cruise." He tapped the brochure in the palm of his hand. "It's like I told you, surfing is only one small piece of this mission. There are only a handful of surfers who don't understand that, and sadly Justin just happened to be one of the best and the worst."

"That's the way it goes, isn't it?"

He raised his brow. "You're sharp. Don't sell yourself short on the extreme thing. You know I tell everyone that ninety percent of it is mental. Don't let fear get in your head." He flicked my shoulder with the brochure one more time. "Nice working with you, Meg Reed. Catch you next year."

Don't let fear get in your head. Yeah. A great sentiment, but how? I shook my head as I walked away. I'd been wrong about Kyle. I'd been wrong about everyone actually.

# Chapter 33

I followed the sun up the sidewalk toward town. Someone who looked like Matt was chatting with a group of surfers. I walked up and tapped him on the back. When he turned around, my face fell. Not Matt.

"Sorry," I mumbled. "I thought you were someone else."

"Who do you want me to be?" the surfer flirted.

"No one. I thought you were my friend." I started to walk up the hill.

"I'll be your friend." He grabbed my hand and planted an exaggerated kiss on it.

At that very moment I spotted Matt up the hill. He stared at me, glared at the surfer kissing my hand, and marched out of my line of sight.

I pulled my hand away. "Sorry, I have to run."

The surfer called after me. "Hey! Give me your digits. We can hang out."

I called behind me as I ran up the hill. "Can't. I'm taken!"

That was a lie, but I was hoping it wouldn't be soon. What were the odds that Matt would pass by when some guy was flirting with me?

*Bad luck, Meg.*

When I made it to the top of the hill, I was panting for air. I'd run as fast as my short legs could carry me, but there was no sign of Matt. I checked both ways. Where had he gone? How had he disappeared so fast?

He couldn't really think I was flirting with someone new, could he? A new thought popped into my head as I sucked air in through my nose: Did that mean he was jealous? That was a good sign, right? Not that I wanted to play games with him, but I kind of liked the idea that he might be feeling the same way, too.

I ducked into the coffee shop. What a change from a few hours ago. Every table was taken and a line snaked from the counter to the door. I did a quick check for Matt. He wasn't here.

As I passed by a table on my way back outside, someone grabbed my hand. It was Avery. She and Ian sat across from one another. Ian sucked black ice coffee from a straw. Avery sipped a cup of green tea.

"Meg! We were just talking about you." Avery placed her tea on the table and her hand over her mouth like she was trying to keep it down.

"Uh-oh." I stuck out my tongue.

Avery laughed and waved me off. "No, it's all good." She leaned over and asked a couple at a table nearby if they were using the extra chair. "Here, sit." She pulled the chair to their table.

I hesitated. I really wanted to find Matt, but I also had a few lingering questions to ask Avery and Ian.

Matt can wait, I thought as I sat. He's not going anywhere, and this might be my last chance to talk to Avery and Ian.

"How are you feeling?" I asked Avery.

She held up her mug of tea. "I'm keeping this down, so I think that's a good sign."

Ian gave her a look of concern. "The doctor told you to take it slow, though, remember?"

"Don't worry. I'm not going to chug my tea." Avery laughed. "If this was a beer in front of me, maybe that would be a different story, but that's off the menu for the next nine months. Man, being pregnant is kind of a bummer."

I didn't respond. The thought of being pregnant was totally foreign to me, and Avery wasn't exactly making it look like fun.

She rubbed her belly. "As soon as the doc gives me the okay, I can't wait to take this little bean out on my board."

"You're going to surf while you're pregnant?" I asked.

"Of course. I want this kiddo to get a feel for the waves as early as possible."

"But what about balancing and everything, won't that be difficult as you get bigger?"

Avery looked at Ian and rolled her eyes. "This

isn't 1950. Women run marathons while they're pregnant. I think I can handle surfing."

She had a point. Although I had to admit that there was a small part of me that wouldn't mind jetting back in time to the 1950s sometimes. Minus the fact that I'd probably never be doing a job like this. It was much easier to romanticize what life might have been like over sixty years ago.

"Did Justin even know that you were pregnant?"

Avery's eyes welled with real tears. "No, I never had the chance to tell him. I planned to wait until I figured out what I was going to do. . . ." She trailed off.

"I'm sorry," I said with genuine concern. It was nice to see her show some raw emotion for the first time.

She brushed a tear from her eye. "It's okay. He probably would have freaked out on me anyway. Maybe it's better this way."

I wanted to say more, but the moment was lost. Avery folded her arms across her chest and stared out the window. I turned to Ian. "Congrats on your big win."

He showed me the medal around his neck. It looked like something from the Olympics.

"Is that real gold?" I asked.

"Nah, Kyle's cheap. I think that's just sprayed on."

"Hey, speaking of Kyle, is everything okay with you two?"

Ian tucked the medal under his T-shirt. "Yeah, why?"

"I heard you arguing yesterday. It sounded like you were thinking of severing ties with King of the Hook."

A look passed between Avery and Ian that I couldn't decipher. Avery nodded as if giving him approval to speak.

"Nah, Kyle was right. I was just freaking out after Justin died."

"So you weren't going to start your own competition with Justin?"

"Nah, that was his dream. I'm heading out on a world tour for the next few months."

"World tour? Wow. That sounds awesome."

Ian chomped on a piece of ice. "You know it. Can't pass up the chance to catch some big waves around the globe."

"What about you?" I asked Avery. "What are you going to do now?"

She took a sip of her tea. "I'm not going to be traveling the globe in search of good surf, but I have a few ideas."

"Like vlogging for *The O*?"

"Maybe. Your friend Matt is going to put in a word for me. I have some other ideas, too. Maybe some modeling. I've been trying to get in with that ESPN reporter who's here. I'd love to do commentary for them."

"Yeah, that would be great." I didn't mention that I already had a job offer from ESPN.

"Did you hear the news about that nerdy dude?" Avery asked.

"You mean Sherman?" I could hear the defensive tone in my voice, but he had a name after all.

"Yeah, I think that's the one. He killed Justin. Can you believe it?"

"I can." I folded my arms across my chest. "From what I hear, Justin was horrible to him. He'd been bullying Sherman and all the kids who hang out at his shop. That's not cool."

Ian ruffled his already shaggy hair. "Not cool at all, man. Not cool. I tried to tell Justin to leave them alone, but he wouldn't let it go."

"You tried to stop him?" I looked at him in disbelief. "From what I heard it sounded like you were right there with him."

"No way, man. Not me."

"But you were there the morning that Sherman's store was vandalized."

"I already told you, I was helping Avery home. On my way to the clinic I saw Justin egging the store. I told him to chill. He wouldn't listen. I don't get why he was so obsessed with messing with that dude."

Maybe Ian had been telling the truth the whole time. I thought back to the first time I saw Justin harassing Sherman; come to think of it, Ian had been the one who pulled him away.

"I think they had a long history," I said.

"Too bad." Ian sighed. "If Justin could have controlled himself he might not have gotten himself killed."

"I can't believe that nerdy dude did it," Avery said. "He isn't exactly the athletic type, is he?"

I didn't see any need to tell them that I suspected Sherman hadn't done it alone, so I took the opportunity to excuse myself. "Good luck to both of you," I said as I stood. "Be sure to get a copy of *Northwest Extreme*. This feature will be in the October issue. You're both going to be part of the story."

Now to find Matt, I thought as I pushed open the door to the coffee shop and stepped into the sun. Where did he go? It was too early to hit the pub. Could he have gone to the beach?

I stood on my tiptoes to get a better view of the crowded sidewalks. No sign of Matt, but I spotted Gam at Good Dog Company across the street. A mangy dog with black hair lapped at a water dish at her feet. Animals are attracted to Gam.

She caught my eye and waved. I waited for a car loaded with paddleboards to pass, and crossed the street. "You found a friend," I said to Gam.

"Isn't he the sweetest?" The dog leaned into Gam, who stroked his matted hair.

I could think of another description but kept it to myself. "You haven't seen Matt by chance?"

Gam brushed black hairs from her hands. "No.

Why?" Her eyebrows formed into two perfect peaks. "Is something wrong?"

"Nope, not at all."

"If you're sure?" Gam's expression revealed that she knew I was holding back. Thankfully she didn't press me. "How did your experiment go?"

"Experiment?"

The dog nudged her. "Oh, sorry. Did you want some more?" She petted him again. "Your intention. Did our little experiment on focus work?"

I wrinkled my forehead. "You know, actually, I think it did. I set my focus on going with the flow, and things have seemed to flow with more ease now that I think about it." My cheeks warmed at the thought of Matt's kiss. That was definitely in the flow.

Gam clapped. "That's great! I knew it would. Good on you for giving it a go. You can try a new intention if you want."

"Good idea. I'll have to think about what to work on next. Maybe not stumbling upon murders?"

"That could be a good place to start." She glanced at the silver watch on her bronzed wrist. "Oh, look at the time. I need to go find that cowboy of mine."

"What time is it?"

"Almost eleven."

Oh no! I had to check out of the house. Matt would have to wait. I gave Gam a quick hug and hurried up the sidewalk to the rental house. Sure enough, Matt and Jill had the place sparkling. I felt bad for not helping them clean. I would have to buy them both a beer when we were back in Portland.

Packing didn't take long. I tossed my clothes into my bag, left the key on the kitchen counter, and locked up. "Good-bye, Hood River," I said aloud as I lugged my bag down the front porch steps. What a week it had been.

My Subaru sat, unmoved, in the same spot on the street where I'd parked it when I arrived. I appreciated the fact that I could walk everywhere in Hood River. Portland's a very walkable city, too, but nowhere near as small. I threw my bag in the back and decided to drive through town in hopes of catching Matt before leaving.

What would I say to him? For the first time in my adult life I was nervous to talk to one of my best friends. This was uncharted territory for me, and I didn't know how to proceed. I just knew I needed to see him.

I drove slowly, scanning the storefronts. I passed a funky pet store, a bakery and fishing supply store—there was no sign of him. Had he left without saying good-bye? Did he feel differently? Maybe he regretted kissing me last night.

My stomach fluttered with nerves as I drove at a crawl. The car behind me honked. I jumped and waved in my rearview mirror.

*Get a move on it, Meg. He's not here.*

Resigned that my next encounter with Matt would have to wait, I steered the car toward the freeway. There was so much to think about on the drive home, I couldn't believe it when I pulled up to my bungalow forty-five minutes later. I also couldn't believe that there was someone waiting on my front stoop.

# Chapter 34

"Greg, what are you doing here?" I asked as I got out of the car and walked around the back to get my bag.

He jumped to his feet and made it to me in three long, easy strides. "Here, let me get that." He took the bag from my hand and shut the back of my car.

"How do you even know where I live?" I asked, walking to the front door.

"HR. Your address is on record."

"Oh, right."

"I hope you don't mind me stopping by. I want to talk to you about something sensitive. I figured it would be better if we talked somewhere more private than the office."

"Okay." I fumbled through my purse for my house key and unlocked the front door. The apartment smelled stuffy, like it had been shuttered in the heat for the past week. It had. Yuck. I left my keys in the basket by the door and bent over to grab a stack of unopened mail that had piled on the floor. One of the perks of renting a vintage bungalow is all the charming little features it contains, like a mail slot on the front door and built-in cupboards around the fireplace.

"Come on in." I motioned for Greg to enter as I hurried to open all the windows and let some air in.

"Where do you want this?" He held up my bag.

"Just stick it next to the door. Thanks."

"Nice place."

"Thanks. I love it. It's so retro, you know?"

"Retro is the thing with you young ones, isn't it? I don't understand it."

"I have a theory on that, actually," I said as I sat on the couch and motioned for Greg to join me. "I think it's a natural response to technology. We're the first generation to grow up in a technology-focused world, so we have to have some kind of outlet to escape it, hence the 'things in jars' movement."

"Things in jars?" Greg sat in the vintage wing-back chair I'd scored at one of my favorite antique shops. His legs stretched out so long they hit the coffee table. I pushed it back for him.

"Yeah, you know, everything in Mason jars. Haven't you seen that blog? It's beautiful. You can put anything in a Mason jar and make it look good. Anything—candles, fruit, nuts, moss, rocks. Really, *anything*."

"Noted. I'll have to check it out."

"You should. You know we could do a feature on escaping technology for *Northwest Extreme*. I mean,

I think it would tie in well. I could take the angle of how my generation is heading out into nature to escape the constant glare of cell phones and screens in our face. What do you think?"

"Slow down. Take a breath."

I gave him a nervous laugh. I knew I had to confront him about working at *The O,* but I wasn't sure how.

"It's a good idea." Greg continued. "However, many of the kids in your generation who I see out on the trail have their cell phones with them. In fact just the other day I almost ran over a kid who was texting while hiking. Maybe your story should be about how we protect what little wild space we have left from technology. I was reading about how all the major cable companies are fighting to get Wi-Fi in the forests."

"They are?"

"Yep, there's a big push to map every square inch of the planet. Pretty soon—if the big guys have their way—you'll be able to whip out your phone in the middle of the jungle or at the top of Mount Rainier and upload a picture to Facebook. I hate it."

"That's pretty depressing."

"You're telling me. We have to have space where we can completely unplug. What is the outdoors going to look like for the generations behind us if we let technology seep in?"

I'd never seen Greg so passionate about something. He reminded me a little of Pops.

"We should do a story on this." I sat up a bit on the couch and reached for my phone. "Let me take a couple notes."

Greg snickered. "Classic. Let me take a picture of that: Discussing how technology is invading our wild spaces on your phone."

"Right." I laughed and held up my phone. "I forgot. My phone is toast, but we should do a story on this topic, though."

"It's all yours." Greg grabbed my phone. "What happened?"

"Uh, let's just say I had a little mishap with it." I could feel heat rising in my cheeks.

He tossed the phone back to me. "Expense a new one. You need it for social media, right?"

"Thanks. That would be great." I bit my bottom lip. Should I ask him about working at *The O,* or should I follow Matt's advice? I just couldn't believe that Greg was dangerous.

"Of course." Greg grinned. Then his face clouded. "That's not why I'm here, though. We need to talk, Meg."

I swallowed. "That doesn't sound good." Did Greg know that I'd seen the picture?

"It's not." He cracked his knuckles and sat closer. His eyes focused on his knees.

"Is this about my dad?"

His head swung up. "Yeah, I'm afraid so."

"Greg, I'm really confused and honestly I'm not

sure who to trust. Can you please tell me what you know?" I hated the pleading tone in my voice.

"I wish I could, Meg. That's why I'm here. I've gotten word from a good source that your friend Matt has been poking into things he shouldn't. He needs to stop. Now." Greg held my gaze. His face was cold. "If he doesn't, you could both be in danger."

"Why? I don't understand."

"You don't need to understand. You just need to convince your friend to stop whatever it is that he's doing. I tried to tell him myself, but he won't listen to me. He seems to be under the impression I'm not on your side."

"Are you?"

"Meg, there's a lot I can't tell you, mostly because there's very little I know or understand myself when it comes to this situation, but I promise you, I have your back."

He sounded and looked sincere, but I didn't know who to trust.

"What can you tell me?"

"Someone at *The O* approached me last year and suggested that I hire you. They thought you'd be safer at *Northwest Extreme*. That's all I know. I agreed to watch out for you, and I have been ever since. I'm not going to stop. I have your back, Meg. Always."

"Who? Who at *The O* approached you?"

Greg shook his head. "I don't know."

"How can you not know if they approached you?"

"I never met the person. It was all arranged through e-mail and phone calls, but we never met face-to-face, and they never gave me a real name."

"Why did you agree to do it, then? How did you even know it was legit?"

"They had some convincing evidence they shared with me." Greg held up his finger. "Don't ask. The less you know the better."

I stood. "Why do people keep saying that to me? The less I know the better? That doesn't even make sense. I'm so tired of all this secrecy."

Greg pushed to standing and walked over to me. He placed his hand on my shoulder. "I know, Meg. I can only imagine how hard—and confusing—this must be for you, but your dad went to great lengths to protect you. I know your friend Matt cares about you, but he's doing more harm than good. He's on someone's radar now, and someone is not happy to hear that the Meth Madness file has been touched."

I looked out the window. Greg stepped to the side.

"Listen, I'm going to take off. You'll talk to Matt, right?"

I nodded.

"Meg, I'm sorry. I really am, but there's nothing else I can say. I guess this is one of those times that the past is meant to stay in the past."

Sheriff Daniels had said the same thing this morning. Tears began to well in my eyes. I really didn't want him to see me cry. I blinked hard.

Greg walked to the front door. "See you at the office tomorrow. I'll be eager to read your feature."

As soon as the door shut behind him, tears spilled from my eyes. *Pops, why did you have to do this to me?*

# Chapter 35

After I recovered from Greg's warning, I spent the rest of the afternoon finishing my feature. I was going to deliver a story early. A small victory given the swirling questions I had about what Pops had been mixed up in before he died. Greg said Pops went to great lengths to protect me. What did that mean? What did I need protection from?

I had to e-mail Matt and Jill to see if they were free for a beer. I wanted to thank them for cleaning the house, and more than anything I wanted to see some friendly faces.

Jill wrote back right away. "Ecliptic in twenty?"

"Done."

Matt didn't respond. Maybe he wasn't checking his e-mail.

Ecliptic was a relatively new pub that had opened on Mississippi Avenue, not far from me. I changed into a pair of capris and a pink wrap shirt. The early evening air held the promise of fall. I drank in the scent of honeysuckle and hops as I pulled into the parking lot.

Jill was already seated at a picnic table with a large sun umbrella when I arrived. She held up a pitcher of beer. "Over here, Meg!"

I joined her at the table, noting there were four pint glasses. "Did you hear from Matt? I can't text him because my phone is dead." My heart skipped a beat as I said his name.

"No, he hasn't texted, but that surfer I met lives here. He and his friend were already going out tonight. I hope it's okay, but I invited them to come join us."

"You are practically smitten." I helped myself to a pint.

"No," she scoffed. "But it is fun to flirt."

"Especially when those surfers are so easy on the eyes."

"Exactly." She clinked her pint glass to mine. "To eye candy."

"To eye candy." I laughed.

She leaned across the table. "So before our eye candy arrives, tell me. Did something happen between you and Matt?"

I choked on my beer. "Why do you say that?"

"He was acting weird this morning."

"Weird? How?"

She flicked my arm. "Something did happen, didn't it?"

I blushed.

"Did you hook up?"

I think I turned as red as a fire engine wailing in the distance. "Maybe."

"Maybe? There's no *maybe* in hooking up. You either did or didn't. Meg Reed, I'm your best friend, you need to dish right now."

"We kissed. That was it, but I think it freaked him out."

"Why?"

I shrugged. "I don't know. I haven't talked to him since. What did he say this morning?"

"It wasn't what he said. It was how he was acting. He kept glancing out the window and checking his phone like he was looking for someone."

"That is weird."

"Don't sweat it, Meg. Matt adores you. One kiss isn't going to send him running."

"I don't know. Why wouldn't he text you back? He always meets us for beers."

"I'm sure he has a reason. Don't let this become something it isn't in your head." She reached across the table and patted my hand.

Her dreamy surfer and his friend arrived. Saved by surfers. Thank God.

We finished off the pitcher and they ordered another one. I enjoyed Jill's new guy. What a difference from the buttoned-up Will Barrington. But even the distraction of athletic, laid-back surfers and delicious beer couldn't get my mind off

Matt. Was kissing him a mistake? Had I ruined the relationship with the nicest guy I'd ever known?

Jill and the surfers decided to move on up the street for pizza and more beer. I declined. I couldn't concentrate on anything. I wouldn't be much fun, and I didn't want to bring Jill down on the first date she'd had in months.

"He's awesome," I whispered in her ear as we parted ways. "Have fun and don't let that eye candy out of your sight."

She squeezed my hand. "Thanks! See you this weekend, and don't worry about Matt, okay?"

I gave her my best brave face and headed for my car. I wish I had Jill's confidence. I had a bad feeling that something had gone wrong with Matt and me.

All the way home I debated about sending him another e-mail. Maybe he hadn't gotten the first one. That can happen, right? Things get lost in the vastness of cyberspace.

*Doubtful, Meg,* I told myself as I parked in front of my bungalow. More like he doesn't want to see you.

My worst fear had been confirmed. I'd ruined my relationship with Matt, and I had no idea how to repair it.

Once inside, I flopped on the couch and flipped through the channels until I landed on ESPN. Maybe the Universe was trying to tell me something. Was I destined to go to New York?

I must have dozed off because I woke a while

later to fading light outside and a soft knock on my
front door. Wiping drool from my chin, I stretched
and tried to shake off the groggy feeling from my
unintended nap. When I opened the door I saw
someone speed off down the street on a bike. Matt?

"Hey!" I called.

He didn't turn around.

Was it Matt? There were so many bikes in Portland, I couldn't tell. Maybe I had dreamed that
someone was knocking on my door. I turned to go
back inside and noticed a bouquet of flowers on the
stoop. Okay, maybe not.

I bent down to pick up the bouquet. It was
arranged in a pale-pink vase with pink lilies, roses
and peonies tied together with a pink polka-dot
ribbon. It was the most beautiful flower arrange-
ment I'd ever seen.

Matt left me flowers! My chest thumped. But why
hadn't he stayed?

I took the flowers inside. They smelled heavenly.
I breathed in the scent of the fresh-cut roses and
ran my finger along their delicate petals. Matt sent
me flowers!

Matt sent me flowers! I grinned from ear to ear
as I rested them on the coffee table. He did love
me. Whew.

A card fell onto the table. I hadn't noticed it
tucked into the ribbon.

He left me a love note, too? This night was getting better by the minute.

*MEGS.* My name was written in his block-letter

handwriting on the front of the creamy envelope.
I used my pinkie to pry it open, not wanting to
rip it.

Inside there was another handwritten note. I
clutched it to my chest for a minute before reading
it. This was my first love note. How romantic!

My stomach gurgled to life as I read the note. My
heart felt like it was in my throat. Man, I had it
bad. Bad.

*DEAR MEGS,*

*WHEN I RODE BY THE FLOWER SHOP I
SPOTTED THIS IN THE WINDOW. THE
WOMAN AT THE COUNTER SAID SHE
CALLED IT "THINKING PINK." PERFECT!*

Perfect, indeed. Thinking pink. I smiled and
held the card to my chest again. Matt knew me
so well.

I read on.

*PLEASE ACCEPT THESE FLOWERS AS AN
APOLOGY.*

An apology? I didn't like the sound of that. My
heart sped up a bit.

*I'M SORRY TO HAVE TO DO THIS TO YOU,
BUT . . .*

Do what to me? Do what? The card shook in my hand. I wasn't sure I wanted to read on. Was he breaking it off with me before we'd even officially gotten anything started? This was not what I expected. Not at all.

*Chill, Meg,* I told myself. Don't panic. Keep reading.

*I HAVE TO TAKE OFF FOR A LITTLE WHILE.*
*THINGS ARE COMPLICATED.*

Complicated? My throat tightened. What did that mean?

*I'LL BE IN TOUCH WHEN I CAN.*
*IN THE MEANTIME TAKE GOOD CARE*
*OF YOURSELF.*
                    *LOVE,*
                    *MATT*

That was it? That was my love note? He was telling me he was leaving.

I threw the note on the coffee table.

Had I pushed him away? Had one kiss freaked him out so much that he was leaving town? And what did taking off for a little while mean? Because of me? Because of his job? Because of Pops?

Could this have something to do with Greg? Had Greg forced him to get out of town?

My mind spun. I felt sick.

I wanted to text Matt. Why did my phone have to

stop working now? It probably wouldn't matter anyway. I could tell from the curt tone of his note that it wouldn't do any good. He made it clear that this was good-bye, at least for the moment. I just wished I knew why.

# Chapter 36

The next few days passed in a haze. I heard that Justin's case was still open. Sherman was sticking to the story that he was responsible for Justin's death, and no other arrests had been made. I wasn't sure what that meant for Jordan. Unless Sheriff Daniels and his team found hard evidence or a witness who could place Jordan at the scene, it probably meant that Sherman would carry all of the blame for Justin's murder. He would go to jail while his young paladin walked free.

I felt torn about Jordan's involvement. One could argue that Sherman was taking the moral highroad in protecting the kid. But as Sheriff Daniels pointed out, justice wasn't really being served if Jordan had played a role in Justin's death. I wished that the case was tied up, but I guess that the reality of life is much messier and not always so black and white.

I went through the motions at work. I turned my King of the Hook feature in early, and my colleagues greeted me with gushing praise about our successful social media campaign. Everything felt flat. I couldn't stop thinking about Matt. I'd memorized every word of his note, and I was no closer to understanding what it meant.

I hate to admit it, but once I expensed a new phone I did end up texting him. Twice. He didn't answer. That stung even more than his leaving.

The "thinking pink" bouquet he left me sat wilting on my coffee table. I refused to throw it out. It was the only tangible reminder that I had that he cared about me. He did, didn't he?

A cold front settled over Portland and brought with it the first rain in sixty-five days. The heat wave was officially over along with my short-lived romance with Matt.

I tried throwing myself into work. Greg agreed to let me work on a technology in the great outdoors feature. It only reminded me more of Matt. With each sentence I wrote, I could picture him with his sandy hair and iPad, typing away as we drank pints.

Jill tried to reassure me. She invited me out with her new surfer. He was taking her on all kinds of dates that Will Barrington never would have. They went hiking through Forest Park, on a pub-hopping bike ride, and exploring Portland's funky art scene at "Art in the Park."

"You're overthinking this, Meg," Jill said one afternoon as we drank lemonade on my front porch. "Matt adores you. I've told you a thousand times.

Something else has to be up. He'll come back. Don't worry."

I sipped my lemonade and asked her a thousand questions about the new surfer and her painting in hopes of deflecting attention away from myself. It was too hard to talk about Matt. He'd deserted me. Whatever his reason, I was angry now. If he really cared so much about me, he wouldn't have left without saying more.

Jill beamed as she talked about all the fun things she was doing, and how much surfer dude dug her painting. She'd showed him her work. Shocking. That was a huge step. Despite my own melancholy, I was thrilled for her. It was about time that her love life had turned around. Why did it have to coincide with mine falling apart?

Gam invited me over for dinner one night about a week after Matt left. She made my favorite home-made meatballs and marina sauce.

"Want to tell me what's bothering you?" she asked as she dished up steaming bowls of pasta and took them out to her deck overlooking the Columbia River.

It was hard to believe only a short time ago, I'd been farther east on the same river.

"Are the rats gone?" I asked her, trying to deflect the conversation away from me.

She clapped her hands together. "They are!" Handing me a bowl of hand-shaved Parmesan cheese, she frowned. "I do feel sorry that I had to help them along to their next incarnation, but I asked my spirit guides for some understanding on what they were here to teach me. You won't believe what I found."

"What?" I sprinkled cheese on my pasta.

Gam looked out onto the smooth river. The sun danced on its subtle current. Her deck was a spiritual oasis. Wind chimes dinged together, letting a calming melody envelope the enclosed space. A hummingbird flapped its tiny wings at a lightning-fast pace as it drank from one of the many feeders on her deck.

"You know every animal has an important teaching to offer us."

"I know. I remember the cougar card I kept pulling last spring."

Gam nodded. "I should have asked for guidance sooner on why the rats were showing up, but when I did, I was completely stunned at the power of the Universe. If we can go to center and really listen, there's always a profound message waiting for us."

I took a bite of the rich pasta. I had tried going to center about Matt and nothing profound had showed up for me.

"The rat spirit animal comes to remind us that it's time for new beginnings and change."

"Uh-huh, and?"

Gam smiled. "They also symbolize spring cleaning. Cleaning out the old to make way for the new."

"Are you making way for something new, Gam?"

She pursed her lips into a serene smile. "I think I am."

I sat up and put my fork down. "Gam, what are you saying?"

"Sheriff Daniels asked if I was ready to take things to the next level."

"The next level?"

"He wants me to move in with him, Margaret."

I didn't know how to respond. "That's great, Gam. If that's what you want?"

She put her finger to her chin and gazed out at the water thoughtfully. "I think it may be, but I'm letting my spirit guide me."

"Would you want to leave all this?" I motioned to her collection of chimes, sundials and plants. "Would you want to leave the river and Mount Hood?" Gam found her spot on the shores of the Columbia because when looking east from her deck she is greeted by a stunning view of Mount Hood. She calls the mountain "the tall one." On sunny mornings she meditates outside and claims that she can feel the mountain's energy calling to her.

"It would be hard to leave the river and my mountain." She turned to look at Mount Hood and placed her hand over her heart. "But at my age, there's no reason to wait on love."

"Where does Sheriff Daniels live?" I asked, stabbing my pasta. I wished I didn't have to wait for love either.

"Gresham." Gam smiled. "Even closer to my mountain."

"Gresham?" I grimaced. "You wouldn't want to

live in Gresham, would you? What do you even know about Sheriff Daniels anyway? I mean, Gam, I love you, and I want you to be happy, but you've hardly been dating him very long. Moving in with someone is a big step."

She patted my arm. "Margaret, I can tell that you're feeling protective of me. I appreciate your concern, but I'm seventy-three."

"Exactly! You've lived alone since Grandpa died. Do you really want to live with someone again? Can't you and Sheriff Daniels just hang out and visit each other now and then?"

Gam threw her head back and laughed. "Visit each other now and then! Yes, that could work." She started to say something else but stopped herself. "Eat. Your pasta is getting cold."

I dug into the tomato sauce with its fresh basil and gobs of garlic. It was just as I remembered it. Whenever I stayed at Gam's place she always made me spaghetti, meatballs, and her homemade chocolate cake. Maybe I was overreacting, but moving in with Sheriff Daniels was a huge step, and I wasn't entirely sure I trusted him. I trusted Gam. She'd always been a pillar of strength and a centering force in my life. She'd made wise decisions in the past. But I had a funny feeling that, despite her assurances she was following her intuition, she wasn't. She was following her heart.

We ate in silence. After Gam had polished off a hearty helping of pasta, she pushed her chair back and folded her hands in her lap. "Now, Margaret, shall we have a little chat about Matt?"

I choked on a noodle. "Matt?"

Gam raised a well-penciled eyebrow.

"How did you know?" I asked as I coughed, trying to get the noodle down. "Is it that obvious?"

She didn't answer. She got that faraway look in her eyes. They shifted focus from me to someplace off in the distance. I knew this meant she was tapping in. After a minute she nodded and placed her hands to her heart center. "They want you to know that sometimes love requires radical acts."

"What does that mean?"

"What it means to me and what it may mean to you are two very different things. Take some time and sit with that message." She scooped up our dishes and stood. "Now, how about a slice of chocolate cake?"

I'm sure the cake was as delicious as always, but I couldn't taste it. This must be what it felt like to be lovesick. I didn't like it, and I was ready to be over it.

That night when I got home, I thought about Gam's advice: Love requires radical acts.

Fine. I could do radical.

I found my laptop bag and unzipped the middle pocket. I hadn't touched it since I'd returned home from Hood River. Sure enough what I was looking for was exactly where I'd left it. I pulled out the business card for Ryan's boss at ESPN and booted up my laptop.

Before I could change my mind, I typed the subject line: INTERESTED IN A JOB, wrote an introductory e-mail, and hit send.

If love required doing something radical, I couldn't imagine doing anything more radical than moving to New York.

## Meg's Adventure Tips

**Rule one—Cover up.** When heading out on the water or spending a day under the baking sun, it's important to protect yourself from the elements. Wear lightweight, loose-fitting clothing that breathes easily. Many outdoor clothing manufacturers are designing lines with built-in sun protection. Look for brands that offer a UPF (Ultra Protective Factor) of 15 (good) to 50 (excellent). Protect your face and scalp with a hat, and be sure to shield your eyes from the sun's glare with a pair of UV sunglasses. Lastly, apply a waterproof broad-spectrum sunscreen with an SPF of 15 or higher thirty minutes before going outside. Don't forget that you'll need to reapply often, especially if you're sweating or in the water, so pack an extra bottle in your beach bag and slather it on your skin!

**Rule two—Hydrate, hydrate, hydrate.** Heat exhaustion and heat stroke are very real dangers in the summer months and hot climates. They can strike quickly, so it's imperative to know the signs, stay hydrated, and seek shade. The Red Cross advises to look for these signs of heat exhaustion:

- Cool, moist, pale, ashen or flushed skin
- Headache
- Dizziness
- Nausea
- Weakness or exhaustion
- Heavy sweating

If you or someone you know begins exhibiting any of the above signs, get out of the heat immediately. Drink small amounts of liquid, apply wet compresses to the skin, and remove clothing. If symptoms don't improve, call EMS before heat stroke develops.

**Rule Three—Watch the wind.** Windsurfing and kiteboarding can be safe enough for young children or thrilling enough for adrenaline junkies. Regardless of your preference, here are some ways to make sure you return back to the beach in one piece. Experts recommend always surfing or boarding with a friend. Don't be like Meg and get separated from the pack. Stick with the group or your bestie, and avoid any danger areas with things like jagged rocks. Areas for beginners are usually well marked. When in doubt, ask another windsurfer. They'll tell you where it's safe. Watch the wind. Know the blow. Twenty-five-knot winds will bring out the thrill seekers for bumping and epic air-catching rides. It's a blast to watch their high-flying stunts, but don't attempt to take on crazy winds as a newbie. Familiarize yourself with flat water and a nice light wind—eight to ten knots. Once you've mastered calm waters, then you can crank it up and go for the gust!

## Meg's *Silenced in the Surf* Scenic Tour

Follow along on Meg's adventure in Hood River, Oregon—one of the windiest cities on the planet. You'll find big winds and surfers catching even bigger air on the banks of the mighty Columbia River.

### Stop One—Hood River, Oregon

This charming town is an easy day trip from Portland, Oregon. Follow I-84 east from Portland for approximately sixty miles. Hood River is situated at the foot of Mount Hood. This adventure lover's paradise is surrounded by organic apple, pear and cherry orchards and hillside vineyards. Deemed the windsurfing capital of the world, this small, bustling tourist hub brings in visitors from every corner of the globe for kiteboarding, paddle boarding, kayaking, windsurfing, mountain biking and a bevy of other outdoor sports. No matter the season, Hood River finds a way to celebrate its bounty from cherry blossom festivals to cider pressing to hop fests and swims across the channel. Meander through downtown Hood River's many shops and restaurants, or stop in the History Museum of Hood River County for a look at Native American art and a glimpse back at the region's rich history. You just may decide to stay for a week.

## Stop Two—Waterfront Park

Any trip to the windy city requires a stop at Waterfront Park. Get a close-up view of all the action from the park's sandy beaches or under the shade of a tree. The launching area for windsurfers and stand-up paddleboarders is sure to be packed with colorful sails on a summer day. Watch from the safety of the shore, or try your hand at watersports by taking a lesson or renting a board from one of the nearby surfing schools. If you're in the mood for more of a traditional park experience, stroll along the Columbia River on the park's riverfront path. There are a number of benches perfectly positioned with stunning views of the river and Washington cliffs, where you can pause and take a moment to "be one with the river," as Gam would say. Among the park's many amenities are a swimming area, a children's playground designed to blend in with its natural surroundings, covered picnic shelters, and large, grassy areas. Pack a picnic and spend the day soaking up the sun.

## Stop Three—Full Sail and Double Mountain Brewing

Meg stopped at two Hood River pubs, but there are even more to sample in this outdoor lover's mecca and throughout the gorge, so pace yourself and take a tasting tour. Full Sail, her first stop, is a fully employee-owned microbrewery. Gam would most definitely approve of their work–life balance philosophy, and Meg is a huge fan of lingering over a pint on their incredible outdoor deck. Despite the fact that Full Sail has grown into a beer empire, shipping its award-winning ales all over the country, they have stayed connected to the community of Hood River, supporting local charities and farmers and finding ways to make the brewing process greener.

Double Mountain Brewing (Meg's second stop) is another favorite hangout for locals and visitors. Their downtown taproom is always hopping with events, live music, beer release parties and plenty of flowing taps. Give Meg's favorite—Hop Lava—a try. A refreshing treat after a long day on the river.

**Stop Four—Naked Winery**

The Naked Winery takes a witty approach to wine. At their tasting room in downtown Hood River you'll be welcomed with open arms whether you're a wine aficionado or novice. Forget fancy food pairings, you'll be offered Goldfish crackers and chocolate to cleanse your palate between tastings. Meg's all in for that! Don't let their irreverent attitude or laid-back style fool you. They produce seriously delicious blends that have been met with rave reviews from fans and critics alike. Made from handpicked grapes from around the Northwest, their blends just may make Meg a wine lover after all. Time will tell, but in the meantime make sure to add a visit to the Naked Winery to your Hood River itinerary.

**Stop Five—The Fruit Loop Tour**

Meg didn't have a chance to take the Fruit Loop tour in this book, but she promises that it is the best way to experience the Columbia River Gorge. The scenic tour winds through over thirty organic fruit stands, farms and orchards. Along the way you can stop and pick apples, peaches, pears, fresh-cut flowers, berries and vegetables. The thirty-five-mile loop will take you past lavender fields, alpaca and chestnut farms, wineries, eateries and unique shops. You can purchase homemade pies, syrups, cider and gifts, or stroll through rows and rows of family vineyards while sipping a perfect Oregon Pinot. Be sure to pack some gallon-sized buckets in your backseat. You'll return with a bounty of fruit and vegetables sure to last you until your next visit to Hood River.

Please turn the page for an exciting
sneak peek of
Kate Dyer-Seeley's next
Pacific Northwest Mystery

**FIRST DEGREE MUDDER**,

coming in December 2016
wherever print and e-books are sold!

# Chapter 1

My feet squished inside my drenched kicks as I limped through the damp grass. *I'd like to give Billy a swift kick in the shins,* I thought cranking the volume on my phone to high. Maybe Dean Martin's "King of the Road" would give me a final boost. Doubtful. I didn't feel like the king or queen of the road. Quite the opposite.

The rest of my Mind Over Mudder teammates were nowhere in sight. Thank God. I checked behind me twice, just to make sure. I probably could have taken the shortcut straight to the barracks, but I didn't want to risk being seen. That might have been a mistake. The historic grounds gave off an eerie aura, especially the dilapidated army hospital Building 614, to my left. It was rumored to be haunted. I understood why. Built in 1904 during an influenza outbreak, the three-story brick building had served hundreds of infantry men over the decades.

I shuddered to imagine the torture some of them must have endured. Was that a moan? A prickly feeling ran down my spine.

I think that's a moan, I said aloud as I glanced up at the broken top story windows. Something ghoulish floated past.

Run, Meg!

I willed myself forward, not caring about the blisters on my heels or the chafing under my sports bra. It felt like I was breathing under water. I didn't care. I crested the hill and turned onto Evergreen Boulevard.

Relax, Meg. It's just your mind playing tricks on you. I had read one too many ghost stories when researching the history of Fort Vancouver and its surrounding grounds. The hospital had been abandoned for years, but people swore that strange things were amiss. Faucets were said to turn on in the middle of the night, bathroom doors banged shut for no reason, faces, like the one I'd just seen, appeared out of nowhere in the windows. The place was haunted. Definitely haunted.

You're fine now, I told myself, slowing my pace.

I followed the flour on the sidewalk that marked the route of our morning run. It took us past the Fort's parade grounds complete with an old-fashioned bandstand and Officer's Row—a row of stately Victorian officer's houses. That's when I saw the creepy old lady again. I'd seen her watching us from her ground floor apartment before. The twenty-two mansions that make up Officer's Row were now used for a variety of purposes. The Grant House had become one of Vancouver's premier restaurants and the Marshall House a favorite spot for weddings. The remaining properties had been converted into commercial and residential space.

Yesterday when I jogged past the creepy old lady's apartment she peeled back one lace curtain and watched me and my teammates. It was unsettling to say the very least.

I stopped to tie my shoe under an ancient oak. Its leaves looked parched from summer's endless sun. My throat commiserated with the tree. I could use an ice-cold glass of water right about now. Pushing myself to standing all the hairs on my arms stood at attention as a creaking sound came from the creepy old lady's front door. She appeared out of nowhere on the wraparound porch.

Were my eyes playing tricks on me? Where had she come from? I jumped back in surprise. Her glossy eyes bore into me. She wore a faded pink bathrobe and appeared to be old enough to be one of the original members of the Hudson Bay Company.

"Hi." I offered a tentative wave.

She didn't move.

I tried again. "Good morning."

Her eyes remained locked on me, but she gave no indication that she'd heard my greeting.

Was she a ghost?

I had no intention of waiting around to find out. I plowed ahead, crossing Evergreen Boulevard, and practically hurdling the waist-high wooden fence that ran the length of the grassy parade grounds. My feet revolted as I stumbled down the hill. It felt like someone was sanding my heels with sandpaper.

Pick up the pace, Meg.

The only thing that kept me upright was the promise of a hot shower and the fact that a ghost might be in hot pursuit. I needed to get to the barracks and get out of these shoes. Mud and sweat oozed from every pore. Thankfully I'd learned my lesson after the first day on the training course and ditched my cute pink tank top and capris for old raggedy sweats and a t-shirt. Everything ended up discolored from the mud. There was no point in trying to look cute while under Billy the Tank's watchful eye and blaring bullhorn.

I cut through the grass, something Billy definitely frowned on. "Reed!" he bellowed in his bullhorn when he caught me sneaking around the back of the barracks last week. "When you take a shortcut you're only cheating yourself."

That was fine by me. I happily owned cheating on myself.

There was a single light on in the otherwise deserted collection of buildings down the hill. The reserve encompassed three hundred and sixty-six acres of land. It included Fort Vancouver, Pearson Airfield and Museum, the barracks, army hospital,

Red Cross building, Officer's Row, an old chapel, stables, and non-commissioned officer's houses. The grounds are considered the Pacific Northwest's most important historical site. And this morning I couldn't shake the feeling that there were whispers from the past surrounding me.

My target was the barracks' building where the single light glowing golden yellow looked like a welcoming beacon. Billy and his business partner Dylan had leased the barracks to use as base camp for their three-week intensive training class Mind Over Mudder. They promised that by the end of the session (if you survived which at the moment looked doubtful for me) that not only would you be in "fighting shape" to finish a mud run, but that you'd also drop pounds and pant sizes. So far the scale hadn't budged when I stepped on it, and I was so exhausted at the end of the day that I felt like dropping dead.

Using the wooden railing, I placed one hand over the other and slowly hauled my body up the ramp. The rotting wooden slats buckled. Please hold, I said a silent prayer to the Universe. The last thing I needed was to crash through the ramp.

Compared with the other buildings the barracks were in great shape. Everything had sat empty since the army abandoned its post in Vancouver decades earlier. The National Park along with a trust had begun renovations on the massive site. The barracks were first on the list, and Mind Over Mudder the first and only tenant at the moment. A sharp splinter lodged itself in my palm. It protruded from my mud-chapped skin. I stopped and yanked it free. Ouch!

Yet another reason to love this training program, I sighed as I opened the front door and stumbled inside. Every muscle in my body quaked. Billy had promised us that muscle pain was a sign that our metabolism was revving up and we were replacing fat with muscles. "Embrace the quakes" was his motto. Easy for him to say. Billy aka "the Tank" was the fittest person I'd ever met. That was saying a lot given that I write for *Northwest Extreme* Magazine and am constantly surrounded by hard bodied adventure junkies.

Billy instructed us to call him Tank on the first day of training. He looked like a tank. His stout body bulged with muscle mass. There wasn't an ounce of fat on his body. Let's just say that he was a bit intimidating when he sounded the whistle around his neck, wearing skintight army shorts and a sleeveless shirt specifically designed to show off his enormous muscles.

I scanned the dimly lit hallway to make sure the Tank wasn't here. By my estimate they should be on the course for another thirty minutes. That should give me ample time to shower, soak my aching soles, and hightail it out of here before anyone was the wiser.

The barracks have an ominous vibe even when

they're packed with my teammates and coaches. Shuffling down the long empty hallway made it feel even creepier. Like the army hospital the barracks are said to be haunted. The top floor was used for gun testing. There are still bullet holes in the walls upstairs, and it was said that you could hear phantom gun shots.

A loud thud sounded below.

I jumped and let out a scream.

My heart pounded in my chest. Relax, Meg. It was probably one of my teammates who had the same idea.

I continued on, checking over my shoulder to make sure no one was behind me. The locker rooms were located in the basement. Not exactly where I wanted to be at the moment, but I hobbled down the hardwood stairs anyway.

When I was a few feet away from the locker room doors they swung open nearly smacking me in the face.

I jumped again.

Was it the ghost? How were the doors opening? One of the rumors that I'd heard about the haunted buildings was that doors were known to open and close at will.

I backed up.

At that moment someone barreled through the doors and knocked me off my feet.

"Hey!" I caught myself on the wall.

The guy leaped over me and raced down the

hallway before I could get a look at his face. I had a pretty good guess who it was. Tim Baxter, one of my fellow teammates. I recognized his bulk and black hooded sweatshirt. What was he doing in the locker room and why was he in such a hurry?

I pushed to standing. "Tim, where are you going?"

He paused at the front doors.

I noticed a package under his right arm. "Tim!" I called again. "What's going on?"

He froze. I thought maybe I'd made a mistake. My contacts were thick with sludge. I don't see distances very well even when my contacts are perfectly clear. Dirt had formed a thick filmy layer, making my vision blurry. I blinked twice.

The door slammed shut. Tim or whoever had run into me was gone.

Weird.

I brushed myself off and continued into the locker room. Steam enveloped the front area where three massage tables sat empty. Long mirrors stretching the length of the room were completely fogged over. It smelled like stale sweat, moldy wood, and eucalyptus. Someone, probably Tim, must have left the steam room doors open.

Using my hands as a shield I made my way past the massage tables and into the shared steam, sauna, and whirlpool room. Doors on either side of the room lead to the men's and women's changing rooms and showers.

My cheeks burned with heat. Muddy sweat dripped

onto the floor. The wet air filled my lungs, making me cough.

I fumbled through the dense layer of steam. My hands landed on the cedar steam room door, which was indeed wide open. Someone had propped it open with one of the locker room benches. Really weird. I pushed the bench away. It made a sound like nails on a chalkboard on the tile floor.

My feet slid across the wet floor. I landed on my tailbone as the steam room door swung shut. Awesome. Two falls in a matter of a few minutes. That had to be a new record for me. At least my phone was safely secured to my arm. I just got a new phone after a little accident with my old phone. Smart phones aren't cheap, especially for a girl on a tight budget. I couldn't risk damaging this one, so I undid the Velcro strap around my arm and placed my phone and earbuds on a bench nearby.

Steam bellowed from underneath the door. It reminded me of dry ice on Halloween. Whoever turned it on must have cranked the heat to full blast. I braced myself as I opened the door to shut it off.

I couldn't see my hand in front of my face, but I knew where the dials controlling the heat and steam were. The steam room and I had become besties over the past few days. Nothing soothed my training aches and pains like the moist warm air.

I found the thermostat and switched it off. Then I climbed onto the cedar slatted bottom bench and drank in the steam. My breathing steadied as I sunk onto bench. This is exactly what I needed, I thought.

The steam began to evaporate after a few minutes. I opened my eyes. My contacts were like glue. Blinking as hard as I could, I tried to loosen their grip. It didn't work. They felt like sand. I might have to ditch them, I thought as I stood up.

The small cedar room came into soft focus. Someone else was in here with me. I blinked again. "Billy?"

Billy was laying on his back on the top bench with his eyes closed. Why hadn't he said anything? He must be pissed that I snuck out early.

"Listen, Tank, I'm really sorry I took the short-cut. My feet are killing me this morning. I have like a thousand blisters."

Billy didn't respond.

"Tank, I'm a reporter, remember. I'm here for a story. It's not like the rest of my teammates." I stood. Spots danced in my vision.

Again Billy didn't respond. I moved closer. Suddenly I knew why he wasn't responding. Billy wasn't resting.

As I came closer, a horrific sense of dread came over my entire body. Billy was dead.

You would think that I would have learned my lesson by now. But no. Signing up for Mud, Sweat, and Beers was entirely my idea. I wanted to prove myself as a serious member of the *Northwest Extreme* team after returning to Portland from a whirlwind week in New York.

It might be hard to believe (it still was for me) that I turned down a job offer at ESPN. ESPN! What was I thinking? Did turning down their generous offer make me wise beyond my years, or a total idiot? I wasn't sure, but I was sure that I belonged in Portland.

New York had been exactly as I imagined it— busy and crowded with a constant pulse of people and energy. I loved it. I loved watching throngs of businessmen and women in sharp, smart suits and fancy shoes, navigate sidewalks and honking taxis. No one honks in Portland. Cars *always* yield to pedestrians. Merging into the flow of foot traffic in the Big Apple was as challenging as trudging up deserted wooded backcountry trails in the Pacific Northwest. I almost got run over twice. Thanks to a bystander with quick reflexes I was spared being mowed down by a speeding Uber driver.

Fortunately I'm a quick study and the social media team at ESPN gave me a quick course in how to blend in like a New Yorker. My first rule was to *never* look up. Apparently no one in New York stares at the massive skyscrapers that tower over the city. I couldn't help myself. Some of them seemed as high—if not higher—than Oregon's majestic peaks. I found myself bumping into strangers as I walked with my head tilted up trying to catch a glimpse of the sky through the giant columns of steel and concrete. They were as impressive as the Cascade Mountains and equally intimidating.

My new friends also advised caution at crosswalks. I wasn't in Portland any longer. That was for sure. After two near misses, I learned to stop and wait for the light to change before crossing any street. In no time I began to feel like a bona fide New Yorker. And the fashion. Swoon. I could definitely get used to the big city wardrobe.

Very few Portlanders wear suits. Not true in New York. I appreciated the city's sophisticated style. I usually feel overdressed in my vintage A-line dresses at *Northwest Extreme* where most of my coworkers arrive in shorts and hiking gear. Many of them don't even bother to shower. Fashion in Portland had been defined by an influx of hipsters who sported shaggy beards, knit caps, flannel shirts, and skinny jeans.

New York brought out the girl in me. I have a serious addiction to pink. I've tried to temper it with my outdoor apparel, but in New York I embraced my love of all things pink, wearing my favorite cashmere cardigan and flared skirt with strappy pink sandals to happy hour and sporting a pink polka dot 1950s number to lunch. I even chopped off my hair on a whim. One afternoon I passed by an upscale hair salon. Without a moment of pause,

I walked in the doors and asked the stylist for a modern pixie cut.

The social team at ESPN was a blast. Unlike at *Northwest Extreme* where most of my colleagues were older than me by a decade or two, everyone at ESPN's new satellite office was my age. Hanging with my fellow Millennials made for an eventful week and required copious amounts of coffee in the morning to deal with the hangover from hitting the club scene every night. New York was alive no matter the hour. No wonder they call it "the city that never sleeps." I didn't sleep at all during my stay.

I'm pretty sure that was due in part to trying to make a major life decision. As flattered as I was by ESPN's offer, and as enamored as I was with the city, I just couldn't quite picture myself living in New York. Maybe I wasn't as athletically inclined as the other writers at *Northwest Extreme*, but I'd come to really enjoy my job and the outdoors. There was something about the wide open space on the west coast that I couldn't bear to leave. Portland was home, and everyone I loved was in Portland.

At the end of the week, I packed my suitcase and turned down ESPN's offer. The entire cab ride and flight home I debated with myself. Had I made the wrong choice? What if I never got another opportunity like this?

But when the pilot announced we were starting our decent into Portland, I pulled up the shade and looked out the tiny window. We circled over evergreen trees as far as my eye could see. Mt. Hood stood like a mighty snow-capped pillar at the base of the deep blue waters of the Columbia River. The vast clean sky seemed to stretch to the ocean. I had what Gam calls a "knowing." I had made the right decision. I was home.